Find out more about Charlie Huston and other Orbit
authors by registering for the free monthly newsletter at
www.orbitbooks.net

By Charlie Huston

Already Dead
No Dominion

NO DOMINION

CHARLIE HUSTON

www.orbitbooks.net

ORBIT

First published in the United States in 2006 by Del Rey Books,
an imprint of The Random House Publishing Group, a division of
Random House, Inc., New York
First published in Great Britain in 2007 by Orbit

ISBN: 978-1-84149-527-9

Papers used by Orbit are natural, recyclable products
made from wood grown in sustainable forests and certified in
accordance with the rules of the Forest Stewardship Council.

Typeset in Fairfield by Palimpsest Book Production Limited,
Grangemouth, Stirlingshire

Printed and bound in Great Britain by
Mackays of Chatham plc, Chatham, Kent
Paper supplied by Hellefoss AS, Norway

Orbit
An imprint of
Little, Brown Book Group
Brettenham House
Lancaster Place
London WC2E 7EN

A Member of the Hachette Livre Group of Companies

www.orbitbooks.net

To Bob Wilkins
and the Friday night
Creature Features

Thanks for keeping me up late
and scaring the crap out of me.

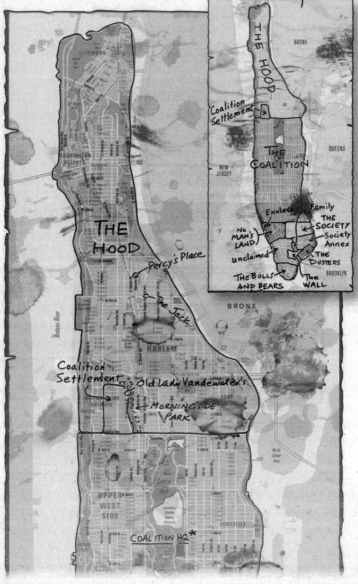

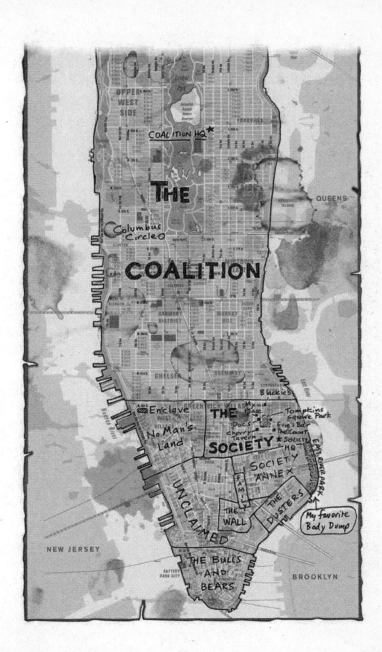

THE GLASS IS BREAKING.

That's not the surprising thing; the surprising thing is that it didn't shatter when he threw me against it. Shouldn't come as a shock. This place, they went through a few front windows the first year they were open and decided it was more cost-effective to lay out the extra cash for the safety glass. Save them from having to replace it every time there's a brawl in here. Which is pretty regular I'd imagine. Any case, I'm not bitching. Wasn't for the guy who had the bright idea, I'd be on the sidewalk right now, my good leather jacket cut to ribbons and my face sliced up in all kinds of new and interesting ways. But now it's breaking, it is most definitely breaking. I'm sure about that because my face is jammed up against it. The big question for me is whether this is the kind of safety glass that bursts into thousands of tiny pebbles when it breaks or the kind that turns into shards. Pebbles would be fine. Shards, not so much. The window creaks. Tiny fissures appear in front of my eyes.

OK, time to stop worrying about the glass, time to start worrying about getting this guy off of me. I can't expect any help from the bartenders or the crowd, not after they watched him pound on the bouncer with that pool cue. And I don't see any helpful officers of the law rolling up outside at this point. Not that I have any intention of being here when the cops show up. So, I guess it's just me and him. That's OK, I can go this one alone. Not like it's new to me or anything. I just wish he really was on PCP; if it was just PCP he'd be pretty easy to deal with. But this? This is gonna take grace and style, maybe even a little tact.

He shoves my face harder into the big front window. People out on the sidewalk flinch as they see my features squashed yet flatter against the glass. The glass creaks again. The fissures grow another millimeter. He's still screaming, babbling insanity at the top of his lungs, howling so loud I can barely hear Boxcar Willie on the jukebox:

> *You load sixteen tons and what do you get?*
> *Another day older, and deeper in debt.*

Ain't that the fuckin' truth.

He's enraged that my face won't just explode through the damn glass the way he wants it to. He rears back, and before he can slam my face forward, I've slipped to my right, spun, twisted my arm free of his grasp, winced as a clump of hair is torn from the back of my scalp, planted my right foot in the hollow behind his right knee, hammered my elbow into the back of his neck and sent him face first through the window in my place. The sidewalk audience scatters as he hits the pavement. I step through the dagger-edged hole he left behind. Shards it is.

He was spazzing the second he came out of the bathroom.

Before that, I hadn't even noticed him. Why should I? Not like I'm working; not like there's any reason I should be doing anything but paying attention to the booze in my glass, the cigarette in my mouth, the pool game in front of me and the girl by my side. Especially the girl. Girl like this, most everyone in the place is paying attention to her. Want to be invisible? Hang out with a girl like Evie. All that red hair, the body that not only won't quit but works weekends and holidays, too. That smile. She's the kind of girl guys like to look at, but most aren't sure how to go about approaching her. Too bad for them. They miss out on the best part, they miss out on how cool she is, how funny, how sharp, how down-to-earth. Anyway, a girl like Evie on your arm and you turn into a shadow, just the lucky fuck taking up space next to the best view in the place.

So a night like this, when it's so cold out Evie is wearing her leather pants and that tight old thermal top with the Jack Daniel's label silk-screened across the front, a night like this where she's glued to my hip and every guy in the place wishes he was me, is it any surprise I didn't smell him the moment he came through the door?

Most nights I would have picked up his scent right off. Couldn't miss it. After all, he smells just like me, only different. But what with the Early Times I'm pouring down my throat and the Luckys I'm sucking on and Evie rubbing up against me, I just can't be bothered. Still, he couldn't have been in here all that long. Sooner or later I would have smelled him no matter how distracted I was. It wouldn't have meant trouble necessarily; we would have eyeballed each other a bit, sniffed each other's asses like a couple of big dogs, but there wouldn't have been any trouble, not in here, not where everyone can see us. That shit just doesn't happen. As it was, I was lining up a neat little combo that was gonna let me run out the rest of the table and he came out of the john and started spazzing out.

This wasn't your run-of-the-mill junkie-who-just-shot-up-in-the-can stumbling around. He came out of there like the Tasmanian Devil: spinning, arms flailing, kicking anything that came in range, sending tables and people flying; a full on spaz. A space quickly opened up around him while he whirled and gibbered and foamed at the mouth. The bouncer, a nice enough guy goes by Gears, came over and tried a little sweet talk.

—OK, man, settle down, settle down. Take it easy. Got yourself a dose of some bad shit, but we're gonna take care of you. Got some 911 on the way, gonna get you to an emergency room and get that shit out your system. Just take it easy.

Moved in slowly, arms spread wide, talking soft. Might as well been trying to soothe a rabid dog. The guy stopped spinning long enough to jump at Gears and swing his arm like a club. Guy was freaky fast. Gears got lucky when he fell on his ass out of the way. Guy's arm hit the backside of a bench made out of two-by-fours and a couple of them cracked. Then he went back to spinning. By this time folks are starting to clear out, and I'm starting to pay attention. Gears gets back on his feet, muttering something about *fucking PCP*, grabs himself one of the cracked and twisted house cues from the rack and goes after the guy. But I've taken a good whiff by this point and I know the guy ain't on PCP. Gears would be lucky if that's all it was. I mean, I don't know what he's on, but I know he doesn't need it; he's dangerous as hell to start with.

Gears waits 'til the guy has spun his back to him, and brings the cue down on top of his head. It makes a nice noise, but before Gears can get too proud of himself or maybe think about bringing the cue back up for another swing, the guy has turned around, snatched the cue away, kicked Gears's legs out from under him and gotten busy finding out how hard it is to break a pool cue by pounding it on someone's face. That's when I figured I should do something. Not that Gears is so big a friend. I barely know him except to call him by name when I come in the place, but The Spaz is out of control, causing the kind of scene that's bad for business. If I don't deal with him, the cops will. That will get very ugly very fast. Nothing causes a scene like when cops start putting bullets in a guy and the guy refuses to go down. Sure, Gears and the law and the press may just chalk it up to a PCP freakout, but there are other people who will hear about it. And some of those people will want to check it out. And I don't want those people around. Not down here. Not in my neighborhood. So I jump on the guy's back. Figure I'll get him to the floor, put a sleeper hold on him and drag him out of here. Make up some story for the crowd about how I know him and I'll take care of it. Get him out before the cops come; get him someplace private and get rid of him before he can make another scene like this one. That's the thing to do. Except he shrugs me right off his back, picks me up off the floor and throws me at the window. And when I bounce off the glass instead of going through it the way he wanted me to, he grabs me by the hair and tries to shove my face through the glass. Lucky for me, strong and fast as he is right now, he's a lousy fighter.

Once he's on the sidewalk I handle it pretty much like I wanted to inside. Knees in the middle of his back, pin him to the scummy pavement, arm around his windpipe and cut off the O_2 until he goes asleep. He does a fair amount of thrashing around, and I have to hold on good and tight to keep from getting bucked clear, but once I'm locked on to him I'm not going anywhere. When he's nice and sleepy I toss him over my shoulder and point at one of the bartenders who's come out to watch how the story ends.

—Get me a cab, will ya?

—Ambulance is on its way.

—Let 'em deal with Gears. This guy, I know him. I'm gonna take him back to his halfway house. See if I can keep him out of the shit.

—What about the cops? What about the window?

—Hey, come on. I got the guy out of the place. Give me a fuck-ing break.

—Yeah, sure.

She flags a cab.

The cabbie's none too happy about me piling in with blood-drippy guy, but he sees I'm in no mood for debate and just gives me a dirty rag to put over The Spaz's face. Before we pull away, Evie runs up and passes my pack of smokes and my Zippo through the window.

—Want me to come?

—Nah, I got it covered.

—Meet you back at your place?

—Yeah. Maybe a half hour at the most. You gonna be OK?

—Don't start.

—Right. Sorry 'bout this.

—'S OK. Nobody can say you don't know how to show a girl a good time, Joe.

The Spaz tries to come to in the cab. I pinch his esophagus and he goes back under before he can cause me any more trouble. I have the cabbie take me down to the Baruch housing project just below Houston. It's a couple blocks outside what I'd usually call safe turf, but no one really has a claim on it, so it seems like a good place for an impromptu dump. I manhandle The Spaz up the steps to the pedestrian bridge that spans the FDR to the East River Park. It's nearly two in the morning on a Tuesday. Cars whiz by below, but the lights on the park playing fields were shut off hours ago. My eyes penetrate that darkness just fine. Too cold for any homeless people to be camping out. I do see what looks like a couple junkies sitting on a bench at the far end of the park, but they're facing the river. I pause at the top of the concrete stairs that lead down to the park.

The Spaz is still alive, alive and reeking of blood. I think about that blood; how I'd like to tap a couple pints of it and stick them in my fridge at home to replenish my rapidly shrinking supply. But his blood won't do me any good, won't do anything but make me hellishly sick and kill me. I know that because of what I smelled back at Doc Holiday's; the smell of the Vyrus, the same smell I carry with me. Nonetheless, I'm just hard up enough to give him another good sniff. Hell, maybe I was wrong, maybe it was some other Vampyre's scent I picked up in there, maybe this guy really is just whacked on PCP. I inhale. No, no such luck.

He's another sad fuck like me. But there is something about him, something about his scent that's a little off. Must be whatever he was taking in the bathroom. No surprise I guess. Whatever he's on would have to be some mean shit not to be neutralized by the Vyrus the moment it entered his bloodstream. Sure would like to know what it was. Be nice to try something like that sometime, something for a distraction. Christ, I drank over a fifth of bourbon tonight and it barely gave me a buzz. The Spaz stirs in my arms. Time to deal with the problem at hand.

I snap The Spaz's neck and shove him hard down the steps and watch him tumble to the bottom. The broken neck won't kill him outright, not like it would a normal person. A normal person, you break their neck, the medulla oblongata stops communicating with the body and all those autonomic functions like your lungs inflating and your heart pumping just stop. But the Vyrus reprograms your body, hyperoxygenates your blood and does a bunch of other stuff I can't really follow. The Spaz won't be getting up or anything, but there's enough O_2 in his brain to keep him lucid for the next several minutes. Probably a good thing for him that he's high.

I pop a smoke in my mouth, light it and head back across the bridge. I have to walk all the way to Avenue B before I can find a cab, but I still make it back to my place just a few minutes later than I wanted.

We don't get to sleep in.

Evie's a bartender. She's used to crawling into bed around dawn. Even on a night off she has a hard time falling asleep before the sun hits the horizon. Me, I got my own reasons for being a night owl. But we're up early the next day. Early for us, anyway, say just after noon. Evie's got an appointment.

I reach for a smoke as she crawls out from under the covers.

—What's the deal today?

—Viral load results.

—Right.

I sit on the edge of the bed, smoking and watching Evie through the open bathroom door. She rinses her mouth and spits toothpaste into the sink, then walks back into the bedroom.

—You been feeling any different?

—Nope. Nausea, vomiting. The usual.

—Yeah.

She squats next to her big black leather bag on the floor. Her back is to me. She's wearing panties and one of my old wifebeaters. I look at her ass while she digs in the bag.

—How much did you drink last night?

She keeps looking through the bag.

—A lot less than you.

—It's different.

—I know.

She finds a pill bottle in the bag and fishes out a capsule. Then she goes back in the bag until she finds another bottle and takes two capsules from that one. She tosses all three pills in her mouth and holds her hand out to me. I pick up the water glass from the bedside table, hand it to her, and she washes the pills down.

—Aren't you supposed to take the Kaletra with food?

She's squeezing herself back into last night's leather pants.

—I'm not hungry.

—Not hungry how?

She peels off the wifebeater. I stare at her pale, freckled tits until she covers them with the Jack Daniel's shirt.

—Just not hungry.

—Not hungry like you're not hungry, or not hungry like a side effect?

She stands in front of the mirror on the back of the closet door and starts raking a brush through her hair.

—Not hungry like I don't want to fucking eat anything, OK?

—Sure. OK.

I get up, go into the bathroom and close the door. I look at my-self in the mirror. It's a bad view. I splash some water on my face. I flush the toilet needlessly. I open the door, go back to the bed and get another smoke from the pack on the table. Evie has her hair pulled into a ponytail. She shrugs her way into her big, black biker jacket; all zippers and snaps. I light my smoke.

—You gonna be warm enough in that?

She holds up a hand.

—Enough.

—Just asking.

—And I'm just saying, enough. I know you're concerned. I know you care. That's great, I really appreciate it. I know it's not the nor-mal thing for you. But you have to get out of my ass.

She steps closer to me, bends over and gives me a kiss. Then she picks up her bag and starts up the stairs that lead to the ground floor rooms.

—It's just I want you to take care of yourself, baby.

That does it. She stops on the steps, drops her head, exhales loudly and turns to face me.

—I am taking care of myself, Joe. I'm taking care of myself the way I want to. That means if I want to have a couple drinks and risk raising my blood sugar, I'm gonna do it. That means if I'm not hungry when I'm taking my meds, I'm not gonna force myself to eat. OK? That OK with you? Because if it's not, you know what you can do. No strings attached, Joe. That's your motto, right? You weren't there when I got the disease, and I don't expect you to be there when it kills me. In the middle, you want to be more involved in my life, you want to have a say? All you gotta do is involve me in yours, that's all it takes. Until then, stop with the fucking nagging. I get enough of that shit from my mom. I don't need it from my goddamn *boyfriend*.

And she pounds up the stairs, slamming the front door good and loud on her way out.

I flop back on the bed and take a big drag off my cigarette. I blow the smoke at the ceiling and smile. I can't help it, I just love it when she calls me her boyfriend. And she only does that when she's mad.

I know, pretty fucked up, provoking your HIV-positive girl until she's pissed enough to forget that you're not really supposed to be a couple and calls you her boyfriend. But then again, our whole relationship is pretty fucked up. Start with the fact we don't have sex. She beats herself up about that pretty good. Carries around this big ball of guilt about me being stuck on her even though we don't fuck. I get it. It's not like it's rocket science or anything. She's terrified of giving me her disease. Condoms, dental dams, there's no amount of protection that'll make her feel safe enough to get more intimate than necking, dry-humping and hand-jobbing each other on occasion. It's too bad that I can't tell her that there is no way on God's green earth that she could ever get me sick. Nobody could. There isn't a bug on this rock that could put a dent in me. It's too late for that, I'm already as sick as a man can get. Pretty much. Once the Vyrus set up shop in my bloodstream, it made me uninhabitable for anything else. Any regular viruses or bacteria or germs come calling, they're gonna get their asses kicked but good.

So I don't mind the not-having-sex thing. That's not true. I mind the not-having-sex thing a hell of a lot. Just watching her get dressed this morning was enough to drive me half crazy. But I can deal. I can deal because I have to. Not because of what she's sick on, but because of what I'm sick on. I don't know if the Vyrus can be sexually transmitted, but I'm not taking any chances. I'm not taking any chances of infecting Evie with an organism that will colonize her blood and strip-mine it for whatever components keep it happy. A bug that is always hungry for more. A bug that, when your blood is tapped out, will send you hunting. And you'll hunt, man, you will hunt. Because the alternative, the pain that will rack you and twist your body and eventually boil your insides? It'll make anything Evie may have to go through in the next couple years look like child's play. That's just a fact.

Nevermind that if she was infected with the Vyrus it would cure her of the HIV. Nevermind that she could go on living pretty much just as long as she wanted to, as long as she kept the Vyrus fed. Nevermind that we could be together that whole time and fuck to our hearts' content. It doesn't matter. It's still not the kind of thing you tell the woman you love. It's not the kind of choice you ask someone you love to make. If you're a man, you make it for them.

And now I guess we've settled what I am. Or at least what I'm not.

So yeah, the relationship is all fucked up. No reason why it shouldn't be, it matches the rest of my life that way. Besides, yours any better?

Not that Evie knows any of this. Not that Evie knows shit about me. Three years running and I'm still keeping secrets. It's what you'd call a sore point between us, her not knowing enough. Can't blame her for being curious, girl's got reasons to be. Like why I rent two apartments: the one-bedroom upstairs and this studio below it. Why I nailed the studio door to the door frame and installed a panel in the lower half that I can kick out in an emergency. Why the little spiral stair that leads from the upstairs living room to the studio is concealed by a secret trapdoor. And why, with all that space up there, I do most of my living down here in the basement where the only window has been drywalled over. She's willing to accept it when I tell her it's because of my work, cuz of some of the enemies I've made. But she'd sure like to know more about that work. She knows I'm kind of a local tough guy, a guy who collects some debts, does some unlicensed PI work, that kind of thing. But it doesn't seem to warrant the security in this place, the secret room, the multiple locks, the alarm. What can a guy do? He can't tell her about the Van Helsings running around with a hard-on for people like me, those self-righteous busybodies looking to sprinkle me with holy water and drive a stake through my heart. Not that the holy water would do anything, but the stake sure as shit would. Hell, a stake through the heart will kill anyone. They don't really need it; a few bullets will do just as well. But a guy can't explain something like that. In the end she doesn't buy it, the whole *I got enemies, baby* thing. She maybe figures it's drugs.

Drugs would make sense. It would explain the security. It would explain my total and complete paranoia. It would explain why I don't have a regular job of any kind. And it would explain the little dorm fridge in my closet with the padlock on it. By now she's pretty certain that if she looked in there she'd find a whole selection of exotic pharmaceuticals that aren't carried by your garden variety, street corner dime-bagger. She *would* find my stash in there, but it's not anything anyone can get high off of, unless they're like me. Just three pints of healthy human blood mixed with the necessary anticlotting agents so it'll keep. Three pints. About seven pints less than the minimum I like to have on hand. Thinking about it makes me feel itchy.

Yeah, drugs would be fine as far as Evie is concerned. The blood? Figure it's a safe bet that would freak her out.

Funny, one of the things that should be toughest to explain is one of the easiest. How I never go out in the daytime? Solar urticaria. A sun allergy. I go out in the sun and rashes will break out all over my body and my skin won't be able to regulate my internal temperature and I'll black out and all kinds of bad shit. She buys it. And why not? She's looked it up online. Besides, it's not far from the truth. I do have an allergy to the sun. But if I go out and start sucking up UVAs, I won't just get all itchy and pass out. Me? The Vyrus will go haywire; tumors will erupt and riot throughout my body and over the surface of my skin. Bone cancer, stomach cancer, gum cancer, brain cancer, prostate cancer, skin cancer. Think of a cancer, I'll get it. Fucking eye cancer. And all of those cancers will have a race to see which can kill me first. Might take fifteen minutes all told. Less if it's a really sunny day. By the time everything runs its course, there'll be nothing left but a big blob of cancer cells. Biopsy that thing and it'll look like a giant, man-size tumor with maybe a couple teeth stuck in it.

I've never seen it happen. But the stories are more than enough to keep me from rolling the dice on a day at the beach. That's why I have to spend the rest of the day indoors.

I kill the time.

I shower and shave. I go through my DVDs and watch *Vanishing Point*. I go upstairs and find some old takeout from the Cuban place around the corner. I listen to some music and try to read a book. All I'm really doing the whole time is thinking about those last three pints and how I need to get some more.

It's been four days since my last pint. That's part of the reason The Spaz almost had his way with me last night. When things are good I like to hit a pint every two days. Keeps me sharp.

Four days? No wonder I've been crabby. I'll need to drink one today if I don't want to start jumping down everyone's throat. Figuratively speaking. Maybe I can get away with just a half.

I also spend a fair amount of time wondering how things went with Evie at the doctor's office. But she doesn't call to tell me. Which isn't a real surprise after the way she left. And that means

I'll need to go by her work if I want to get the news. Which means I better just drink a whole pint so I'm not on edge when I see her. I don't need to be picking any more fights with the only person in the world who gives a shit about me.

Around four-thirty I open the closet. I flip the dial on the fridge padlock back and forth and snap it open. I used to have a key-lock. Then I lost the key. It was the middle of the day and I couldn't run out to the hardware store for a bolt-cutter. I just about chewed through the fucking thing before I got my shit together enough to find a hammer under the sink and use it to claw the hasp free. It can be like that when you're hungry. Simple shit just plain escapes you. Now I got the combination lock. God save me if I ever forget the combo. I open the fridge.

Times like these, opening the fridge is like the third or fourth time a gambler checks his betting slip to see if maybe he really had his money down on the winning horse instead of that nag that finished way out of the money. I know what's in there, but maybe, just maybe, I did something right without knowing about it. Like maybe I laid up a dozen extra pints that are just somehow hidden in the back. Something like that. So I open the fridge. No dice. Wrong horse.

I take out one of the three pints. I take out the scalpel I keep in the fridge. I poke a little hole in the bottom of the pouch and place my lips around it. I squeeze the pouch and a thin stream of cold blood squirts into my mouth. When it's warm it's better. When it's hot, say 98.6 degrees Fahrenheit, it's best. But well chilled is just fine. I try to sip, but who am I fooling? I tilt my head back, hold the pouch upright and poke another hole at the top. It drains in a single rush, flooding my throat. Then I carefully cut the bag open and lick the inside clean. It makes me feel good. It makes me feel alive.

It is keeping me alive after all. Giving the Vyrus something else to gnaw on, something fresh. Keeping it from ranging further and further into the blood-making parts of me. Keeping it from digging into the little blood factories inside my bones and scraping them clean. Keeping the Vyrus healthy and happy so that it doesn't rampage through my brain, randomly hitting switches as it looks for more of whatever it is it wants. It's keeping me alive. But only if you call this life.

When I'm done I tuck the pouch into one of the red biohazard bags I keep in the fridge. There's only a couple empties in there, so I leave it be for now.

The nice thing about winter? The sun goes down early. I love that. Add in all the overcast days and those three months are my favorite. I pull on a sweater, lace up my boots, grab my jacket and scoop keys and change from the top of my desk. I also flip through a thin fold of bills: just over a hundred bucks. I got another grand stashed in the toe of a shoe, but that's for emergencies. And it won't cover half the rent on this place, which I'm two months overdue on. Blood ain't the only thing running short around here.

Depending on who I'm doing a job for, I might get paid in either one: blood or money. But I haven't had a job for a while now. I can hustle for the blood, dig up a pint here or a pint there on my own. But, in a way, money is riskier. I knock out some guy, drag him in an alley and tap his veins, I know I'm gonna come away with a pint or two. But as to what's in his wallet? The kind of guys who look like they might be sporting a good roll are the ones you least want to hit. Those are the ones that might make noise after the fact. Don't want a guy like that finding holes poked in his arms after he's been rolled, asking his doctor what the hell that's about. And there's just no point in robbing a man if you're not gonna tap him as well. Just no percentage in the risk if there's no blood. I mean, money is money, but blood is blood.

And don't even think about a real robbery. Walk into some liquor store and point a gun at someone? Try to do a little house-breaking? Anything like that leaves behind a profile and physical evidence. Start getting a file at the precinct, an MO in some computer database. Show up on the cop radar and you can just cash in. No blocked up windows in the holding cells. No blood in the chow line. Just a matter of maybe a week before you starve or get hit with some rays.

What I need is a real gig. A deal that will pay off big in both categories. I need something besides all the nickel-and-dime crap I've been hitting for the last year or so. The year since I pissed off the Coalition and they stopped dropping their loose ends on me. I never realized just how much I relied on the scraps from their table 'til they were gone. But I sure as shit miss them now.

For the thousandth time I think about giving them a call. Ringing up Dexter Predo and telling him I made a mistake. Telling him I can make it right; I'm ready to toe their line. I think about it. But the phone stays right where it is.

Fuck those assholes.

I walk out of my place and down the block to Avenue A. I hit the deli around the corner for a pack of Luckys and a beer. I cross the avenue, find a bench in Tompkins Square and drink and smoke and think about my problem. My problem is jobs.

My work comes to me by word of mouth. Problem is, word hasn't been getting around much lately. No straight citizens show-ing up with a deadbeat dad to track down, none of the smaller Clans calling to have a Rogue swept off their turf. Just me picking up bouncer shifts at Niagara and some arm-twisting for a couple shylocks. Shit work. Fucking Coalition. When I finally bit back at those guys, I maybe bit a little too hard; bit clean through the hand that fed me.

The Coalition is the only game when it comes to booking a heavy gig, but they always got to rub your face in the fact when you come calling. Kind of makes you resent them for being the only Clan that has the juice and the resources to drop a couple grand and a dozen pints on a guy on anything like a regular basis. And Predo? He just plain hates me. That's what happens when you land in the middle of the Coalition spymaster's plans and end up screwing them up all to hell. He hates you. He wants your head. He has papers on his desk he thinks it will maybe look good holding down.

I suck down the last of my beer, toss the empty in a trash can and start walking. The Coalition is the only outfit that could hook me up regularly, but there are other Clans, and you never know when they might have some dirty work lying around. And I may have been avoiding this play for a good long while now, but the two pints left in the fridge are a pretty compelling argument to bite the bullet. So I head east, toward Avenue C and Society headquarters, biting that motherfucker all the way.

—Hey, Hurley.

—Joe.

—Read any good books lately?

—Fuck yas.

—Yeah, I like that one, too.

It looks like your average Alphabet City tenement, but it's not; it's a fortress. I don't know exactly what kind of security or how many partisans they got holed up here, but Hurley is all they need. He stays in front of me, slouched against the door frame, threatening to bring the whole building down if he leans a little harder.

—Sumtin' on yer mind, Joe?

—Terry around?

—Yeah.

We stand there, me on the threshold, him blocking my way. I want in, but I don't think I could ever want anything badly enough to try and force the issue with Hurley. Guy's been around at least since Prohibition. I can't begin to calculate how tough a Vampyre thug has to be to last as long as he has. As for him, he's in no hurry to move himself. He could stand there all night waiting for me to get down to business and never move an inch. It's not that he's possessed of Zenlike patience, it's just that he's too stupid to ever get bored.

—Think I might talk to him?

—Gotta appointment?

—An appointment?

—Yeah.

—Since when does Terry make appointments?

Someone steps out of the shadows behind Hurley.

—Since I took over security.

I look him up and down.

—Evening, Tom. See you finally got that promotion you been bucking for.

—It wasn't a promotion, asshole. The Society isn't a fucking corporation, it's a collective. I was elected to the post by my peers.

—Yeah, sure. Anything you say. I'm sure Terry backing you had nothing to do with it.

He starts to come outside, but stops himself.

—OK. OK. You know, you can say whatever you want, Pitt. Doesn't matter to me. Know why?

—No. Tell me, please.

—Cuz you're just a slob on the outside who's trying to get inside, and all I have to do to get rid of you is this.

And he slams the door in my face.

Well, shit, I'm a bigger pain in the ass than that.

I cover all the buttons on the intercom panel, push them down and hold them there. It takes about a minute for him to open back up.

—Knock that shit off, Pitt!

I take my hands off the buttons.

—Hey, Tom. Terry around?

—You don't have a fucking appointment. No appointment, no Terry.

He slams the door. I hit the buttons. He opens the door.

—Hey, Tom. Terry around?

—Hurley, get rid of this guy.

Hurley comes out onto the porch.

—Time fer ya ta go, Joe.

—Hey, Hurl, that rhymes.

He points at the steps.

—Ya want ta walk down 'em, or ya want ta fall down 'em?

I stand on my tiptoes and look over his shoulder at Tom.

—So if a guy wanted to make an appointment, how would he go about it?

Tom smiles.

—A guy like you? An old friend of Terry's?

—Yeah, a guy like me.

—Well, I'd say all a guy like you has to do is pencil something in for a week past fucking never.

—That's a long time.

—Hurley.

Hurley turns around and looks past Tom.

—Yeah, Terry?

—What's the hassle about?

—Joe here wanted ta come in.

—Well, why's the man standing out there?

—Didn't have no appointment.

—That's cool. Let him in.

Tom spins, dreadlocks flying.

—What the fuck? He's got no appointment.

—No problem, Tom. I'm not really busy right now. Just taking it easy.

—That doesn't matter. I'm supposed to be clearing people in advance.

—Sure, but we got to stay flexible, too.

—But security.

—Sure, sure, we want to be safe. But that's Joe. We all know Joe.

I hold my hand up.

—Hey, Terry, I don't want to cause trouble. I can make an appointment. No problem.

—No, man, no. Come on in.

—You sure?

I take a step toward the door. Hurley moves to the side, but Tom steps in front of me.

—Security is supposed to be my job. And this asshole hasn't been cleared by security.

Terry takes off his Lennon glasses and wipes them on his Monterey Pop Festival T-shirt.

—Yeah, man, you're security and all, but we got to remember this is a community organization. You know, it's all well and good for us to be safe, but we have to be able to respond to the needs of the community. Otherwise, man, what's the point? And Joe here, he's a member of the community. So let's, you know, let's just bend a point here and let the man in.

—Fucking. I was duly elected and I'm taking this shit seriously. I'm drawing a line. No appointment, no meeting. Especially for a security threat like this guy.

Terry puts his glasses back on.

—A line. Uh-huh. A line. OK. OK. I get it. You and Joe have history. Some, you know, some difficult history. Some unresolved conflicts. That's cool. So I tell you what, why don't you and Hurley go do a perimeter check?

—What?

—You know, go, like, check the perimeter. Make sure it's secure or whatever.

—My post is—

—Tom, really, go check the damn perimeter and stop acting like a storm trooper.

Tom opens and closes his mouth a couple times, looks at me, looks back at Terry, looks at me again.

—This goes on the list, Pitt. Right near the top.

And he storms down the steps, making sure to hit me with his shoulder on the way.

—What list is that, Tom?

—Fuck you, cocksucker. Come on, Hurley.

—The list of times you've made an ass of yourself?

—FUCK YOU!

He walks away down the sidewalk, Hurley a few steps behind him.

I turn to Terry.

—It really safe letting him walk around with Hurley?

—He's an OK guy, Joe. Good at his job. Pretty mellow most of the time. It's only when he's around you that he loses his cool.

—Well, that's the only time I see him.

—Think there's a connection there?

—Got me.

He smiles.

—Uh-huh. So. Something you wanted to see me about?

—Yeah.

—Well, come on in, my friend. I'm just brewing up some *chai*.

—Lucky me.

—The thing is, Joe, the thing is, I really thought I'd be seeing more of you. After the last, you know, realignment, I thought we had gotten back some of that trust, some of those good vibes we used to share.

—Thought it'd be just like old times?

He takes a big whiff of the branches and dirt brewing on the stove.

—Well, old times. You can never get those back. But I thought we'd reached an accord, an understanding. Something to build on. But you haven't really been around. Why do you suppose that is?

—Got me, Terry. Maybe because I don't like you?

He laughs as he pours the mess in the pan through a strainer and into a cup.

—Well, yeah, I guess that'd explain it. Sure I can't interest you in some of this? It'll mellow you right out, put you in a good frame for conversation.

—I don't like to be mellow.

—And that, Joe, that is too bad. Too bad.

He picks up his cup, walks across the dingy kitchen and takes the chair next to mine.

—Well then, what is it, my man, what's on your mind?

—A job. I need a job.

You could say Terry saved my life.

You could also say that over two decades back he found me on the bathroom floor at CBGB, bleeding my life away through a hole that had been chewed in my neck. The guy who put the hole in me must have had a real taste for that shit, a real yen for the old-school style. That kind of thing ain't easy, a person's got to be desperate-hungry, or just be the sort who enjoys it. This guy, he'd taken his time with me, buttered me up, picked me out of the crowd as an easy mark. He was right. Nineteen seventy-eight: me, seventeen and living on the street, a hard-ass punk looking for cash, looking to score. He offered me a twenty to suck me off. No brainer at the time. Terry found me right after. Scooped me off the floor and took me to a Society safe house. Not like this deal they got now, but one of the holes they used to skulk around in before they had fully secured their turf. I ran with him for a few years, learned the ropes, saw how some things got done.

Salad days, those.

—Not to make light, Joe, but we're not really an employment agency.

—No shit, Terry. I don't need a career, I need a gig. I need to beef up my stash and make some money.

He shrugs.

—I don't really see where we can help. Now, don't get me wrong; you're hard up, we can, you know, front you a little something to get you by. But our resources are limited. You know that.

—Sure.

—What we do have, we need to use it to help support the cause. World's not gonna change on its own.

—Sure.

—The Society is always looking for opportunities to reach outside, to aid anyone afflicted with the Vyrus, but the pledged membership, the people doing the actual dirty work of trying to integrate the infected population into the noninfected, they have to come first.

—Right.

He takes a big sip of his gunk, ponders a moment, then lays it out.

—Now if things were different, if you were still a member, there'd be a few more options. There'd be, you know, emergency funds and such that could be tapped. But for a Rogue, even one like you, one we like to think of as an ally? Well, the politics of charity are more complicated than they should be.

—That an offer?

His mouth drops open a little.

—An offer?

—You asking me to come back?

He waves his cup.

—Joe. If you wanted to come back in, all you'd have to do is ask, man.

He sips again, watching me through the steam rising off his cup.

—Well I'm not asking.

—Too bad, man. Too bad.

—Besides, you got yourself a security chief. What would you need me around for?

He sets the cup on the table.

—Your ego need stroking, Joe? Self-esteem been suffering? Need an old friend to tell you how much you meant to the cause?

I stand up.

—You're not my friend.

I start for the door.

He talks to my back.

—Actually, I am. More of a friend than you know. And I can prove it.

I stop.

—How's that?

—Have a seat.

I stay on my feet.

—Joe, have a seat, man. And tell me about that deal at Doc Holiday's last night.

I stay by the door.

—Guy was spazzing on something and I took care of him before he could cause more of a scene. Why do you care?

He picks up his cup.

—Because he was one of ours.

—Why should *I* care?

He takes a sip, swallows, smiles.

—Because maybe there's a job in it. For the right man.

I take a seat.

Something happens on Society turf, Terry knows about it. Fourteenth to Houston, Fifth Avenue to the East River, if it happens on those blocks, Terry will hear. Especially if it involves anything having to do with the Vyrus. That kind of stuff is very close to the Society's whole charter: their ultimate goal of integrating the infected with the general population. That's Terry's personal daydream: uniting all the Clans, bringing together a population of *Vyrally infected individuals* that is large enough to have a political identity. He thinks that if he can bring us above ground, we'll be able to get the resources of the world behind finding a cure for the Vyrus. It's a nice thought, I even believed in it for a while myself, then I woke up. We go public, the world community is gonna take note all right. They're gonna take note and start opening concentration camps.

But the man dreams on. And he keeps a tight watch on anything that surfaces down here, anything that might upset his long-term plans. Plans that I sometimes think have nothing at all to do with all that Society party-line BS.

—So everyone saw you ride off with the guy?

—Yeah.

—And the cops were on their way?

—Yeah, but it won't make a difference. The bartenders know they owe me one for getting The Spaz out of there. Anyone else who maybe knows my name knows better than to mention it to the cops.

—What about the citizens?

—What do they know? Big guy dealt with The Spaz. Took him away in a cab. What the cops gonna do with that?

He stares into his cup, looking at the sludge that's settled at the bottom.

—Yeah, yeah, I can see that. Still, I wish you hadn't dealt with him so harshly.

—Harshly? Guy was a troublemaker. Figured you'd be happy to have him off your turf.

—In principle, yes. But he was a pledged Society member. That makes it, you know, just a little more complicated. I mean, sure, we're completely opposed to any overt acts of violence against the noninfected population. Any behavior that will increase anti-Vyral bias when we go public is an issue. But he was pledged, and we have a protocol for dealing with these things. Ideally, we would have, you know, liked to have seen him subdued and brought to us. We could have maybe gotten him down, mellowed him out, found out what was up. Then, you know, depending on the circumstances, there might have been a tribunal kind of a thing, to determine if he had acted irresponsibly. After that, sure, there might have been a punishment phase. But, you know, vigilantism . . . that's never been a tactic we've endorsed.

—Funny, I seem to remember you endorsing plenty of my vigilantism when I worked for you.

He looks at me over the tops of his lenses.

—Be fair, Joe. Technically, that wasn't vigilantism. You were enforcing Society doctrine back then. That's just worlds different from this case.

—I don't remember too many tribunals, Terry. I just remember you taking me aside and whispering names in my ear.

—Well. Well, that's true.

He gets up, walks to the sink and dumps his dregs down the drain.

—But that was a different era. Due process wasn't a luxury we could really afford back then. And we do things differently now.

—Uh-huh. Not whispering in Tom's ear, Terry? That what you telling me? Murder by decree out of style?

He rinses his cup, puts it on the dish rack, leans his hip against the sink and looks at me.

—Look, Joe, let's not dig into some irresolvable past issues. There's no benefit to anyone in going that route. Did we have a different way of doing things back then? Sure we did. But that has no bearing on things today. Living in the past. That's not healthy, that's not how you get things done. And the Society is all about getting things done. Anyone can talk, but it takes action to change the world.

I think about the building around us, the tenement that he has managed to legally purchase through whatever series of blinds and cutouts. I think about the other properties the Society has locked up down here. I think about the partisans he has bunked out in the barracks upstairs, the soldiers he can mobilize. And I think about the way it used to be, back in the seventies when I came on the scene, just ten years after the Society was born, after Terry's little Downtown revolution had forced the Coalition to concede this territory.

It *was* different back then: Coalition spooks everywhere; scrapping with the smaller Clans to keep the turf intact; trying to build our own major Clan out of the fringe elements: the socialists, the women's libbers, the anarchists, whoever else would listen. Terry had the numbers when I got infected, but he had a hell of a time keeping them all pointed in the same direction. I did more than my share in getting them all unified, had more than my share of names whispered in my ear. I know what kind of action it takes to change the world, all right.

—Sure thing, Terry. I got no interest in talking old times. So why don't you cut to the chase? Tell me what you want.

He pushes away from the sink and comes back to the table.

—That's it, man, that's it, right on. Let's get grounded in the now.

He sits down.

—So here's the deal. Let's just say that no one really knows much about this particular situation right now and we can kind of talk about it in pretty simple terms. OK? Talk about it more as a social concern than as a Society security issue.

—Fine by me.

—Great, that's great. So that guy last night, and *spaz* isn't really the term I'd like to use, but, in any case, he was, you know, pretty much a kid. In all senses, I mean. Young in years and also just very recently infected.

—So he was a new fish.

—That's right. And you know how they are, the new ones, they need lots of supervision. I mean, sure, some people, you, for instance, some people take to it right away. Others, they need some help adapting. This one, he was still in the adapting phase. Not even supposed to be out on his own yet.

—OK.

—But he slipped out a couple days back.

—How many days?

—Three.

—He stayed low for three days?

—Yeah, yeah, I know. Doesn't seem like a new fish should be able to keep such a low profile, does it?

—OK. So, what, you want me to find out where he went to ground? Make sure that crack is sealed up? Doesn't sound like a gig that's gonna pay out the way I need.

—Well, thing is, yeah, I'd like to know where the fish was, but that's not really the gig.

—What is?

—That scene you described at Doc's? The way he "spazzed" out? He wasn't the first.

—Say what?

He runs a hand over the top of his head, smoothing loose strands of his long hair.

—We had another case just like it earlier this week. A new fish went kind of haywire. This one had gone through his, you know, adjustment period, but he was only out in the population about a month. Then he just went . . . well, I guess spastic *is* the word.

—What'd you do with him?

—Hurley was there.

—Oh.

—So that was that.

—It'd have to be.

He pulls his hair free of the rubber band that holds it in a pony-tail.

—Yeah. But that's not the whole deal.

He collects his hair, pulls it back.

—What I'm hearing, there's been others.

He redoes the rubber band and fiddles with the new ponytail until it sits the way he wants it to.

—So when I say that I don't think we have to deal with this as a security problem, but as a social issue? I mean social with a lower-case s. 'Cause I think what we may have here is, I don't know for sure, but it looks like kind of a drug problem in the community.

Junkies. They get infected, they go one of two ways. First way, they couldn't be happier to be off the junk. Second way, they can't believe how hard it is to get high.

Sure, the blood is a rush, it's a rush like no other. But it's not the kind of thing you can do recreationally. There's too much demand and not nearly enough supply. With a few thousand of us trying to make it on the island, and all of us needing at least a pint a week to get by, there's just no way to get your hands on enough blood to keep a steady natural high going. You might get your hands on enough to gorge for a week or two, but the havoc you're going to wreak doing it is gonna beat a path to your door. And someone's gonna follow that path. Could be the local Clan looking to get rid of a troublemaker, could be a Rogue looking to get what you've stocked up, or it could be a Van Helsing. Any way you slice it, that kind of deal won't last. So a junkie who wants to keep getting high? It's gonna be a problem.

You pump enough junk, crack, crank, x, morphine, special K, LSD, or whatever else into your veins and you'll get high. But soon the Vyrus is gonna clean it right out. Your everyday junkie has enough trouble keeping himself in dime bags. Now what if that same junkie needs a week's worth of skag just to put him on the nod for a half hour?

Bleach, Sterno, gasoline, formaldehyde, glue, cleaning products of all types; all those standard alternative highs get a run for their money. I've seen a junkie with the Vyrus so desperate for a good old-fashioned high, he shot Prestone into his eye. Didn't give him a buzz, but it sure as shit distracted him for a while. These types tend to weed themselves out of the population.

But if it was out there, if there was a readily available substance out there that could cut its way through the Vyrus and get you dependably high? Everybody would be trying it at some point.

Lot of time on your hands in this life. Hard to punch in on a nine to five. Hard to make a regular living that lets you go take in a movie or grab a bite out. Hard to fill the hours when the sun is up. Something that could make the time pass a little more quickly, I'd give it a shot. And Terry, he's no prude. Check out the aging hippie look he's sporting and you got to figure he tried it all back in the day. But he has other concerns.

Terry's trying to change the world. That takes time. And it takes subtlety; so he says. Not only is a bunch of guys spazzing out in public bad for the cause, it's also more than a bit perplexing. These are new fish, for Christ sake. How the hell are they tapping into this shit? There's some new way of banging DMT, or some new cocktail of industrial solvents out there, word should have gotten to Terry before the fish stumbled across it.

—So you want to know what it is and who cooked it up.
—That's it. Just, you know, the skinny on where these kids are getting it.
—And that's it, just the info?
—Well, yeah, what else would there be?

I fiddle with my Zippo, snap it open and closed.
—I just don't want you thinking that I'm gonna be *dealing* with anyone who might be making this stuff.

He strokes his chin.
—I'm not sure I follow. What's your point?
—The point being, I don't kill for you anymore, Terry.

He scratches the back of his neck.
—Wow. That hadn't really occurred to me. Like I said, Joe, I see this as a social issue. That's why I feel comfortable asking you, as an associate in the community, to look into it. Because I know we share many of the same concerns.

He stops scratching.
—If it turns into a security issue, well, we'll deal with it in-house at that point.
—Fine by me.

I stand up.

—Guess I'll get to it.

He stands.

—All right. All right, Joe. That's good to hear. It'll be good having you doing some work with us again.

—Yeah, sure.

He walks me to the door.

—And, you know, like I say: a *social* issue. Just between us for the moment. Till we know what we're dealing with.

—Any way you want it. You're paying.

—Great. Great.

He leads me down the hall to the tenement's entrance and opens the door.

—So, hear from you in a couple days?

—Sure.

—All right.

He slaps me on the shoulder.

—Good to see you, Joe.

—Yeah, you too, Terry.

I go down the steps and cross the street. On the opposite sidewalk I look back and Terry is still standing there in the open doorway. He gives me a big smile and a wave.

—Keep the faith, Joe.

I lift my hand slightly and he pops back inside and closes the door.

At the end of the block I turn the corner and see Tom and Hurley coming in the opposite direction. We walk toward each other, Tom pretending like he doesn't see me. Hurley takes up three-quarters of the sidewalk, and I know Tom ain't gonna budge off the rest of it. I step into the gutter to let them by.

A little smirk creases Tom's face.

—That's right, asshole, better make some room.

I let them go past.

—How's that perimeter, Tom?

They keep walking.

—Everything secure?

Walking.

—You pick up Terry's dry cleaning while you were out?

He keeps walking, but throws me the bird over his shoulder.

Tom's got it in for me about as bad as Predo does. Those guys ever came across me dying in the streets, they'd kill each other fighting over who got to sit closer to watch me go. Whatever, doesn't change the fact that he's a world class punk. And about as easy to get a rise out of as a thirteen-year-old's prick. But I keep doing it anyway. Man's gotta have hobbies.

Terry can social me this and security me that, but what it boils down to is he doesn't want anyone to know I'm looking into this. Not even his own people. Especially not his own people. Fair enough. Terry wants this done quiet, he knows what that costs. He knows me digging around on Society turf without an explicit license from the council could get hairy. And he'll pay for that. Slippery as he may be, Terry always comes across when the bill is due.

So me, I'm feeling pretty good about things. A gig that should take care of my rent and empty fridge at the same time? What's not to feel good about? I even got a couple leads. I can go poke around Doc's, see if anyone noticed if The Spaz had company that night, do a little sniffing around in that vicinity. Might turn something up. But I'll save that for later. Right now I got another idea. Someone in this town's figured out a new way to get high. And if getting high is involved, I know the man to talk to.

—Hey, Phil.

—Aw shit. Aw fuck.

He tries to duck off into the crowd. I hook the collar of his shirt and tug him back.

—I said, *hey Phil*.

He turns around, adjusting his collar, flipping it back up James Dean style.

—Oh, hey, Joe. Didn't see ya there.

—Yeah, well, it's dark in here, so I see how that might happen.

—Yeah, dark in here. Couldn't see ya cuz of all the dark.

He smiles at me, lifts his drink to his mouth and tilts the glass just enough to wet his lips. He'll drink like that all night. Has to, he'll only buy the one drink. When no one's looking he'll snatch up any glasses left unattended and suck them dry before the owners can turn from the jukebox. But that one drink he paid for, he'll nurse that all night. It's like a badge of honor he can show a bartender or doorman if they question his right to be here. *Hey, man, I paid for my drink and I got a right ta finish it.* Only way he'll toss that thing down is if someone offers to buy him another.

—Buy ya a drink, Phil.

He brings the glass up, vacuums the contents and nods.

—Yeah, that'd be great. I was about to offer, but sure, thanks.

A waitress bustles past and I lift my chin. She gives me a harried half smile, too busy right now to work the charm for a tip.

—What? What?

—Double bourbon, rocks. And . . .

I look at Phil. He glances at the bar, cataloging the bottles on the top shelf.

—Oban neat.

She starts to leave. Phil grabs her arm.

—And a water back.

She nods and starts to leave again, but he still has her arm.

—And no ice in the water.

—You don't let go my arm I'm gonna piss in the glass.

He lets go of her arm.

—Jeez, what a bitch. What crawled up her cooz?

—You, Phil.

He giggles.

—Yeah, yeah. Sure like to, Joe. She's a piece.

He brings up his glass again, tilts it, lowers it, and looks into it sadly, having forgotten already that he emptied it. He reaches between a couple sitting at the table next to us and sets the glass down. He looks at me.

—Sure could use a drink.

He's trying to sad-puppy-eye me. Problem is his eyes are betraying him. The pupils are screwed up to the size of pinheads, the whites marbled red, his irises, usually muddy green to start with, are a sickly diarrhea shade, and I'd swear there's sweat breaking out across the damn things.

—Jesus, Phil, what the fuck you on?

He bounces up and down on his toes, his enormous blond pompadour swaying.

—A bender.

—Of what?

—Uh, the usual, man.

His eyes scan the ceiling, searching for the contents of his bloodstream.

—Bennies, couple bumps of crank, little freebase.

The cocktail waitress appears with our drinks. She hands me my whiskey.

—Double bourbon, rocks.

And offers Phil his.

—Oban neat, water back, no ice.

Phil looks at the glasses.

—I didn't order those, I ain't paying for those.

I hand the waitress some cash.

—I got it, Phil.

He smiles and takes the glasses.

—Thanks, Joe. I was about to offer, but thanks.

The waitress takes off. Phil guzzles the water.

—Jeez, needed that.

He squeezes between the couple again to set the empty on their table.

—Well, see ya 'round.

He turns to go and I snag him again.

—What's the hurry, I just got here?

—Sure, sure ya did, Joe, but I got a thing I got to get to.

—What's that?

—A, you know, a thing.

—No problem, Phil. We'll have a little talk, then you can go to your thing.

—Sure, sure. Um, hey, but I gotta hit the can first. Take a leak.

—Fine by me.

He just about sighs with relief. I put my hand on his shoulder.

—In fact, why don't I go with you? We can talk in private. Long time since we had a private chat.

His free hand goes to his face, covering the crooked nose and the scarred cheek I gave him last time we had a private chat in a bathroom.

—Hey, no, that's OK, I can hold it.

The couple at the table are collecting their coats.

—Here, we can sit here, let's talk here, Joe.

—Sure.

We sit at the little table. I stare at him and he stares down into his expensive Scotch, turning the glass around and around with his fingertips.

—How many days you been on the bender?

He jumps.

—Uh, what? Oh, uh . . .

He starts counting on his fingers. Finds them inadequate to the task.

—Couple weeks maybe.

—Not too healthy.

He carefully weaves the fingers of his right hand into his pomp and scratches his scalp.

—Well, healthy, you know? I mean, healthy? Not really my MO.

I smile.

—Nah, guess not.

He draws his fingers clear of his hairdo and wipes greasy pomade on his tight black jeans.

—So?

—Yeah, Phil?

—So, ya got something to ask, Joe? Cuz if you're just looking to break my chops or bounce me off the walls I, not that I'm looking forward to it or anything, but if that's the plan, I kinda wish ya'd just get it over with cuz I really want ta get on with my evening and see if I can't maybe score a little something to keep me going a little longer.

—Going for the record or something?

—No, no, just, you know me, just that I got my hands on this bag of bennies and I, you know, don't have such great self-control so I kind of just did 'em 'til they were gone and by then I'd been up however long and I thought I'd keep the party going, but, jeez, I been up so long now, when I come down the crash is gonna be murder and I really don't want to deal with it if I can, like, put it off.

—Sound reasoning.

—Yeah, that's what I thought.

—Speaking of drugs, Phil, you hear of anything new?

—Anything new?

—Like a new product going around?

His ears literally prick up.

—New? Something new going 'round? Ya on to something new? What's the deal? It like an up? There a new up out there, Joe?

—Settle down. This'll be something for people like me only.

He screws up his eyes, trying to focus.

—People like you? Like what, like nonusers? Shit, man, I'm not into the light stuff. You know me.

I lean across the table.

—Focus for a second here, Phil. I'm asking if you've heard about a new drug out there.

I point my finger at my own chest.

—Something for people like *me*.

I point the finger at his chest.

—As opposed to people like *you*.

He concentrates, looking from my finger to me to his own chest, then back at me.

—Oh! Oh, shit! Oh, yeah! Oh, I get it.

He points his finger at me.

—Some shit for people like *you*.

He points at himself.

—But not for people like *me*.

He grins.

—I get it.

He wets his lips with Scotch and his eyes wander off.

I slap the table.

—And?

His eyes come back around.

—And? Oh, right. Yeah, yeah, I heard about that shit. The new deal, the shit the new kids are into. 'Course I heard about that shit, who ain't? Shit, Joe, where ya been, under a fucking rock?

—Wish I could get my hands on it, whatever it is. Try some of that shit.

—It'd kill ya.

—Me? Naw. Never.

—It's cutting through the Vyrus, Phil. It'd kill ya.

—Well, OK, sure, maybe, ya put it that way, maybe. But if anyone could hack it, it'd be me.

—'Spose it would.

We're walking down A, leaving Niagara behind us. Phil wants to score and the place is dry.

I could just beat it out of him, give him a good one every time his mind starts to wander, but with the amount of speed he's pumped into his system the past two weeks it could take a lot of slapping around. Not that I'm opposed to slapping Phil. Not that I'm opposed to beating the hell out of him for that matter. A worm like Philip, he was pretty much born to be slapped. Christ, he was any more of a Renfield he'd be stuffing his face with flies and cockroaches. God only knows how Phil ever found out about the Vyrus, probably by being somewhere he shouldn't have been, but he's been existing on the edge of the community for some years now. Really, it's kind of a miracle none of us have killed him yet. Guy's right hand's been keeping secrets from his left for so long he doesn't even know which is which at this point. But he won't fuck around with me anymore, not after the last time. He used up his last Fuck-With-Joe-Pitt Coupon about a year ago. I made his face look different when he cashed it in. He tries to play me again and I'll take it clean off. So we walk down to the Cherry Tavern.

The guy working the door takes one look at Phil and me and shakes his head.

—Uh-uh. We're full up.

A couple teenage girls come giggling up. He glances at their fake IDs and waves them in.

He's in his early twenties, his arms and chest pumped too big for his legs. He's all high on working the door at this East Village meat market, enjoys being the man who decides which guys get in for a crack at all the underage pussy he lets in, and which do not. Me and Phil, we're a little long in the tooth for this place.

Me, I'm very long in the tooth for it, but I don't look it, wearing my age as well as I do and all. Far as he's concerned we're a couple trolls who are gonna fuck up the ambience. I could do some things, I could grab his balls and give 'em a yank, I could bounce his skull off the door, I could just put a hand on his shoulder and squeeze until he gets the point. Instead I pull out a twenty.

He plucks it from my fingers.

—Happy hunting.

The Cherry has turned the corner about four or five times going from shit-hole to hot spot and back again as a new crop of NYU kids comes in each year. Right now it looks to be on the downward curve. It's doing a brisk trade in binge-drinking hipsters, but they're not fucking in the bathrooms. I drag Phil to the bar and order three of the specials: shot of house tequila with a Tecate back. We work our way through the hormones to the back of the bar where we find some open space and take a seat at the tabletop Ms. Pac-Man machine.

I put two of the specials in front of Phil.

—Drink up.

—Thanks, Joe. I was gonna buy, my round and all, but thanks.

He takes a sniff at one of the glasses. He pulls a face.

—Jeez, Joe, not the best stuff.

—Yeah, well you know the Cherry, not big on the fifteen-dollar Scotches.

—Yeah. Place is a dump.

He downs one of the shots and follows it with beer. I do the same.

—So talk to me, Phil.

His eyes are dancing over the tightly packed crowd, searching for anyone who might be holding. I snap my fingers in front of his face.

—The new shit. I've been under a rock, so tell me about it.

His eyes never leave the kids in their low-slung jeans, Pumas and hoodies, trying to spot the telltale hand clasps of drugs being passed off. But he talks.

—Yeah, the new shit, it's like all the rage. Not, you know, thick on the ground or anything, but, like, the thing with the cutting edge crowd, the new kids are bringing it in.

—New fish found it?

—Yeah, that's the vibe I'm getting. Like this isn't the kind of thing the old farts, no offense, Joe, but not the kind of thing the old farts are into. That a monkey fist?

He's pointing at a bulge about the size of an eight ball of coke in the tight pocket of a girl's cords.

—Not my specialty.

—It is, it's a monkey fist. That chick's holding. Watch my beer, I got to go talk to that chick.

I grab his wrist before he can get up.

—Not yet.

—C'mon, man, I got to get in on this.

—Sit. Drink. Talk.

He watches her edge into the bathroom followed by a couple of her friends.

—Aw, man, gonna be nothing left.

I push the last shot of tequila in front of him.

—Drink.

He downs the shot.

—Anyway, not the kind of thing for the senior circuit is what I'm hearing. Taboo shit, scandalous and exotic. Frankly, shit piques my interest in the worst way.

—You see anyone do it?

—Naw, naw. All happening behind closed doors like *Reefer Madness* or something. Stories you hear, about these intimate rave kinda scenes with everyone hitting the new shit and freaking out and fucking wolves and bats and shit. You know, that kind of thing.

Right. Bat-fucking. That kind of thing.

—Where you get these stories? There aren't enough new fish around for a scene like that.

The girl in the cords comes out of the bathroom, monkey fist significantly depleted. Phil rolls his eyes.

—Aw, man, aw shit. I knew it. Fuck.

—Where you getting these stories, Phil?

—I don't know, around, you know, just, in the air. Shit like that, it's just in the air.

—In the air and I haven't heard about it? Terry Bird hasn't heard about it?

He chugs beer, some of it overflows his mouth and runs down his chin. He wipes it with the back of his hand.

—In the air for people like me, man, people looking to score. You, Joe, you got a one track mind; you're like this worker bee always trying to, like, you know, get what you need, always working a *job*. May as well be nine to five. And Bird, he's like the establishment down here. May still be fighting the good fight with the Coalition, but far as the kids are concerned, he's pretty much The Man himself. New fish aren't looking to fight the power, they're looking to maybe have a good time, enjoy life while it's, you know, youngish. Think they're gonna come above ground to chat it up with a guy like you?

He's looking at me now, talking to me without watching the room. I stare at him. He snatches up his other beer, takes a drink, tilting his head back to break eye contact.

—Anyway, that's, like, about it, I guess. All I got anyway.

—Uh-huh.

—Yeah, that's it.

He drinks some more beer.

—That was quite a speech.

A little more.

—Where you get a speech like that, Phil? All them ideas?

He finishes the beer, shrugs.

—I dunno.

He points.

—Hey, hey, that look like—?

I cover his hand with mine.

—I said, *Where'd you get a speech like that?*

He tries to tug his hand free of mine, but I keep it pinned to the table.

—Speech? Jeez, Joe, that's no speech, that just the speed rapping, just the old oral diarrhea. Just, like, whatever garbage rolling around my head getting cleared out by the speed. You know that.

I press down on his hand.

—Who you been talking to, Phil?

He clenches his teeth.

—Talkin' to?

—Phil, I'm gonna crush your hand. You'll never cut another line again. Who you been listening to?

He's grabbed onto my wrist with his free hand, trying to pry himself loose.

—Um, yeah, well, yeah, I could have been list'ning to someone, to this guy.

—What guy?

—Guy goes by, *The Count.*

I lift my hand. He snatches his back and massages it.

—Jeezus, Joe, didn't have to do that. Could have broke the damn thing. Ain't ya had enough fun whalin' on me over the years? Ain't enough enough?

—Where do I find this guy?

—Got me. I mean, really, *got me.* The guy ain't like no friend of mine or nothin', he's just a guy who's around who I crossed paths with a couple times.

—Set something up for me.

—Aw c'mon. That could take all night. I got things of my own to deal with, I got a high to maintain here and you already got me off my schedule. As it is I don't know how I'm gonna score, gonna have to rely on the kindness of strangers or something to get by, and now you want me to invest my few remaining energies in taking care of your business? That ain't right, Joe, you know that ain't right.

I stand up and dig the last of my cash out of my pocket. After the drinks here and Niagara and the twenty for the doorman, there's about forty left. I drop it in front of him.

—Score.

He scoops the money up.

—Sure thing, don't gotta tell me twice.

—Score, and then get me my meet. I want it set up tonight.

—I don't know, man, could be tough on short notice. Like I said, not like he's a pal of mine or anything.

He's looking sadly at the bills in his hand, rubbing them back and forth against one another.

—Forget it, Phil, that's all there is. Get me the meet. I'll talk to you later tonight.

He gives up, tucking the cash into his jeans.

—Sure thing, Joe. You got it. Just tell me where to meet you and I'll be there.

—I'll find you.

—Uh, sure, sure OK. Um, where ya gonna find me?

—You'll be at Blackie's, right?

—Sure.

—I'll find you there.

I make my way out of the place, leaving behind the low fog-bank of cigarette smoke, the fake wood paneling and the aroma of puke that drifts from the can every time someone opens the door. Leaving behind Philip, hip deep in his element.

* * *

The Count.

There's one born every minute. Or every couple years anyway. Seems there's always someone coming down the pike calling themselves The Count, or Vlad or Vampirella or some shit. Some asshole geeked on the whole vampire scene and wanting to play the role to the hilt. Whatever, I'll meet this guy and talk to him. Won't be the first time I've grilled a dude in a red satin-lined cape. Sad to say, it won't be the last.

It's close to one. Blackie's won't open 'til the regular bars close at four. I wander past Doc's. A sheet of plywood has replaced the window I sent The Spaz through last night. I think about going in to talk to the bartenders, see if they saw anything I didn't, but it's pretty packed. I'll save it for later. I walk to the corner of 10th and A. Take a left and I can stop by my place and grab some more cash, dig into that emergency fund. I stand on the corner for a minute. But I'm just putting shit off. I know where I need to go now, and my money's no good there anyway. I walk one more block down A, take a right on 9th, and cross over to Avenue C.

When I come through the front door of Hodown, Evie glances up at me from behind the bar and gives me a look. She's weeded back there. I slip past the pedal steel, fiddle and harmonica trio jamming on the tiny stage, collecting empties from the tables. I take the bottles behind the bar, dump them in a plastic garbage can with a couple hundred others just like them, and start washing glasses. Evie nods at me as she shakes a martini. Fifteen minutes later the glassware situation is looking better, so I go back around to the fun side of the bar and take a seat.

Evie's still serving the crowd. It's not a bad bunch. This late at night in the middle of the week it's mostly waiters and waitresses getting off their shifts at the ten thousand cafés and bistros that opened down here in the last decade. Or it's regulars coming in to work on their liver disease and listen to the music. She pops open a Lone Star, slides it down the bar to me. A half hour later things settle down and she comes over.

She wipes her hands on the bar rag tucked into her studded belt, picks up my smokes from the bar and sticks one in her mouth.

—Got a light?

She hardly ever smokes.

—What happened today?

She picks up my Zippo and lights the Lucky herself.

—No big deal.

—Good. What'd the doctor say?

She looks at the band.

—You hear these guys before? Corpus Christi?

—Yeah. I heard them before. What's the doc say?

She takes a drag, coughs on the smoke.

—Said. Cough! Said. Cough! S'cuse me.

She takes a sip of my beer and stops coughing.

—Doctor said my viral load was up. Said the HIV is showing again.

I try to touch her hand, but she moves it. She stares at the band, holding the smoldering cigarette unsmoked.

—OK. Then what's next?

A guy at the other end of the bar tries to catch her eye. She doesn't see him.

—Well, it's the second test showing a load, so that means we have to test to see if I've developed a resistance to the Kaletra.

—And if you have?

—We try other drugs.

—So when do you get the resistance test?

The guy at the bar is waving his hand.

—I get the resistance test after I take the recommendation from my doctor to my insurance company and they say I can have it, and if it comes back inconclusive I have to get them to approve a different test, and if that's inconclusive we start shooting in the dark, trying different meds, but since Combivir and Kaletra are the Health and Human Services-recommended treatments, I'll have to get every new drug we try approved first, and that will take Jesus knows how long, and they all have a different set of side effects so, instead of just puking all the time, I might start putting on something charmingly known as *back fat* or losing my hair or, you know, experiencing sudden heart failure.

She hands me the cigarette.

—Here, take this. I gotta go help this asshole.

She crosses over to the guy who's been waiting for his drink. I stare at the cigarette she was smoking. She comes back, plucks it from my fingers, puts it to her lips, then pulls it away and hands it back to me.

—Sorry. Didn't mean to blow up on you.

I take a drag from the smoke.

—What can I do?

She tucks some loose hair behind her ear.

—Honestly. There is something.

—What?

—Do you know your blood type?

—Um.

I take another drag.

—No. I guess not.

—Well, if you could find out that would be cool.

—What's up?

—The doctor. He's says I should start, this is so gruesome, he says I should start laying in a supply. For later. If I need transfusions. I can't save my own obviously, so I need to find donors. I'll get credits or something in the blood bank. So if you could find out. And then, if you're a match.

She laughs.

—If you're a match maybe you could give me some of your blood. Man, that's about the most fucked up thing I've ever had to ask.

She looks at me.

—You OK, Joe?

—Yeah. I'm fine.

The infected population is pretty stable. And it's that way for a couple reasons. One of the reasons is that it's hard to infect anyone. It's not just a matter of a couple bites on the neck. Somehow your infected bodily fluids need to mingle with someone else's bodily fluids. The amount of mingling is up for debate. But seeing as how the Vyrus can't survive outside the human body, it's kind of tricky to get it from one person to another. It's also not clear if it exists in any fluids other than blood. Not that I've done a lot of research into this stuff. My education stopped when I was about twelve. Biochemistry's not my strong suit. I'm just getting by on the introductory lectures I got from Terry way back when. But I'm not special in my ignorance. Nobody has done any real research into this stuff. Way I understand it, researching a virus under the best of circumstances is a pretty tough proposition. But when the facilities at your disposal aren't much more than a high school chemistry set, you're doomed to operating in the dark.

Not that people don't try.

The Coalition took a crack at it. They got their fingers into a very big pie called Horde Bio Tech, Inc. Took a shot at taking over the whole deal. Wanted to use their labs to start cracking the Vyrus. Didn't work out for them. That was at least partly my fault.

OK, mostly my fault. That's why me and the Coalition don't get along so well anymore. That's why Predo has shifted me from his barely tolerated list to his torture-maim-and-kill-on-sight list. Anyway, they got as close as anyone's gotten to having a chance to really dig into this thing. The Coalition Secretariat has built up some big piles of money over the decades, centuries, whatever. Money like that creates cracks. And they have become very adept over the years at working their fingers into those cracks and widening them. Once again, that's the way Terry tells it. And I got no better way of knowing. But that kind of brings up the second reason why Vampyres aren't cropping up like mushrooms: The Coalition doesn't want them to.

The Coalition operates on a charter that is the exact opposite of the Society's: They want to keep the Vyrus under wraps. They've been around for a long time, long enough to have a historical perspective of sorts, and they've already decided that no one is ever going to accept us as anything vaguely resembling normal. It's pretty much the only thing I agree with them about. So while their grip on Manhattan may have slipped since the sixties, they still draw some lines, and one of the biggest is about keeping the numbers down. Not that they need to convince anyone. We all get it. This is a pretty delicate ecosystem here. It's an island for fuck sake; the food supply, as it were, can only support so many predators. But in this case, the problem isn't that the prey might be hunted to extinction. The problem is that when you get right down to it, we're not predators, we're *parasites*. And we are vastly outnumbered by the true masters of the territory. So it's in all our interests to keep the numbers as they are.

And that's why I know Philip is an asswipe.

I think about what an asswipe Philip is while I walk to my place. I think about Philip and all this other crap because the alternative is to think about Evie. The fact that she's not getting better. The fact that she may be getting much worse. And, yeah, the fact that she's hoping I'll be able to donate some of my blood to help her if she gets really bad down the road.

Philip. Think about Philip.

At my place, I duck downstairs and grab the emergency cash. I didn't need it at Hodown, but at Blackie's everyone needs cash. I stand there for a second and look at the bed, still messed from last night. Evie didn't want to come over tonight. Not after I told her I had to go take care of some business and didn't know when I'd be home. Not the kind of thing a girl wants to hear from her guy the same day she finds out her terminal illness has taken a turn for the worse. Not the kind of thing I wanted to tell her. But I need to knock out this job for Terry, need to get the monkey off my back. I don't take care of that, I'm not gonna be any help to her anyhow. And I want to, I want to help.

I go in the closet. It's not blood I need this time. It's a gun. I unlock the gun safe and take out the .32 snub. I check that it's loaded and tuck it into the back of my pants. I don't have any reason to think I'll need it, but it's late, and I'm irritable, and I might want to pistol-whip Philip with it. Him or this Count clown.

I lock up and go to Blackie's.

I push the button next to the anonymous door on 13th. I stand there, knowing someone inside is peeping at me to see if I look OK. The door opens. It's Dominick.

—Hey, Dom.

—Hey, bud.

He glances up and down the street, checking to see that no cops are nearby, then holds the door wide for me.

—C'mon in.

Blackie's is a pit. It was probably once the super's apartment for this building, now it's as scummy an after-hours joint as you're likely to find. It's 4 a.m. and the place has just opened. Lucky me, I'm one of the first in. There's only the one tiny room, but Blackie managed to crowd it with the bar, a few tables, a couple couches, a pool table and an old-school jukebox that plays real 45s. It takes me two seconds to look over the four or five losers in the place and see that none of them are Philip. I go to the bar and order a beer and a bourbon on the rocks. The beer is a can of Bud that comes out of an Igloo cooler at the end of the bar. The bourbon comes out of a bottle that says Maker's Mark, but it ain't. I give the bartender a twenty and she gives me back six and asks me if I need anything else. The anything else being a dime bag of coke that costs twenty-five bucks and wouldn't get me high even if I didn't have the Vyrus. I pass. With nothing else to do, I do the usual: sit out of the way, drink and smoke.

An hour passes. The place fills up, but it never gets loud. There are only two rules in Blackie's: no loud voices and no cursing. The loud voices I get, there are occupied apartments right above us. The cursing is Blackie's thing. Guess it makes him feel better about running a shitty after-hours coke den. A couple people try to sit at my table and coke-rap my ear off. I stare them down and they leave. Blackie himself shows up at some point: a potbellied black guy in his late fifties sporting ostrich skin boots, a black cowboy hat, and ropes of gold chain draped around his neck. He takes his stool at the end of the bar.

Blackie came to fame back in the day when he opened the first topless club in the East Village. He ran whores and did a brisk business in hijacked booze out the back. He also owned a piece of five or six other bars scattered around the neighborhood. That was then. He lost the club years ago and it was made into a rock venue. His whores left him. The other joints he sold off piece-meal. Now this place is all that's left of his empire. And it proba-bly makes more money than everything else put together ever did. He knows me from when I used to bounce at Roadhouse. He'd come in and pass me a heavy roll of C-notes and a tiny .25 automatic with pearl handles. I'd hang onto that shit for him 'til he left, the cash in case someone tried to rob him, the gun because he didn't want to shoot no one if they tried to rob him. I'd pass it back to him at the end of the night and he'd peel off one of the hundreds and hand it to me.

I eye him as he chats with the bartender, looking him over to see if he still carries that bankroll. There's a baseball-sized lump inside his black Levi's jacket. Take that off him and my money problems are all solved. He catches me looking, shows me a couple gold teeth, touches his index finger to the brim of his hat and tells the bartender to buy me a round. I nod my head and forget about robbing him.

I drink the free drinks and inhale more Luckys. The place chokes with smoke, a James Brown tune whispers from the juke, everybody does key-bumps of shitty coke or just cuts lines right on the peeling Formica tops of the tables. A light by the door flashes from time to time and Dominick takes a look out the peephole and either lets in the person on the stoop, or doesn't. I take a look at my watch. Fucking Philip. Boy is cruising for a bruising.

I get up, collect my cigarettes, lighter and jacket. I give Blackie another nod and head for the door. Dominick comes over to let me out. Just as he's about to check the peephole and make sure a cop car isn't sitting outside, the light flashes. He peeks and shakes his head.

—Hang on a sec, let me get rid of this guy.

He opens the door and Philip tries to dart in.

—Hey, Dominick, hey.

Dominick puts a hand in the middle of his chest.

—Uh-uh.

—Uh-uh? What uh-uh?

—Uh-uh you ain't comin' in.

—Why? Why the fuck not?

—Cuz ya can't follow the rules. You talk too loud and you curse and you ain't coming in.

—What the fuck are you talking about I don't follow the fucking rules!?!

Dominick starts to close the door.

I tap him on the shoulder.

—It's OK, he's with me.

Philip sees me for the first time.

—Hey, oh, hey, Joe. You still here? Thought you might have left by now. Getting close to sunup, you know.

He winks at me.

—Sunup. *You* know.

Dominick looks at me.

—You sure you wanna vouch for him?

—Yeah, let him in.

He holds the door and Philip comes in.

—Yeah, Joe's my pal, he'll fuckin' vouch for me.

—Watch your mouth, Phil.

—Sure, yeah.

Dominick still has the door open.

—So you goin' out?

Philip shows me sad eyes.

—You leavin' now, Joe? Too bad. Wanted to buy you a drink or somethin'. Take care and all.

I nod at Dominick.

—No thanks, Dom, I'll stick around a little.

He sighs and closes the door. Guy opens and closes the door from 4 a.m. to 10 a.m. and tells people to keep it down and not to curse. Think he'd like his job a little more.

I catch Phil at the bar.

—So, Phil.

—Oh, Joe, hey. Decided to stay? Sure that's a good idea? Like I say, getting light soon. Know how you hate to be going home when the sun's up and all.

—Yeah, thanks for the concern. I'll stick around a little longer.

The bartender comes over. I order another round for myself. Phil stands there and waits, but I don't order one for him and he finally gives in and asks for a cup of water. Two bucks, the cheapest thing you can get here. The bartender takes a plastic cup over to the Igloo and pulls the little drain plug at the bottom of the ice chest, filling the cup with melted icewater. Philip looks at it.

—That sanitary?

The bartender plucks the dollar bill and four quarters from Phil's palm and tosses them in the cashbox.

—Like you care.

Phil picks a flake of something black out of the water.

—Jeez, what the fuck's his problem?

Blackie looks at him and clears his throat.

I lead Phil to the table I was occupying.

—Watch your mouth.

—Yeah, yeah, I know. Language, language.

We sit.

He stares into his cup, making sure there are no other contaminants floating around.

—Two bucks for some water, you'd think they'd at least give you a bottle or something.

—Phil.

He looks up.

—Yeah?

—Where's my guy?

He finds another particle in the water and chases it around with his finger.

—Your guy?

—The one you were supposed to hook me up with.

He shows me a speck stuck to the tip of his index finger.

—What's that look like to you?

I grab his finger.

—Phil, where's The Count?

He pulls his finger free and points it over my shoulder.

—He's right there, man. The Count's right there.

I look at the guys playing pool.

—The one taking his shot.

I look at the one taking his shot: twenty to twenty-five, skinny, mop of blond hair, little fringe of blond goatee, and a faded brown Count Chocula T-shirt.

Philip wipes the speck from his finger onto the thigh of his jeans.

—I mean, jeez, how'd you miss the guy? Told you he's called The Count.

Philip makes the introductions.

—Hey, hey, Count. This is my man Joe. Joe, this is The Count.

The Count flips his fingers at me, not offering to shake.

—Hey, Joe. 'S up?

—Wanted to have a word.

He looks over his shoulder at the guy racking the balls on the pool table.

—I got another game.

—I can wait.

He smiles, points at my watch.

—But not too long, right?

—No, not too long.

He twirls his pool cue.

—Yeah, got the same condition. Let me knock this guy off and we'll go someplace.

I watch him play. He's sharp on the table. Smooth. Keeps up a patter with a couple girls sitting on one of the couches. Between shots he takes a clove cigarette from one of their mouths without asking. He drags on it and passes it back, steps to the table and casually sinks the eight. The loser comes over to shake and The Count passes him his cue.

—Take the table, man. I got to go.

He looks over at me, flashes a finger, asking for another second, and chats up the girls as he puts on his fake fur-lined cord jacket, plaid scarf and furry Russian hat. Before he comes over to me he's flipped open his phone and entered both girls' numbers into it.

—Thanks for waiting, man.

I get up. Phil gets up.

—So cool, where to, guys?

I put a hand on Philip's shoulder and press him back into his chair.

—Stay, Phil.

He starts to rise again.

—But.

I point a finger.

—Stay.

He stays. We go.

—Hey, girlie. No, I'm up. Yeah, right, as if. I don't know, just heading for my crib. Right now? Girlie, you know I want to, but I got a thing I got to do. That ain't right. That ain't right. Girlie, you know I don't rock like that. No doubt. There was any way, I'd be there. Yeah? Yeah? You are such a bad girlie. You know you are. Yeah. Sure. That's it. Later.

The Count snaps his cell phone closed.

—Sorry about that. She's not my regular thing, but she likes to think she is. I could shine her on, but the girl is just so damn dirty, I don't want to lose the hookup. Know what I mean?

—Sure, I know.

—Right you do. This is the place.

It's an old brick building, right next to the El Iglesia de Dios Church on 6th between B and C. The place is turreted. Oxidized copper plating details the roofs and gables.

—You live here?

—Yeah, I know, all castlelike and such. Didn't plan it that way.

I eye the renovated lobby through the glass door.

—I was thinking about the money.

He takes out a set of keys.

—Oh, that. Well, I got like a trust fund I draw on. Money's no thing.

I look at my watch: almost five forty-five. Mid-January: sunrise just after seven. I look at the sky. There's a heavy overcast. Even if I'm out right at seven, there shouldn't be enough UVs hitting the street to do me any real harm. The Count catches my eye.

—Don't sweat the sun. You get stuck here, you can hang. I got some chicks staying with me. All like to party.

—No thanks. We'll talk. I'll go home.

—Cool by me.

He opens the door.

We take the elevator. The Count looks down from the numbers as they light up.

—Thanks for getting rid of Philip, man. That guy, he starts tagging after you and there's just no way to lose him.

—You hang out with him much?

—No chance. He just always shows up. Something's going on and he hears about it. One of those guys. Nothing wrong with him. He's just, he's such a . . .

—Renfield.

—Yeah, he is. Didn't want to say. Thought he might be your friend or something.

—He's not my friend.

The elevator stops, the doors open and he leads me down the landing on the fourth floor. A door at the end of the hall opens while he's still fiddling the key into the lock. A twenty-something girl in a pink leather miniskirt and black camisole top, her blond hair done up in pigtails, jumps into his arms.

—Hey, baby.

She wraps her legs around his waist and plants her mouth on his. They make out for a couple seconds, then The Count pulls his face away.

—Brought a friend.

She looks at me.

—Hey, friend.

I nod.

She jumps down.

—Well, don't stand around, come join the party.

She spins and skips back inside.

The Count goes to lead the way and his phone rings. He looks at the number.

—Got to take this. You go in.

He opens the phone and starts talking. I go in, the door shuts behind me.

The apartment is a loft. An assortment of partitions have been used to separate sleeping areas. One defined by two Chinese screens collaged with pictures clipped from fashion magazines, one by roll-down bamboo blinds, and the last by an assortment of cast-off doors clearly rescued from the street. The communal space is about one-third disaster-area kitchen and two-thirds disaster-area couches, beanbags, TV and stereo.

The girl with the pigtails drops into one of the beanbags and a handful of Styrofoam pellets squirts out of a splitting seam in its side.

—Careful!

Another girl, this one a brunette, in nothing but beige Ugg boots, panties and a scarlet poncho, comes out from behind the wall of doors.

—You'll pop it.

Pigtails stretches her foot toward the TV and starts changing channels with her big toe.

—It's already popped.

Poncho kneels next to the beanbag and presses on a piece of silver duct tape that's peeled away from the seam.

—It's not popped all the way. You keep bouncing on it and it's gonna pop all the way.

—So what?

—So I'm not gonna clean up all the fucking foam BBs.

—So what?

—So they stick to everything and they're a pain in the ass.

—So what?

—So stop jumping on it.

—OK. Where's the remote?

Poncho stands.

—Don't know.

She looks around for the remote and sees me.

—Hello.

I stand there.

—Hi.

She takes a long look.

—Do I know you?

—No.

—Uh-huh.

She nudges Pigtails with her foot.

—Darlin', who's he?

Pigtails glances at me, but keeps flipping channels with her toe.

—Don't know.

—Uh-huh. And where'd he come from?

Pigtails finds something she likes and tries to adjust the volume with the heel of her foot.

—Came with The Count.

Poncho looks at her.

—The Count's here?

—Yeah.

—Where?

—Here.

I point at the door.

—He's in the hall. On the phone.

The door opens and he comes in. Poncho smiles at him. He smiles back. She walks slowly past me and plasters her body against his.

—You're cold.

—It's cold out.

—You got something for me?

He kisses her.

—Nice. You got something else?

He holds up the phone.

—Just got the call. It's on its way.

She melts against him. Pigtails springs up and starts jumping on the beanbag and squealing.

—It's on its way! It's on its way!

A redhead in Sleeping Beauty PJs lifts the bottom of one of the bamboo blinds and ducks out.

—We scored?

Pigtails jumps higher.

—The Count is here and it's on its way!

Poncho points at me.

—And who's your friend?

The Count wraps an arm around her and leads her toward a couch.

—Baby, don't you know? That's Joe Pitt.

The beanbag explodes and a cloud of Styrofoam BBs covers the room. Pigtails falls on her ass.

I brush BBs from my shoulder and try to figure what the hell this is all about. These four living here. Under the same roof. It doesn't make sense. Why? Because the whole place reeks from the Vyrus. They've all got it, every one of them. Four new fish under one roof.

—You know how it is. It's a small world out there. You hear about people.

—How come I never heard about you?

The Count sits on a tired gold velvet couch, Poncho leaning against him, rolling Drum cigarettes in her lap.

—Why would you? Me, I'm just a new fish. You, you got a rep.

A rep I've got.

—Say I wanted to know about you. What would be the story?

Poncho places a cigarette between The Count's lips, strikes a wooden kitchen match on one of the buttons of his fly and lights the smoke.

He takes a drag, pecks her on the cheek, and exhales.

—The story would be pretty boring, man.

—I'm easily amused.

He laughs.

—OK. OK, man. Well. Until recently I was a student at Columbia. That was like a mom and dad thing, made them happy that I went Ivy League. But my life is down here. Got this place, got my bars, got my ladies, all of it down here. So by day, I'm Mr. Pre-

Med to keep my moms and dads happy, keep the trust fund flow-
ing and the lifestyle living and all. By night, I'm doing my thing. I
mean, my thing before things changed.

I pull out my Luckys and find the pack empty. The Count
pokes Poncho.

—Offer the man a smoke, babe.

She licks the seal on another Drum, walks over to me and puts
it in my mouth. I catch her wrist as she's reaching toward my
crotch and take the Ohio Blue Tip from her fingers.

—Thanks, I can light it myself.

She shrugs and settles back in next to The Count. I light up.

—So when did things change?

—A year ago, little less than that.

—How'd it go down?

He took off his coat earlier, but he's still wearing the big Russian hat. He takes it off now, sets it on Poncho's head and taps it.
It falls down to her nose.

—I'm not too clear on the details.

—How's that?

He frees the grinning Poncho from the enormous hat.

—Cuz I was mad drunk.

—So tell me what parts you are clear on.

He tosses the hat to the end of the couch.

—Is this what you wanted to ask me about, man? My origin story?

—I just like to know who I'm talking to.

—Not like I know that much about *you*.

—Said I have a rep.

—A rep, sure.

—What is it?

—Depends who you talk to. Out on the street, in the bars, they
say steer clear. But they also say if a person's in real trouble,
you're someone who can take care of things. Course . . .

He chuckles.

—Course, that's not what Tom Nolan says.

I blow smoke.

—What's he got to do with it?

—Tom? He's my sponsor.

Pigtails and PJs have been doing something in the kitchen. Now they come over with a tarnished silver tray loaded with a battered coffee service and several mismatched china cups and napkins. They set it on the floor and start filling cups.

I take a last drag off my Drum and drop the butt in an empty wine bottle. It hisses in the lees at the bottom.

—So you're one of Tom's?

—You were asking origins, man. Well, Tom's the one who sponsored me to the Society. He didn't infect me, but he found me after I got sucked. I'd been at the Mercury Lounge. Got mad drunk on Hennessy and Cokes, went outside and stumbled around and got latched by a sucker. Tom found me. Took me to a safe house, got me nursed up, gave me the 411 on what was going down. Saved my life.

—Hell of a guy.

He stirs sugar into his coffee.

—Well, let's not exaggerate, man. I mean, he got me pledged and all, and I'm indebted, you know. But he's, man, he's . . . *uptight*.

—He's an asshole.

He shakes his head.

—Not for me to say. I haven't been around long enough to be passing judgment on guys who've been doing all the heavy lifting for years.

Pigtails walks over to me on her knees, carrying a cup and the coffeepot.

—Coffee?

—Sure.

I take the cup and she pours.

—Milk and sugar?

—No thanks.

She stays there in front of me, on her knees, holding the pot.

—You really Joe Pitt?

—Yeah.

—Funny.

—What's that?

—I thought you'd look younger.

—Sorry about that.

She blows at a strand of hair that's come loose from one of her pigtails and settled on her forehead.

—No, that's OK. I still think you're hot.

I sip my coffee.

Poncho leans forward and snags the back of Pigtails' miniskirt with her index finger.

—Settle down, girl. The man doesn't want to play with you.

Pigtails scoots backward on her knees, smiling at me.

—But he can. He can play with me anytime he wants.

She sets the coffeepot on the tray and starts whispering in PJs' ear. The two of them burst out giggling, scramble into the bathroom and close the door.

The Count waves his hand at the door.

—Sorry about them.

—No problem. So, Tom found you.

—Found me, schooled me, sponsored me, pledged me to the Society.

—But you're not one of his boys?

He finishes his coffee and takes another cigarette offered by Poncho.

—Look, bro, what is it you want to know? Tom my buddy? I already told you not. You mean, am I one of his partisans? Also not. Exercising authority is not my thing. If there's a referendum at large in the Society, do I vote how Tom thinks I should? Yep. Guy brought me in, he's entitled. He needs some cash, wants me to donate to the Clan coffers, do I go the extra mile? Sure. I can afford it. Do I have him up to my place, let him sit in my favorite chair, have my ladies make him some coffee, put those ladies at his disposal? No. Never done that. But here you are. So what's that tell you?

—Tells me you want something.

He points his cigarette at me.

—That, now that, bro, you ask what your rep is? That is your rep right there. Your rep is, *don't take nothing from nobody no how.* Surprised you took the coffee and the smoke.

—Didn't want to be rude.

He laughs, slaps his knee.

—Yeah, that's it, that's the shit. That Slick Willie lone-wolf style. That's the rep. See, see, me, me? I couldn't do that. I'm not saying I'm a mama's boy or anything, but I am, you know, used to having some comforts. In terms of lifestyle, I'd just as soon be like you, Roguing it. But the truth is, I'm not cut out for it.

Poncho strokes his cheek.

—Poor, soft baby.

He nods.

—Pretty much. As it is, I got my Society membership to keep me safe down here. And I got my trust fund to keep me comfortable. 'Course, don't know how long I can make that last. Told my moms and dads I needed to take a year off. Hard to go pre-med when you can't take classes during the day. Pretty soon they're gonna want to know my plans. What am I gonna tell them? *Uh, I don't know, hang out, drink blood, party.* So, no, bro, I don't want anything from you. I just heard about you, thought maybe you were cool. Philip introduced you, I played it easy and all, but, hey, I was kinda starstruck. Truth. So, my crib, my smoke, my girls. Whatever. You don't want to hang, just want to ask your questions and take off, that's cool. It's all good.

I set my half full coffee cup on the floor at my feet.

—What about drugs?

—Love 'em. But they don't really work anymore.

—Uh-huh. What about this new thing?

He fiddles with his cigarette, licking the tip of his finger and rubbing the saliva on the side of the smoke where the cherry has started to burn unevenly.

—This new thing?

—A new high. Something the new fish are into.

The intercom buzzes. The bathroom door bangs open as Pigtails runs out and presses the button to buzz whoever it is into the building.

The Count stands up.

—You cool if I take a sec?

—Sure. Visitor?

He grins.

—Delivery.

Pigtails is jumping up and down again.

—Delivery! Delivery! Delivery!

The Count steps into the hall and closes the door behind him.

I stand up, look at Poncho.

—Can I get another of those?

—Sure.

She holds out the cigarette. I take it and she offers me a match. I shake my head and light it with my Zippo.

—So what about you, how long you been on the scene?

—Less than a year.

I snap my Zippo open and closed against my thigh.

—Society?

—Oh yeah.

She holds out her hands to the other girls and they run over and jump on the couch with her.

—We're all Society here. Not a Rogue in the house. 'Cept you.

—Yeah. Except me. Who brought you in? You don't mind me asking?

—We don't mind.

—So who was it?

She puts her arms around the girls' shoulders.

—Tom.

—Uh-huh.

I point at Pigtails and PJs, who have put their heads together behind Poncho's and are once again whispering.

—And them? Tom?

—Oh yeah. Tom. We're all Tom's in here. 'Cept you.

—Yeah. Except me. Guess I must just be the lucky one.

The door opens and The Count comes back in. Pigtails bounces off the couch and runs to him.

—Score! Score! Score!

Figure a score for me, too. Figure I get to see firsthand what the shit is and then I can go fill Terry in and that will make this about the easiest job I ever had.

The Count returns to the couch, Pigtails riding on his back. He shrugs her off and she plops onto the cushions. He's carrying a large, padded manila envelope. He opens it with a little flourish and produces a pint IV bag of blood.

Shit. No score. Just a late snack.

He sits. Poncho takes an IV needle and hose from beneath one of the napkins on the coffee tray and hands them to him. He carefully inserts the needle into the valve. A drop wells up and leaks out at the opening. And I smell it. Even in this loft, stinking of the three of them, I smell it.

—Don't drink that.

The Count looks up.

—What?

—Don't drink it. It'll kill you. It's infected. Can't you smell it?

He tilts his head to the side.

—Drink it? We're not going to drink it.

Poncho pulls a napkin from the tray, revealing four paper-wrapped syringes beneath.

The Count picks one of them up.

—Don't worry, there's enough to go around. If you're still curious about the new shit, I mean.

The Vyrus will kill you. It will eat you alive from the inside out. There is nothing you can do; sooner or later, it will get you. But no matter how desperate you may be, you will never latch onto another infected. I've had infected blood in my mouth; it was acid. And while the Vyrus can't survive outside the human body, blood taken from a Vampyre will make you sick as hell, and then kill you. The Vyrus may be dead in there, but some remnant of it will remain, some husk that will twist your insides and make you wish you were dying.

But this is different, altogether something else.

—The Vyrus can't survive outside a living body.

The Count stays focused on what he's doing, inserting the needle of one of the sterile syringes into the IV valve on the hose.

—If you say so.

—The Vyrus dies outside a human host.

Poncho and Pigtails are sitting on either side of PJs, who is reclining on the remaining beanbag. She has her sleeve rolled up and Poncho is swabbing her arm as Pigtails holds a piece of rubber surgical tubing at the ready.

The Count draws the corrupted blood from the hose into the syringe.

—So?

—The Vyrus is alive in that.

He pulls the syringe free, holds it upright and gently taps an air bubble to the top.

—That's kind of the point.

He presses slightly on the plunger and blood squirts out of the needle and dribbles down its length. He takes a cotton ball from the coffee tray and wipes the dribble away.

The dribble emits a thick stink of Vyrus. PJs moans in response, her eyes fixed on the needle as The Count kneels between her spread legs.

—OK, baby?

She nods, breath short.

He puts the tip of his index finger to the tip of her upturned nose.

—Here we go.

Pigtails ties off PJs' arm with the tubing and slaps a vein to the surface. It's a nice dark vein, thick and purple under her pale skin. He braces the vein with his thumb and slides the needle in.

A bead of PJs' own blood rises to the surface of her skin. She squeals softly from the back of her throat. The Count presses the plunger, forcing the poison into her vein. Poncho holds PJs' head between her hands. The syringe empty, the Count draws it free, places a cotton ball over the hole in PJs' arm, and releases the tubing. Instantly, PJs jerks. Pigtails leans over her and grabs hold of both her arms. The Count places the used syringe back on the coffee tray and wraps his fingers around her legs just below the knees. PJs shivers, her mouth goes wide, the sound in her throat grows louder. She starts to tremor and the three of them hold her limbs and head firmly as she shakes. The sound rises in pitch, peaks, stops, her eyes roll back in her head and her muscles go limp. The Count and Pigtails release her and Poncho strokes her cheek and kisses her brow.

Pigtails claps.

—Now me!

—How does it work?

—Really, really well.

—Not what I meant.

—I know.

The girls have all had theirs, Pigtails shaking only the slightest bit and Poncho not at all. The three of them are sprawled on the thick, white synthetic fur rug next to the couch. An occasional moan comes from their lips, a muscle twitching here or there, as they stare blindly at the ceiling.

The Count goes from one to the other, checking their pulses. Satisfied, he looks at me.

—What do you know about blood?

—It tastes good.

He starts stripping the paper from the last syringe.

—What do you know about the Vyrus?

—It tastes bad.

He rolls up his sleeve.

—Yeah, that's what I hear. OK, so I'm pre-med, yeah? But that doesn't really mean shit. All it means is that pops is a doctor and he and moms want me to be a doctor and I scored well on my SATs and went to the right prep school and got into Columbia and declared myself a biology major and I'm taking the classes I'm supposed to. But that doesn't mean I'm very good at it or anything.

—I'll take your word for it.

—You should, bro, you should. So, I got what you said. I heard the same thing, the Vyrus can't survive outside a body.

He picks up the IV bag, still more than half full.

—But here it is.

He holds the bag close to his nose, an expression on his face like a man smelling a piece of really stinky cheese.

—And it's alive in there.

—How?

—Don't know. But it doesn't last.

He fits the needle to the valve.

—We get the stuff and we need to hit it right away. When the Vyrus in there dies, it's over. So you do the math, process of elimination and all, and you know where the high lives. It lives in the Vyrus.

He draws the blood into the syringe.

—But you got to get it right. Too much, you will freak fucking out. Wait too long, 'til the Vyrus peters out: sick as shit or worse. Could be someone out there has developed a preservative, a medium that keeps the Vyrus together for a limited amount of time. How they got the idea to stick it in their arm is beyond me, but I'm sure glad they did.

—Where do you get it?

—A guy.

—What guy?

PJs is slowly coming out of it, stretching, rubbing her face, touching her skin. The Count goes to the kitchen and comes back with a bottle of water. He holds her head up as she takes a tiny sip. It's been no more than a half hour since she went down.

—What guy?

He presses his fingers to PJs lips and she kisses them. He chucks her under the chin and goes back to the couch.

—Look, bro, we got a good thing going here. This.

He holds up the syringe.

—This is so good. You have no idea. And our hookup is solid. But he's a *hookup*. That means all I have is a pager number. He either calls me back or he doesn't. And when he does call me back, if he's holding, he just sends a delivery guy. Some guy who doesn't even know what he's carrying. The delivery guy, he's a civilian, not infected, not even a Renfield. He just thinks he's carrying dope. Different guy every time.

—How did you get the hookup?

He swabs his arm with an alcohol-drenched cotton ball.

—All this sterilization, not really necessary. Not like we can get infected, right? Just makes it better, part of the ritual.

—The hookup.

He picks up the tubing.

—From another fish. Look, can we talk about this later?

—Who was the fish gave you the hookup?

He slaps a vein.

—I heard you were at Doc's last night.

—So?

—I hear a kid freaked out. A fish.

—Yeah.

—You see that?

—Yeah.

—He probably hit too much. Or waited too long and the Vyrus was dead.

—What of it?

—Well, that was the kid who got me the hookup.

He holds the tip of the needle at the vein.

—I don't want to be a bad host or anything, but I'm gonna hit this shit now. You don't have to go. Stick around. The girls come out of it, they'll set you up. You can see what it's all about.

I look at my watch. If I stay any longer I'll be here all day. He's pressing the tip of the needle to his vein. I reach over and grab his wrist.

—Any idea where the hookup is? Where it comes from?

He looks at my hand on his wrist, up at my eyes.

—Hey, man. I been a good host, right? You mind moving that?

I take my hand away.

He nods, smiles again.

—Thanks. All I hear, the only rumor I ever hear, is that it comes from Uptown.

I'm standing up, slipping on my jacket. I freeze.

—Uptown. The Coalition?

He shakes his head.

—No, no. Up. Town. Above One-ten. All the way up. The Hood, bro. And that's what I know. Now, you can stay, go, whatever, but I'm gonna zone out here.

He puts the needle in, pushes the plunger, and unties the tubing. Before he can pull the needle free, he's out.

PJs squirms over to him and removes the syringe from his arm. She leans her head against his thigh, looks at me and holds up the syringe.

—Do me again.

I walk out the door.

How you die, one of the easiest ways, one of the very easiest ways, you go off your reservation. Go outside the territory you know and you may as well be cutting your way through the Amazon. Sun comes up, you got no safe house. Run into the local Clan, and you will, they'll chop you down, a Rogue on their turf. Go to ground, find some hole to hide in, get caught without blood and try to poach something, you won't just be chopped, you'll be put out in the sun. Do not go off the reservation. You're a Rogue lucky enough to have an arrangement with a Clan, do not leave that turf.

Above One-ten. That's way off the reservation. That's Hood turf. Haven't been up there since I was a kid. Since I was a kid from the Bronx. Since I was something you might consider human.

* * *

—Hey, Lydia.

—Pitt?

—Yeah.

Silence on the other end. Then.

—Where'd you get this number?

—You gave it to me.

—That was a while back.

—Guess I'm lucky it still works.

—Yeah, you are.

I sit at my desk, spinning my Zippo around and around on my heavily doodled blotter.

—You still there, Pitt?

—Yeah.

I spin some more.

—You called me, Pitt.

—Yeah, I did.

Spinning.

—Just wanted to say hi, or something on your mind?

I stop spinning.

—You still have people in the straight world?

She grunts.

—Straight's not really my thing.

—Not like sex-straight. Uninfected. I hear you still have a public face.

—Yeah. Heard that, did you?

I tap a Lucky on my thumbnail.

—You used to do gay rights and stuff.

—I used to fight against ignorance. I still do.

—Sure, sure. I know you got that covered in the Society, but out there, in the world, you still do that?

—Yeah. I still got a face. Me, some of the other members of the Lesbian, Gay and Other Gendered Alliance still have faces. We still work out there.

—AIDS?

—What?

—You work with AIDS people?

—*AIDS people?*

—People who are sick. HIV positive.

—I do some needle exchange. Talk to sex workers sometimes.

I balance the Lucky on top of the Zippo.

—Got a destination with this, Pitt?

I pick up the cigarette and light it.

—Say I had a friend who was sick.

—You got a friend?

—Use your imagination.

—OK.

—This friend is HIV-positive, medication isn't working, could be trouble with her insurance company, that kind of stuff.

—OK.

—There other options? This person needed to get meds and whatever, there other options?

—Well, there are exchanges, mostly run online. People with meds they don't use anymore, or they have understanding doctors who write them scrips for whatever, they swap meds. Try things the HMOs would never allow. But it's all pretty catch as catch can, you know.

A flake of tobacco gets stuck to my tongue; I spit it on the floor.

—So you want a number? Some web addresses for your friend?

—Sure.

I find a pen. She rattles off numbers and letters. I draw a series of boxes on the blotter, one inside another.

—Anything else my friend could try?

—Depends.

—On what?

—Your friend got money?

—Why?

—There's a black market for meds. You have the money, you can get anything. Experimental stuff that's not even approved yet. Anything.

—No, no money.

—Hunh. You know . . .

—Yeah?

—You could ask the girl. For money.

  The girl.

—No.

—She'd give it to you. The girl would give you anything you needed. You know she would.

—Not the girl.

—Sela says she asks about you all the time.

  I look at the butt end of my smoke, watch as the cherry consumes the little LUCKY printed on the paper.

—Sela talks to her?

—All the time, she's like her personal trainer now. The girl got her to move up there, wanted her close.

—That's Coalition turf.

—I know. Sela renounced the Society.

—She renounced?

—Had to. She would have Rogued-it up there, but you know the Coalition: *No dogs allowed.* Pledged the Coalition.

—Jesus.

—She loves the girl. Only way she could stay close to her. Figured better to join the Coalition so she could keep an eye on her.

—Terry must have shit.

  She laughs.

—Not half as much as Tom.

—Fuck him.

—You fuck him, Pitt. He's not my type. Fucking fascist.

—Still not getting along?

—It's not just me anymore. I hear you were around to see Terry.

—Yeah.

—I hear you didn't have an appointment.

—Yeah.

—Picture how that kind of stuff goes over with the members. Terry's always been open-door. You need to talk to him, he's there. Part of his appeal. Part of why so many of us trust him. Now Tom wants all contact to go through his security desk. Not popular at all.

—So how's he keep the job?

—He's got his supporters. Younger members mostly, guys mostly, machos that like the idea of *a strong and independent Society*.

—Younger members. I hear there's been a lot of that going around lately.

I hang on the line while she doesn't say anything. I hear a click-ing sound, like maybe she's flicking her thumbnail against her front teeth. The sound stops.

—We got a little off the subject, Pitt.

—Just saying, seems there's a lot of new fish in the pond.

—Hadn't noticed. Anyway. You have a friend who's sick and needs help, I'm happy to give you some advice; that's something I do anyway. Society politics, that's for members only.

—Just passing the time.

—I know what you're doing. I may have helped you out once, done something that wasn't strictly by the book, but don't think I'm not a believer. I'm Society, Pitt, through and through. Got it?

—Sure.

—Good. So. You want me to talk to Sela, have her talk to the girl?

—No.

—It's your business, but if you've got a friend who's HIV-positive, money always helps. The girl would love to do something for you. This isn't the time to get stuck on your pride, Joe.

—Thanks for the advice, Lydia.

—I'm just saying. If you want to help your friend, then help.

—Like I say, thanks, for the numbers and such. I owe you one.

—Right. Whatever you say, Pitt.

Lydia's alright. She may have fallen for the Society line, she may be a pain in the ass PC crusader dyke, but she's alright. She helped me with that Coalition mess last year. She helped me with the girl. The girl and her fucking sick-ass father and . . .

I need to stop thinking about this stuff. I think about this stuff, that means thinking about the thing that took out the girl's father. The thing that shouldn't exist. The thing that was in the same room with the girl, that got a look at her. Don't think about it. The girl's OK. She's got Sela as her angel. Sela, the baddest pre-op Vampyre on the Island. Anyone tries to mess with the girl, Sela's gonna improvise a sex change on their ass. The girl's OK.

And I got other problems now.

I manage a couple hours' sleep. I don't dream about the girl, so that's good. But I do dream about Evie. Normally dreaming about Evie is as good as it gets, but these aren't those kind of dreams. These are the other kind. When I wake up I have hours to go to sundown. And still no idea how I'm gonna get my ass above One-ten.

Figure I call Terry, tell him the trail leads Uptown, he'll have some way of getting me across Coalition territory. I go to the Hood with Terry's blessing, things won't be so bad. The Society and the Hood have a relationship. Both Clans were born out of the same revolution, both were snapped off from the Coalition. So yeah, figure that's how to go about this. Except for the way Lydia got all touchy at the end there. She's Society, sure. But she's not rank and file. That queer alliance she put together within the

Society has some pull, and she often pulls it her own direction, has her own ideas about how things should be done. She clammed up tight when I started talking new fish. Figure that means something's up. As if I hadn't already got that. But now I figure it's something to do with Terry and Tom. Something to do with the way Tom is trying to put a wall around Terry. And this thing with the new high? Figure that's Terry's angle, figure it has something to do with his play, whatever it turns out to be. Fine. But if that's the case, if this is an angle, if it's *Terry's angle,* it's worth something. And not just whatever he's planning to slip me. So figure I don't want to go to Terry for help getting Uptown. I got time before I need to fill him in on my findings. Let him wait. I work this alone? I could end up with the angle, make it pay out, get me some serious money maybe. Money I can use not just for fucking rent, but for Evie.

Got to be that way.

Cause there's no way in hell I'm going anywhere near the girl.

—Hey, babe.

—Hey.

—How you feeling?

—Fine.

—Good.

I'm upstairs in the big apartment, wandering from living room to kitchen to bedroom to bathroom. Picking up odds and ends of garbage: take-out bags piled on the counter, cards for locksmiths and dog-walkers slipped under the door, an empty Kleenex box on the back of the toilet, stuffing it all into a huge, green plastic garbage sack.

Over the phone I can hear a TV in the background, something with a laugh track; just that and her breathing.

—What're you doing?

—Watching the tube. What about you?

—Cleaning.

—Excuse me?

—Not with a mop or anything. Just picking up trash upstairs.

—Cleaning the fake apartment.

The channels flip in the background: a commercial, a music video, an infomercial; faster and faster, and then the TV is silent.

—You left me hanging, Joe.

—I know.

—Had a pretty bad fucking day.

—I know.

—And your response was to bail.

—I know.

—One thing about you.

—What's that?

—When I really need you, you always come through. Makes it so I can take the other shit, you know?

I take a white grocery bag that hangs off the back of the bath-room door, serving as a wastebasket, and stuff it into the sack. It's full of lipstick-smeared tissues and old tampon wrappers.

—Yeah, I know.

—If that's not gonna be the case anymore, if it's getting too stiff now, I need to know. You can't take it the rest of the way, I need to know now. It's OK. But I can't be counting on you if you're not going to be there.

I flip the lid down on the toilet and sit.

—I hear you, baby.

—Do you? Are you sure? I thought you did, but disappearing on me like you did last night, that made me wonder if you get it.

I feel my breast pocket for my smokes. I left them downstairs.

—I get it.

—Then you need to tell me, Joe. I need you to tell me what it's gonna be. I'm sick, and, this, this is it, this is the way it's going to be. It's not going to get any better than this. It might not get really bad, but this is as easy as it will ever be. If you want to stick around, I need you to do some things. I need you to find out what your blood type is so I know if you can help me with that. I need you to back me up when I have a day like yesterday. I need you to. Oh shit, Joe. Just. I need you, you know? To be there.

She's crying. She talks through the tears. It's all very matter of fact. By now she has plenty of experience talking while she's crying.

I listen to her blow her nose.

—I got to go somewhere for a couple days. Take care of. Something. I don't know if I'll be able to call. When I get back.

I feel for my smokes again. Still not in my pocket.

—When I get back, I'll be there.

—Yeah?

—Yeah, baby. Don't worry, I'm practically there already.

—OK.

—OK.

—And. Joe. A couple days, that's Saturday night.

—Uh-huh.

—I'm taking the night off. I'm doing a reading. Reading some of my stuff at Housing Works. A benefit kind of thing.

—Uh-huh.

—You go with me?

—You know I will, babe.

—It's important.

—I'll be there.

—OK. Thanks, Joe.

We stay on the phone a while longer. Until she's not crying anymore.

Just before sundown I'm looking at the fridge. Two pints. This low, I shouldn't even be thinking about drinking one of those after

I had one yesterday. But I could get stuck Uptown. Could take them with me, just in case. Then again, drink one now, it'll give me a little extra edge for the trip, give me an extra day maybe if I get stuck. That's the ticket: drink one, leave one in the fridge. Last thing I want is to come home late and not have any food in the house. I pop the fridge, guzzle a pint and stuff the empty in the biohazard bag.

OK, good to go. Now, where to?

I need a name. I need a name and a ride. I can't roll up there and just start walking the streets sniffing the air for the Vyrus. What am I gonna do, grab some slob from the Hood and start pummeling him until he gives me something I can use? Besides, just being white up there is gonna make me stand out. I need a name, someone to start with.

Christian might know someone up there. He doesn't go much above Houston, but back before he got infected he used to ride the whole city. He could also give me a lift up there. But crossing Coalition turf on the sissy seat of his Harley with a dozen top-hatted, howling-mad Dusters on hogback isn't the subtle play I'm looking for. When a renegade Clan of Vampyre bikers crosses onto your turf, you're bound to notice. Scratch Christian.

Chubby Freeze might have a name. He's also about the only brother I'm tight with. That could mean something when you're talking about dealing in the Hood. But it'll be someone on the fringe. Chubby's porn business keeps him in touch with the kind of people who are in touch with my life. But he's not of the world. Any names he gives me will be a couple steps removed from what I need. And he won't be able to help me with transport. Chubby's not in the know enough to see the dangers involved with getting from 14th to 110th.

There's really only one name. I'm running circles around it, but there's really only one guy who might be able to help me here. One guy who doesn't have any skin in the game, who won't be looking for a payday for giving me some information, who won't be looking for ways to stick it in my back if he sees an angle. But he'll sure as hell find a way to make me pay. And whatever he wants, I'll have to come across with it.

So I stuff the final remains of my emergency fund in my pocket, tuck my switchblade into my boot and the .32 into my waistband, lock up tight, and head west to see Daniel.

—Simon.
—Daniel here?
—Naturally. Where else would he be?
—Can I talk to him?
—Certainly. I'm sure he'll be happy to see you, Simon.
—Don't call me that.
—You would prefer?
—Joe.
The bony Enclave runs his eyes over me.
—Joe. It doesn't suit you.
—Just use it.
—Of course, Joe.
He gives me one of those oh-so-meaningful smiles these fucks are always giving and leads me inside. The door rolls closed behind us and we cross the warehouse's concrete floor. My eyes adjust to the near pitch black and the Enclave emerge from the darkness. Two rows of about fifty emaciated sickly pale men and women in white sit on the floor facing one another. In front of each is a vessel of some sort; anything from a thimble to a cracked coffee cup to a pewter wine goblet. Two Enclave, one for

each row, work their way down the lines pouring blood into the vessels. One of the servers carries a Pyrex measuring cup, the other an iced tea pitcher with a much-chipped smiling sun enameled on its side. The Enclave accept a tiny amount of the blood, some no more than a teaspoon, some as much as a quarter pint. Several hold up their hand, refusing any at all. Whatever they take, it's all they'll have for a week, maybe longer. Feeding time at the asylum.

These crazy fuckers, sitting here in the dark, fasting, meditating, and practicing their crazy martial arts. And Daniel, lord of the crazy fuckers, thinks I'm one of them. He says that's my *true nature*. But this ain't me. Depriving myself, throttling the Vyrus to the edge of starvation, that's not my idea of fun. Even if I have been there. Even if I have stood at the very limit and felt what the Vyrus does to you, the jolt it sends through your system as it spurs you to feed before it dies. Even if I've felt it and know why they cultivate it, it's not for me. You *have* to be a crazy fucker to try to live like that all the time. And that's what they're doing: trying to live like that all the time, searching for the perfect balance, letting the Vyrus consume them in the slowest increments possible, teasing death out in the hopes that one of them will defeat it, one of them will be annihilated but left whole at the same time. One of them converted by the Vyrus they believe to be a spiritual force, converted and made able to teach the others, able to lead them onto the streets, where they can convert everyone else. Or kill them, whichever seems best.

It's weird shit. Far weirder than I'm willing to believe myself. Or it was anyway. Before Daniel showed me some weirder shit. Before he told me about that thing. The Wraith. Now I'm not sure what to believe. But it's still not for me. No matter how many times Daniel says it is.

* * *

—Simon. Look at you. So healthy and well fed. You're just about glowing.

—Daniel. You're looking fit yourself.

He laughs, unbending his skeletal frame from the floor of his little cubicle in the loft above the warehouse floor. He takes my hand. I feel the heat that pulses from his fingers and palm. I run hot, anyone with the Vyrus runs a little hot; Daniel scorches.

He holds my hand and looks me over.

—Yes. Just about glowing.

—Thanks.

He releases my hand.

—It wasn't meant as a compliment. I was trying to express displeasure.

—Sorry, missed it.

—Oh well, passive aggression was never my strength. With my own children. Did you know I had kids?

—Nope.

—I did. Long time ago.

His eyes drift.

—Two girls. Twins. And a wife. I wanted boys. A cliché. She gave me the girls. And several miscarriages. She died of one in the end. Girls. I could never get them to do as I said. A poor father.

His eyes come back to me, refocus, and he shakes his head.

—Odd. I don't think of them much. That other life, I hardly think of it at all. The sleep before waking. Before I discovered my true nature.

He shrugs.

—Senility at last. Sit.

He points at the floor and I take a seat. He takes a place across from me and rests his back against the wall.

—What's on your mind, Simon? I assume you're not here to reconsider joining us.

—Nope.

—Something else then. Information I suppose.

—Yep.

He waits. I wait. He waits longer and I give in.

—I need a name.

He rolls his eyes.

—A name. You already have two. The one you were born with and the one you gave yourself.

—Someone else's name.

—Whose?

—I don't know. I need an Uptown name. I have to go above One-ten and I need a contact, someone to help me with the territory.

He scratches the ribs that protrude from beneath his skin, his fingers all but disappearing into the gaps between them.

—Above One-ten. The Hood. Luther X's turf.

—X is dead.

—Is he?

I watch his eyes, trying to see if he's playing me. They're unreadable; black stones sunk deep in dark wells.

—He got taken out over two years ago. Coalition assassins. They say. His warlord runs it now: DJ Grave Digga.

—*They say.* Well, I would say the Vyrus was simply done with him, consumed him and passed him into the other world. The real world.

—Tell that to the guy stuck the daggers in X's eyes.

—The instrument is immaterial. The Vyrus has him now.

—Yeah. Right. Daniel, I'm not telling you anything you don't know. You know the X is gone. You know everything. What I need to know is if you have a name, and if you'll share it with me.

He stretches his legs out, crosses them at the ankles and tucks his hands behind his head.

—Long trip to the Hood.

—Yep. That's why I should be getting started.

—What do you need up there?

I could lie. But he'd know.

—I'm looking into something for Terry Bird. His new fish are into something.

He raises his eyebrows.

—Terry's new fish are into something he doesn't know about. How unlike him. What is it?

—They have a new high.

—A *new* high?

I lick my lips.

—They're shooting the Vyrus. Someone found a way to, I don't know, preserve it outside a body, and the new fish are shooting it.

—Oh.

He closes his eyes.

—That again.

I blink.

—Excuse me?

He opens his eyes.

—Nevermind, Simon.

—Did you say, *again*?

He takes his hands from behind his head, draws his knees up and rests his forearms on them.

—There is nothing new under the sun, Simon. It's all as it has always been. There is only one change, and the world is still waiting for it. The world is an egg, waiting to be born, waiting for Enclave to usher it across. Until then, it's all the same old shit.

I lean forward.

—Sure, sure, you'll transmute yourself into ectoplasm and lead your crusade and we'll all be turned into pixie dust and join the cosmos. But you said, *again*.

—Did I? Funny. Well, as I also said before, *senility at last*.

—Daniel.

—Simon. Enough. I'm tired. You said you wanted a name.

—I do.

—The Enclave who brought you up, did you recognize him?

—Man, you all look the same to me. All just a bunch of cadavers waiting to happen. You're the only one I can tell apart. And that's just because you look more dead than the rest.

He laughs, lips peeling up over gray gums, mouth open wide, barking laughter.

—*More dead.* You know better, Simon. I'm more alive than you, more alive than anyone else with the Vyrus. Certainly more alive than the sleepwalkers out there on the streets with no idea of the universe's true nature.

I shift, unfolding my legs.

—A name?

He nods.

—A name. Yes. The Enclave who brought you up, he used to be with the Hood. He'll give you a name.

—Good enough.

I push myself up off the floor.

—Simon.

—Yeah?

—I will want something in return.

So much for a clean getaway.

—What's that?

—We talked the last time you were here.

—Uh-huh.

—I told you something.

—You told me you thought you were failing.

He looks at the floor, running his fingers over a nail head that sticks up from the floorboards.

—That's true, I am. But I told you something else.

Fuck.

—I don't remember.

—Don't be like that, girls.

—What?

He looks up.

—Did I?

He taps his forehead.

—What did I say?

—Nothing.

He watches me out of those holes in his face.

—Senility. Strange. Well.

He stands.

—You should go.

—What about?

—Hm?

—You said you'd want something for the name.

—Yes. Yes. Come see me, Simon. Come see me more often.

—Daniel, I'll try, but. I'm pretty busy most of the time.

He puts his hand on my shoulder. The heat radiates through my jacket.

—Come see me, Simon. It's what I want.

Like I said, it'll cost more than blood or money.

—OK. I'll come.

—Good. Good. Now go downstairs and get your name.

I start for the stairs.

—Names. Simon, that reminds me.

—Uh-huh?

—You had a perfectly good one: Simon. It suits you. It says something about you. Why did you change it?

—Lots of infecteds change their names.

—I know. But why did you?

—I don't know. Terry said a new name was a good idea.

—And why the name you chose?

—Shit. I was seventeen. I was just turned into a Vampyre. Joe Pitt. I thought it sounded cool.

He laughs again.

—You're right. It does. It does. Well. Careful in the Hood. And come see me when you get back. *Joe*.

—Yeah.

The Enclave who showed me in is waiting for me at the bottom of the stairs, sitting on the last step.

—Daniel said you know the Hood turf, said you'd have a name of someone I could talk to up there.

—He means Percy.

—OK. Where do I find him?

He leads me to a work area under the loft. Some benches with tools for doing basic repairs on the warehouse, a sink, a stove with a huge boiling pot on top. He finds a pencil and paper and writes down an address on 150th, near Jackie Robinson Park. I look at the scrap of paper.

—What do I tell him?

—Nothing. I'll let him know you're coming.

—How you gonna do that?

He gestures to the warehouse.

—We don't have much, but I do know how to use a pay phone.

I slip the paper into my pocket.

—Any tips on how I can get up there?

He stands on tiptoe to look into the pot, then reaches for a giant wooden spoon and gives the contents a stir.

—You could do what the Duke suggested.

—The Duke?

—Ellington.

—Yeah, what was his idea?

He smiles.

—Take the A train.

—Been saving that one up for a rainy day?

He shrugs.

I look at his skin, trying to find some evidence that he was ever anything but pasty white, ever a guy that could have been with the Hood. Can't find it.

I point at the pot.

—By the way, what's cooking?

—Bones.

—No kidding? Thought you guys already ate.

—One of us failed last week. We'll crack his bones and eat the marrow tonight. You could stay.

—I'll pass.

I leave him there, stirring his pot. At the warehouse door, I pause. I turn around and look back up at the loft. Daniel is at the top of the stairs, watching me.

I remember what else he told me, what he told me last time, after he told me that he's failing. He told me someone would have to replace him.

Well, fuck that, that's none of my fucking business whatsoever.

I haul the door open and walk out into the night, leaving the smell of steaming bones behind.

The A train. As if I couldn't have figured that for myself. As if I haven't been trying like hell to avoid it.

I come out of the Enclave warehouse onto Little West 12th and think about the A train. All this territory around here is no-man's-land. This is the turf no one wants because it's too close to the Enclave. I can grab the A at 14th, but that will put me right on the Coalition's southern border. They'll have spotters. Better I go to 4th Street and catch it there. Stay in no-man's-land, where no one is watching. Once I'm on the A, I'll have more than enough opportunities to get caught out.

The Coalition doesn't like anyone riding the rails under their turf. The major stops, Grand Central, Penn Station, Times Square, Columbus Circle, you come walking out of one of those stations and you're nailed. They got spotters living in apartments, watching over the exits. Slobs that never go out. They just sit there at the window all night, snapping pictures through telephoto lenses, changing videotapes in their cameras and flipping through facebooks to see if they recognize anyone. Rent is paid by the Coalition, along with an allowance to cover takeout from the local diner. Once a week an enforcer comes in, picks up the video and the film and the logbook, and drops off a fresh pint. The smaller stops, they got guys there, too. May only be every other stop, but you don't know which ones. Just like you don't know which train one of their enforcers will be cruising, looking for interlopers. If I get on at West 4th and ride express to 145th, I don't have to worry about those spotters above ground. But from 14th to 110th, anywhere in there I could end up with an enforcer on the train. How do I know all this? Because the Coalition wants everybody to know. It's their way of saying, *Stay off the grass. Trespassers will be prosecuted.* And if they let you know about the spotters and the patrols, that means they're only the tip of the iceberg.

The A train. Thanks for the help.

I take a cab to West 4th to save time. I think about telling the cabbie to turn the thing around and take me uptown, but that's a worse play than the subway. On the train I'll only have to worry about the patrols, and there can only be so many. In a cab, going through rush hour traffic, there are too many chances of getting spotted from the sidewalk or another car. Too random. So the Duke Ellington Express it is.

I get out of my cab at 4th and Sixth. It's dark and cold, but the lights inside The Cage are on and a half dozen guys in sweats are playing three on three. I stop and light a smoke and watch. I'm in a hurry, but this is a long fucking train ride and I can't smoke down in the hole. There's a small cluster of people standing next to the tall chain-link fence watching the showboating street-ballers inside. They whip no-look passes at each other or lob alley-oops. No one plays D. I finish my smoke and light another. 4th to 145th? Even on the express that's a two-smoke ride.

It's no-man's-land. I can take the time for the smoke. No one comes onto this turf. No one risks walking across it, let alone hunting or doing business on it. No one risks doing anything that might offend the Enclave. Piss the freaks off and they come for you. End up eating *your* fucking marrow.

Eating your marrow?

Doesn't it have something to do with blood? Shouldn't they get sick if they eat another Vampyre's marrow? I mean, even if you boil those bones, the Vyrus has been in there. Shit. That's weird. And what did Daniel say? *That again.* What the fuck was that about?

Color me pensive. Color me lost in thought and avoiding getting on the train, lighting a third cigarette without even thinking about it, because that's my story. That's my excuse for why I don't smell Tom until the fucker jams the barrel of his gun in my back.

—What is it, Pitt? Old dog syndrome? New tricks just don't sink in? Can't get it through your head to stop fucking around on my watch?

He shoves the gun a little deeper into my backbone, hurrying me east on 4th toward Washington Square Park and the Society border.

—Hadn't heard no-man's was part of your beat now.

—Fuck off. You know what I'm talking about. Shaking down pledged members on Society turf, going into their homes and grilling them on Society business.

—Where you get that?

—Think you're the only one who can pump Philip Sax for information? Get out the rubber hoses and that pussy opens up and spills everything. Didn't even have to lay in to him. We did anyway, just to teach him a lesson, but we didn't have to.

He's alone. Tom's not the brightest bulb, but he knew better than to follow me over here with a troop. Enclave would have had his ass for that. But he'll have partisans waiting across the border. We set foot on the far curb of Washington Square East and I'll be bracketed by his boys right away.

—Not even Terry's gonna be able to help you on this one, Pitt. Poking on our turf without our say-so. Poking into official Society business. And then crossing over to report to those assholes? Fucking-A, I knew you stooged for the Coalition, but Enclave? That's just sick. Fronting for those mujahideen motherfuckers.

—Got your head on a swivel, Tom? Keeping your eyes peeled? One of those motherfuckers hears you talking about them like that, they'll find you in your safe house and flay you alive with their teeth.

—Fuck off. Fuck off and walk.

I glance back at him.

—Seriously, you ever see them in action? Scary shit. Like Bruce Lee on speed. Only like if you had to cut off his head or something to kill him. Saw two of them spar once. One got his arm torn off, kept coming. Other arm came off, kept coming. Got his leg wrapped around the other guy's neck, brought him down and scissored him. Squeezed the guy 'til his eyes about popped out. Whole time he's spraying this white gunk from his stumps. That was sparring. Scaaaaary shit.

—Shut the fuck up.

I glance back again as we cross Washington Square West. His eyes are zipping side to side.

The light is against us at Fifth. I step off the curb as a battered and graffitied delivery van whips around the corner. Tom grabs my left arm and pulls me back into him, the gun getting pinned sideways between us. He knows right away he's made a mistake. Poor him.

He tries to keep his grip on my arm while he gets the gun barrel jammed back where it belongs. And he is a strong fucker. But Mr. Two Pints In Two Days is stronger just now. And faster. I go left, twist my arm free and clip him with my elbow as I dodge into the street and around to the far side of a NYC Parks Department pickup sitting at the curb. He takes a couple steps around it to the right. I go right. He goes left. I go left. He shows me the gun, flashing it low and out of sight from the people on the sidewalk, reminding me who's in charge.

—Get the fuck over here, Pitt.

—Why?

—Get the fuck over here or I'll shoot you.

—Park's full of undercover cops looking to bust the dealers in there. Pull the trigger and they'll be on your ass in a flash. Throw you in a cell. That's if you're lucky, if the Enclave aren't watching. Waiting to see if you're gonna cause a scene.

—Shut the fuck up.

—Shit, Tom, don't you ever bother to put together a plan? I mean a good one.

—Shut the fuck up.

—Know what Terry calls you behind your back?

—Shut!

—*Halfcock.*

—The!

—I assumed it was cuz you're always going off that way.

—Fuck!

—But maybe he knows something I don't.

—Up!

—If you get what I mean.

He gets it.

He comes storming around the hood of the truck, shoving the pistol into one of the huge pockets of his army surplus jacket, those dirty blond dreads flying behind him.

—Gonna kick your fucking ass. Gonna beat your fucking face like I beat it before.

He did beat my face pretty bad that time. I got a gap between two molars that used to be filled by a third molar before he knocked it out. That pissed me off. So when he comes toward me with his fist raised, I let him tag me once on the neck and grab his sleeve and pull him close so he thinks I want to grapple, and then I use my free hand to whip out the .32 that's still tucked in the back of my waistband because he was too fucking stupid to give me a little pat-down when he got the drop on me, and while he's trying to wrap his hand around my throat I press the barrel against the top of his thigh and pull the trigger.

The shot is muffled by our bodies, but the folks who were just slowing down to look at our little scuffle decide it's best to keep moving along. Tom falls to the ground, hands pressed over the hole in his leg, and I turn around and start walking quickly back toward Sixth. I mix in with the folks a little farther down the sidewalk and listen for the telltale sound of running feet that would mean there actually were a couple cops in the park wasting time on the dime-bag dealers.

I don't bother looking back to see what Tom is doing. He'll be on his feet by now, but he won't try coming after me with that hole in his leg. He'll be moving as quickly as possible back toward the Society border, making for the partisans he has posted there, hoping like hell there are no cops around. Once he crosses onto his own turf there'll be a safe house right around the corner, the place he was planning to take me.

I reach The Cage and walk past it and down the steps into the West 4th Street station, crossing my fingers that Tom didn't get nabbed. I might get away with shooting him, but if he gets busted, if it ends up being that kind of scene, I may as well take this train to the end of the line and get out and start walking 'til I walk right off the edge of the island.

It's just after six. The train is packed tight, the commuters squashed against each other in the aisles bitterly eyeballing the commuters squashed together on the seats. I press through the clot of bodies that always forms around the doors and find a little elbow room at the end of the car, the last car on the train. We pull out and everyone lurches.

We cover the distance to 14th in a couple minutes. A bunch of people spill out of the train to make a connection, but even more cram themselves on. The intercom buzzes static as the conductor shouts at the passengers, telling them not to block the doors. The doors close and we're off. Across the Coalition border.

I stand a little taller than most of the bodies squeezed in here. I use the height to scan the faces. I don't smell anything I shouldn't, just the rank air and the sweat slowly starting to trickle beneath everyone's parkas. There could be a Coalition Renfield on board, but I don't see anything. Fair enough. The real danger starts at 34th, the first stop in Coalition turf.

The train zips through the local stop at 23rd. Somewhere in the middle of the car a man too short for me to see through the bodies is yelling at the top of his lungs, telling the passengers about how he was burned out of his apartment and how he needs ten dollars and forty-seven cents to have enough to stay in a transient hotel tonight. I think about Terry.

Figure Tom's move one of two ways. Either he told Terry I'd been poking around and Terry rubber-stamped his play on me, or he invoked his security authority and made the move himself. Terry might have cleared it, just to keep from admitting that I was doing some clandestine shit for him. Just to keep a cover on whatever his angle is. Figure it's more likely Tom did it on his own. After my lengthy chat with Terry, Tom's smart enough to know something's up. He sure as shit knows Phil is my number one snitch. He probably didn't bother to follow me at first, just went after Phil. Once he beat everything out of him, he would have checked in with The Count.

We jerk to a stop at the 34th Street platform. I get some breathing room as the Bridge and Tunnel commuters pile off and make for Penn Station, but I lose it right away as the Midtown workers heading for Queens and the Bronx come on.

Figure Tom wouldn't have to threaten The Count. Hell, The Count is one of his. Tom just has to ask him what I wanted, what I was looking into. Figure that was too close to the bone. Close to something anyway. Close to all these new fish popping up and the whole shooting the Vyrus thing. After that, all he needed to do was stake out my pad and tail me over to the Enclave. Fucker's definitely got a bee in his bonnet over this shit.

42nd Street, Times Square. The train exhales a rancid mass of drones and sucks in a fresh mass of the same. The doors close. 59th Street and relative safety dead ahead. The A runs express from 59th all the way to 125th, inside Hood turf. After 59th, any enforcers riding the express will be taking a big chance.

Yeah, Tom's definitely got some skin in this game. Then again, it could all be Terry. He might have sent Tom after me himself. Maybe I got too close too fast when I talked to The Count. Maybe Terry's finally gotten tired of having me on Society turf and the whole thing is the start of his play to get rid of me.

Something tickles my nose.

Blood.

Someone in the car is bleeding. Bleeding fresh. Not menstrual blood, not an old cut opening up, but fresh blood. Someone just opened a small wound.

I don't look up. It's the oldest trick in the book, so I don't look up. Could be a nosebleed. Could be a little kid's tooth just fell out. Could be some lady got jarred by the train swaying from side to side and ran the sharp tip of her nail file up under her nail. Still, I don't look up. 'Cause it just as easily could be someone just pricked their hand with a tiny lance and is watching everybody on the train, watching to see who jerks their face toward the source of the blood. The oldest trick in the book.

I keep my head down and scent the air. Someone has stepped in dog crap. A businessman had to puke after his four martini lunch and tried to cover the smell with a fistful of Altoids. Someone just bought a CD player and I smell the new plastic as they tear open the bubble-pack it's wrapped in. Shampoo. Ink from the fat tip of a felt-tip pen as a kid tags a window of the car. Someone had sex just before she caught the train and semen dribbles down the inside of her thigh. Foot powder. Tiger Balm. A Hershey's bar. French fries. A puff of deodorant released as someone unzips their jacket. Hair spray, hair gel, hair mousse, hair cream, hair wax. Over a dozen types of perfumes, twice as many lotions and creams. Once I focus on all of it, once I let that lizard part of my brain that deals with smells start sifting them all out and identifying them, it makes me want to vomit. I bite it back and take another whiff.

The stagnant *menudo* someone had for breakfast carried up from their stomach with a belch. The urine staining the adult diaper of a senior citizen. The mold caking the old paperbacks crammed into the sack carried by the homeless guy. The years of sweat soaked into the rim of a kid's favorite baseball cap escaping as he pulls the bill farther to the side. The smell of spent fireworks clinging to my gun, the stale cigarette smoke that always surrounds me, last night's bourbon still in my throat, the socks I didn't bother to change today.

It's awful. All of it. But nowhere in it do I smell the Vyrus.

Nowhere but in my own blood. I try to stop, try to breathe easy and focus my mind on something else. I bring my head up and let my eyes bob and drift around, lazily taking in the faces around me. There is no trace of the Vyrus in here other than my own, but that doesn't mean I'm safe. The bleeder could be a savvy Renfield, one trained by Coalition enforcers to look for a sniffer. Or it could be worse. It could be a Van Helsing. If it is a Van Helsing, if it's a staker who knows enough to prick his finger and wait to see who takes an interest, he'll be dangerous as hell. A Van Helsing that knows the game? Shit. He won't care about borders and treaties and turf. A Van Helsing will ride this car with me all the way up to the Hood. I get off the train with a Van Helsing on my ass, bring that to Hood turf? There's no punishment that covers that, nothing but getting tumored by the sun.

The train slows, pulling to a stop at 59th Street, Columbus Circle.

The Upper West Side types hurry off the train to rush home and meet their spouses, who are also coming home from work, so they can both kiss their trophy babies before their Jamaican nannies put the little ones to bed so they can go out to dinner and not talk to one another. They are replaced by the far upper Manhattan Caribbeans who have finished cleaning houses and walking dogs and working their shifts at Balducci's and are heading home to fuck up their own children and not talk to their spouses. I watch them. I don't bother with subtlety now, I watch everyone who stays on the train, looking for the thing that is not like the others.

The doors try to close and get caught on one of the overstuffed bags of the homeless guy. The conductor is on the intercom again, screaming through the static.

—DO NOT BLOCK THE DOORS AT THE BACK OF THE TRAIN!

The doors slide open for a moment, but rather than stepping through them the homeless guy adjusts his grip on the bag and gets caught again as the doors slide shut.

—STOP BLOCKING THE DOORS BACK THERE!

They open again and a couple people on the platform take advantage of the opportunity to squeeze in around the homeless guy, who gets stuck again.

—GET OUT OF THE WAY OF THE DOORS BACK THERE! YOU'RE HOLDING EVERYBODY UP! THE TRAIN WILL NOT MOVE UNTIL YOU STOP BLOCKING THE DOORS!

A young guy gets off his seat and tries to help the homeless guy with his bags. The homeless guy jerks away from him, cursing, and the doors close on him again.

—STOP BLOCKING THE DOORS! STOP BLOCKING THE DOORS! STOP BLOCKING THE DOORS!

The kid throws up his hands and goes to sit back down, but someone has already grabbed his seat. The doors open and the homeless guy hefts his bags and lets a businessman on the train. Then he steps clear of the doors as they finally close all the way. Just before they close, just before they seal us in here nice and tight, I finally notice the fresh red stain on the side of one of his bags: the spot of blood from his pricked fingertip. And as the train begins to move, I smell something new in the car, something that smells like me, and I catch the eye of the businessman the homeless guy stepped so easily aside for at that last moment. He's staring at me, not bothering to hide it. And why shouldn't we stare at each other? We're stuck together in here all the way up.

Fucking Coalition. Got a Renfield riding the line doing the homeless thing. I try to remember if he got on at 14th or if he was already on the train at 4th. That would be like the Coalition, to have the sap riding the whole line, dangling out there to get picked off. I wonder if he did the finger-prick trick because he spotted me. Does Predo have that big a hard-on for me? Does he have my photo circulating through his Renfields? Maybe not, maybe it's just standard for them: Let a little blood before Columbus Circle and see if anyone bites. If they do, you block the door long enough for an enforcer patrolling the platform to get on the train. Well, whether he had me from the get-go or not, he must have picked me up when I started sniffing around. Good Renfield, that one. Ever see him again, I'll find out what his blood tastes like. But this guy here giving me the eyeball? He's another matter entirely.

Enforcer. Coalition Gestapo. He'll be well fed. He'll be armed. He'll have some moves. He stands in the middle of the car, glancing at me every now and then to see that I don't do anything rash. Don't know what that would be. My back is resting against the rear of the train. I suppose I could smash the glass on the emergency exit and dive out of the speeding train onto the tracks and hope I don't break my neck or tumble into the third rail. But I'll save that as a final option.

The train is still full, the line dead ends at 207th. I can either get off in the middle of Hood turf with the enforcer on my ass, or ride the line all the way to the end and transfer to a downtown train. Of course, that will mean crossing back over Coalition turf. I don't know if this guy's got any backup on board, but if I'm still on this thing with him and we go back down to 59th, he's bound to pick up some help. At some point before 14th, they'll make a move to drag me off. That or see how far I want to ride. Into no-man's? Lower Manhattan? I don't even want to think about Lower Manhattan and all the tiny, crazy Clans down there. Across the river and into the bush? Who the fuck knows what goes on once you cross the water. Nice choices.

I give him a good once-over. Looks late twenties. Not that that means anything. Got on one of those nice suits Predo has them all wear. Hair slicked back. Not as big as me, but there's a build under the suit.

The train's been racing the line, cutting through the local stations and leaving them behind. The driver's got the pedal down, making up for the time he lost when the Renfield blocked the doors. I see a sign for 110th flicker past. That's it, we're gone, above the line and in the Hood.

The enforcer is staring into my eyes now, trying to put the voodoo on me; give me the willies with his undead badassness. I give it back to him. Fat fucking enforcer. Overfed. Pampered. Coalition paying all his bills, doing all his hunting for him. Sitting tight until Dexter Predo says jump. *How high, Mr. Predo, how high?* I know this fucker. I know what he's got. Fuck this guy. He wants to play eye-kung fu, wants to try and put the fear in me? We can play. We can play.

The train stops at 125th. He keeps his stare on, shooting me all his fantasies about how big the world of hurt's gonna be when he lays his hands on me. I nod my head at him and walk off the train, into the station in the heart of the Hood. Right underneath the intersection of Martin Luther King and Frederick Douglass Boulevards. He hesitates, then jumps off between the doors before they can close. That's right, motherfucker, made you blink.

—OK, guy.

I take the stairs up from the platform one at a time.

—All right, you showed your stones. Now let's go back to the platform and wait for a downtown train.

I come to the top of the stairs and take a look around. They're doing a ton of construction in the station and the whole Uptown half is sealed off behind sheets of plywood painted bright MTA blue. If I want to exit that way, I'll have to go back to the platform and take the stairs at the far end.

—I'm not gonna fuck around with you here, guy. You come back down or I'll haul you down.

The enforcer is still at my shoulder, still talking.

—No shit, guy, you *don't* want to fuck with me. Just turn around and let's get on a train.

Right next to the bank of MetroCard entrances, they got one of those old-fashioned turnstiles. One of the big steel exits that spin like threshers, the tines of the turnstile passing through the bars of the gate.

—Seriously, guy, you don't want to leave this station. You got yourself in enough trouble crossing our turf.

Some kids are fucking around at the MetroCard entrance, a boy outside and his girl inside, making out until she hears her train and has to run to catch it. People bunch up at the other two entrances. I head for the old turnstile.

The enforcer keeps yapping.

—Down here they might not do anything. But you go up those stairs and it will be different. The niggers spot you up there and they will take you apart.

An old lady tries to spin through the turnstile and snags the handle of her shopping bag on one of the bars. I tug it free and she smiles at me. I smile back.

—I'm telling you now, fucker, do not leave this station. Do not leave this station or you will be in a world of shit.

I give him my smile.

—Who you trying to convince, me or you?

I step through the spinning bars. He stays inside.

—Guy, you are fucking up in a big way.

I stand with the gate between us.

—Just come on out and drag me back. Or is there a treaty or something? You step outside that gate, you gonna be abusing the peace between the Coalition and the Hood? That it?

—This is it, you walk over to that entrance and get your ass back in here and get on a fucking train with me now.

I shrug.

—No money left on my MetroCard. Sorry.

He starts to push through the turnstile.

—You stupid fuck.

As he comes through I put out my hand.

—Look, take it easy, man, no need for a scene. I'll go quietly.

—Too late for that, you piece of shit Rogue.

He makes to slap my hand away. I grab his sleeve, yank him forward, grab the bars of the turnstile with my free hand, push him into the set-bars of the gate, and swing the turnstile around, smashing the square steel bars into his back. A few of his ribs make a nice cracking sound. I slam the turnstile against him two more times, trying to force his face through the gate bars. No dice. Then I run for the exit, out the tunnel, and up the stairs.

That was stupid. That was fucking stupid. Making war on a Coalition enforcer on Hood turf was fucking stupid.

But fuck him.

He got what he asked for. Trying to mad-dog me. Trying to make me show yellow and climb back on that train. I look back at the station entrance to see if he's bouncing up the stairs after me. Not yet. Must have given him a good shot to the head. But he'll be up and running. Unless the stationmaster calls the cops from his booth. Could be with an MTA cop right now. That'd be sweet. Let him deal with cops and EMTs and shit. But figure it's best not to count on it. Figure it's best to move.

I'm walking fast. I look up at a street sign and see I'm pointed the wrong way, heading down. I need to turn around, get moving up toward 150th and this Percy guy. I turn the corner onto 123rd. I'll circle the block before I head up so I don't have to go back by that subway entrance.

I turn the corner and two guys wearing huge black parkas with Ecko rhinos embroidered on the breast grab me and shove me against a wall. A black Humvee bounces over the curb, stops next to us and the rear door flies open. The two guys throw me inside and someone shoves the soles of both his Timberlands into my neck, pats me down, pulls my .32 out of my pants and sticks the barrel in my eye.

—That was some stupid shit back there. Some seriously stupid shit.

—What Predo thinkin'? Muthafucka out his brain? Insane in the membrane?

—Who?

—Doan *who* me, muthafucka. Predo. Dexta mothafuckin' Predo.

—Never heard of him.

—*Never heard of him.* That what he said, *Never heard of him,* that what muthafucka said?

The one-armed barber nods.

—Sounded like it, Digga.

DJ Grave Digga nods and looks back in the mirror.

—*Never heard of him.* Mutha. Fucka.

He shifts his eyes and looks at my face reflected just behind his, pinned between the two Ecko rhinos.

—Beat on that muthafucka a little.

They beat on me a little and then they stand me back up.

—I ax you again, what Predo thinkin' sendin' you an' one them fuckin' enforcers up here?

I wipe the blood out of my eyes with the back of my hand.

—What was that name again?

—Shit. Sheeit.

He snaps his fingers and points at the chair next to his.

—Sit his ass down.

The rhinos pull me over and push me into the barber chair.

Digga looks at the barber.

—You done yet?

The barber taps Digga's upper lip and Digga slides his tongue under it, pushing it out. The barber scratches his straight razor over the raised spot, sculpting the edge of Digga's pencil moustache a little sharper. Then he sets the razor aside, squirts some oil from a dispenser into his palm and slaps it onto Digga's face before he whips the smock off his chest, snapping it once to shake loose the hair clinging to its folds.

Digga gets out of the chair and leans close to the mirror, inspecting his face. The barber stands behind him with a hand mirror, angling it so Digga can see the back of his head.

—Nice.

He looks at my reflection again.

—You want a cut? Muthafucka knows his bizniz. Best damn barber in the Hood.

—No, thanks.

—No, you have a cut. Lookin' a little bedraggled, a little raggedy.

He gestures to the barber.

—Clean the man up. Shave and a cut. On me.

The barber comes behind me, rolls down my collar, tucks a piece of tissue inside, snaps the smock and lays it over me.

—Hows you like it?

I run a hand through my hair.

—Just off the ears maybe. Natural in back.

He cuts the air once or twice with his scissors.

—White hair ain't my thing.

I shrug.

—It grows back.

He starts clipping.

Digga leans his ass on the counter in front of me.

—*It grows back.* Hear that? Muthafucka says his hair *grows back.*

Ain't the only shit grown back, huh? Folks like you and us all in here.

He points around the barbershop, taking in the rhinos, the one-armed barber, and the guy in the Timberlands sitting in a chair by the door reading a copy of *The Source*. Timberlands there is wearing my hide, the nice black leather jacket that Evie gave me.

Digga takes them all in.

—We all grow shit back.

—If you say so.

He laughs.

—*If I say so.* Muthafucka. Give it to you, you cool. You busted out in the wrong place at the wrong time, you got yo ass dragged up in my shop, got us Hoodies all about yo ass, an you still cool. Give you that. Give you that.

—Thanks.

—Don't be thankin' me. Shit. Want to do somethin' might help with this situation, you start tellin' me what the fuck Predo thinkin'. Start talking 'bout that 'fore you get somethin' cut off don't grow back.

—Sorry. I missed that name again. What was it?

He crosses his arms and drops his head.

—Mutha. Fucka.

He looks up.

—Cool-ass mutha. What yo name, cool-ass?

I look at the barber.

—Leave as much length as you can on top.

I look at Digga.

—Pitt.

—Oh! Snap!

He claps his hands.

—Pitt. Joe muthafuckin' Pitt. You Terry Bird's bitch. You his pet

Rogue bitch, ain't you? This shit gettin' curiouser an' curiouser. What Bird send you up here for? His hippie ass know better than to send no Rogue agent up here without no transit agreement.

—He didn't send me.

—Uh-huh. You jus wand'rin' up here all by yo lonesome. Sight-seein' like.

—Heard the fried chicken and waffles can't be beat.

The barber stops cutting.

Digga puckers his lips.

—What that you just say?

—Heard about the fried chicken and waffles.

—That's thin ice, bitch. That fried chicken talk is some thin ass ice for a muthafucka to be treadin' on.

—Sorry.

—That right you sorry.

—Not like I said I was here for the watermelon season.

His eyes open wide.

—Uh-uh. You did not. You did not.

He points at the barber.

—You done with that shit?

The barber looks at my head.

—Doan look no worse none than when I started.

Digga flaps his hand at him.

—Leave it, leave it. Lather muthafucka up and give him a scrape.

The barber sets his scissors aside, stirs a brush around in an old coffee cup and starts lathering my cheeks and neck.

Digga turns his back to me and faces the mirror again. He flicks his pinkie over the tips of his moustache.

—*Watermelon season*. That some classic shit. That some good, old-skool, stereotypin', racist humor that is. You a racist, Pitt?

The barber puts his index finger on the point of my chin and tilts my head back.

—Not really. I just don't like assholes.

—Muthafucka!

He grabs the razor from the barber, pushes him aside and tucks the blade up under my jaw.

—Asshole this, muthafucka. You tell me what you doin' up here. *Now,* muthafucka. Want to know what you doin' comin' up here trailin' a fuckin' enforcer behind you. You on Predo's tip or whorin' for Bird, I doan care, you just talk, muthafucka, talk. And doan move yo mouth too much or you slit yo own damn throat 'fore I can.

—Not here for Predo.

—Oh, you know that name now, do ya?

—Not here for Bird.

—Who for?

—I'm here on my own, on my own business.

He adds an ounce of pressure to the blade and the skin splits and I feel the blood start to run.

—*On your own bizniz.* A Rogue out traipsin' 'cross Coalition turf, takin' a spin up ta the Hood on his own bizniz. Bullshit.

—It's my own thing.

—You got someone gonna vouch that shit? You got someone gonna throw down for you on that? You got a brotha gonna back you?

I don't say anything. Got nothing to say.

—That your answer, son? Got no names for me?

The blade slices deeper, the edge raking the cartilage sheath around my esophagus.

I throw the only name I have.

—Chubby Freeze.

He eases slightly on the razor.

—*Chubby Freeze.* That downtown niggah. He vouch you?

—He might.

—Hunh.

He lets go of my head and snaps at Timberlands.

—Chubby Freeze. You got that niggah's digits?

—Ya-huh.

—Blow 'im up. Get that niggah on the phone.

Digga turns to the mirror and adjusts his collar and tie.

—Lucky I di'nt get no blood on this tie.

Timberlands waves his arm.

—Got 'im.

—What he say?

The guy talks quietly into the phone, nods a couple times and then flips it closed.

Digga snaps his fingers.

—Well, niggah?

—Chubby say he cool.

—He vouch?

—Chubby Freeze say he vouch for the man. Say the man righteous to a fault. Say they do bizniz and it always come out right.

—Hunh. Well. Well, well.

He looks me over.

—A vouch from Chubby Freeze. Ah'ite, that somethin'. So, Mr. Pitt, what you doin' up here all by yo'self? What's this bizniz?

—No big deal.

—Uh-huh?

—Just looking for the son of a bitch who's sending bags of Vyrus downtown for the new fish to shoot.

—Huh. No shit.

He holds out his hand and one of the rhinos passes him his Armani jacket. He pulls it on and does the buttons.

—*Lookin' for the son of a bitch.*

He picks up the razor.

—That is some in-ter-es-tin' shit.

He hands the razor to the barber.

—Finish the man up.

He starts for the door, talking to Timberlands as he goes.

—When he done with his shave, toss him in the Hummer and haul his ass up to the Jack. We gonna show muthafucka some shit.

He walks out the door with the two rhinos on his heels. The barber looks at my throat.

—Look there, that all closed up already. Nothin' no how but a scratch that.

He freshens the lather on my face and gives me a shave.

The Jackie Robinson Recreation Center looks like a Civil War fortress: red brick with round turrets at the corners and huge steel doors. The Jack.

Timberlands parks the Hummer on an empty basketball court just inside a chain-link gate. Behind the Jack, a cliff of whatever rock Manhattan is made out of rises several stories above us, Edgecomb Avenue running along its top. It's cold outside the Hummer.

I look at Timberlands.

—How 'bout you give me my jacket back.

He runs his hand down the sleeve, feeling the leather.

—This jacket?

—Uh-huh.

—This my jacket. Why'm I gonna give you my jacket?

—Brotherly love?

He gives me a good push, letting my face open the door for us. He tilts his head at the guy sitting at the check-in desk and muscles me down a corridor of white-painted cinderblock.

At the end of the hall a guy in a cheap black suit and wraparound black shades leans against a door. We stop in front of him. He keeps staring at whatever he's staring at, not bothering to turn his head in our direction.

Timberlands snaps his fingers.

—Open up.

Slowly, Shades rotates his face to us.

—Private party.

—We on the guest list.

Shades unbends a finger and points it at me.

—He ain't.

—He with Digga.

Shades leans his head back, relaxing a little more.

—Already got a main attraction. Don't need an opening act.

Timberlands steps up.

—Say he from Digga.

Shades unrelaxes.

—Digga don't have no free white boy passes.

—This the Hood. This Digga's turf.

—So they say.

The scent is up on them, rank Vyrus pheromones spraying the air. Blood will be spilled. I start looking for a window I can dive through.

—What all this?

Digga and his rhinos come up the hall behind us.

—What all this hostility I see? Where the love?

He stops, looks at the standoff in front of the door, a big smile across his face.

—What the problem, we ain't got the juice to get beyond this velvet rope? Doorman don't like our kicks? We ain't up to the clientele inside?

Shades points at me again.

—He's white.

Digga looks at me.

—Damn! How'd I miss that? Well, shit, you right 'bout that. Still doan see the problem.

—He's white.

—Uh-huh. Well, as to that, know what Luther X used to say? He say, *We all the same color inside.* By that, he mean we all red. Now, I can prove it on you.

He loses the smile.

—Or you can open the damn door.

—Papa won't like it.

—Somebody elect Papa president of the Hood? Somebody give him my job, forgot to tell me 'bout it? Open up.

Shades takes a step to the side.

—I di'nt say move, muthafucka, I said, *open up.*

Shades opens the door.

Digga sweeps his arm in front of me.

—After you.

I walk through followed by Digga, Timberlands, and the rhinos. The door swings shut behind us and we start down a stairwell.

Digga talks to the rhinos.

—You know that fool?

—Uh-huh.

—Get his name on a list.

—Uh-huh.

Below us comes a rumble of many voices and the howl of crazed dogs. The air smells like sweat, chlorine, blood, and the Vyrus.

There are a lot of them. I've never seen so many in one place. There are at least two hundred packed into the old basement baths. Two hundred of them. Two hundred of us. When I lead the way out of the stairwell every face turns toward me. The room goes silent except for the barking of the dogs that echoes off the tiled walls and ceiling. I have an instant vision of what it will be like to be torn literally to ribbons. Then Digga steps up behind me and puts a hand on my shoulder.

—Hey, all. He with me.

He keeps his hand on my shoulder, leading me through the crowd, closer to whatever is at its center. Way is made for him. With his free hand he bumps fists and exchanges backslaps, passing a word with the men and women of the crowd. They are mostly young, mostly hip-hop, all wear the Ecko rhino somewhere on their person, and none are white.

He puts his mouth next to my ear as we press through them.

—Shit, muthafucka, I knew I coulda made a entrance like this, I woulda got me a white boy sooner.

We're approaching the pool. It's drained of water. An eight-foot-high chain-link fence has been strung around it. The barking comes from inside. He brings me right up to the fence. The cement walls of the pool are stained dark maroon with dry blood; a thin sheet of the freshly spilled variety coats the bottom. A man is dragging a dog's carcass to the shallow end and passing it up to waiting hands. Three others have cornered a foaming-mad pit bull in the deep end. It darts at them and they dodge out of the way.

Digga shakes his head.

—Shit.

He calls to the men.

—Put a fuckin' cap in that beast.

One of them waves, pulls a Glock from his baggy pants, and puts a cap in the beast. The bullet slams it into the wall of the pool. Then it gets up and starts barking again.

Digga looks at the ceiling.

—Jezus H. In the head, muthafucka! In the fuckin' head!

The guy puts one in the dog's head. It stays down this time.

The crowd is shifting around us, piling up close, hooking their fingers in the fence.

On one side of the pool a man sits up on the old lifeguard tower. He wears a black suit, wraparound shades, a red fez, and puffs on a cigarette in a long ivory holder. A group of men dressed like the guy from the door stand around the base of the chair. Digga waves to him.

—Papa! What up?

Papa gestures with his holder.

Digga holds his arm up and points at the top of my head.

—You all see my white boy?

Papa ignores him.

—He sweet, right? You want one?

They ignore him.

—No? Well, shit then, let's get to the main e-vent.

The crowd around us rumbles.

Digga whispers in my ear again.

—Tension thick in here, huh, Pitt? Feel that hostility? An' we all black folk. 'Magine what it like when we got the Washington Heights and Spanish Harlem crowds in here. Put the spics in here with the niggahs and it almost always be endin' in bloodshed. An' we all on the same side. Me, I sure as shit glad I ain't white up in this. Can you 'magine what they do to you, you not with me? Oh shit, we 'bout to find out. Look.

He points to the far end of the pool where two more dogs are ready to be brought in. A man is pushed from the steps. His feet slide from beneath him on the blood-slick surface. A couple rhinos jump down after him, get him by the arms and pull him up. The enforcer from the train.

—Hey, Pitt, it your friend.

The handlers bring the dogs together. Another man walks up

carrying a cooler. He opens it and takes out a blood bag and three syringes.

—An' that, that must be the shit you come up here lookin' for.

The dogs are led on long wooden poles hooked to their collars. The handlers take a tiny bit of the Vyrus-infected blood into their syringes and kneel by their dogs while their assistants hold the poles. I watch a rhino as he fills the last syringe with several cc's of the blood. He walks over to the enforcer, who struggles between his guards, eyes fixed on the needle.

Digga gives me a bump with his shoulder.

—That bitch down there, the brindle pit, that my bitch. The rot, he belong to Papa. Tonight was supposed to be some head-to-head action, but seein' as you lead that son of a bitch up here, we thought we improvise. Purse gonna go to the dog gets the killing stroke. Braggin' rights. How you like the look a my bitch?

—Good looking dog.

—Damn right she a good lookin' dog. Want to get something down on this? Make some change while you up here?

—No thanks.

—*No thanks?* You don't believe in my bitch? Don't think she got what it takes? You dissin' my bitch, muthafucka?

—Don't like to gamble.

—Come up here an you don't like to gamble? Coulda fooled me. Well, too late now, muthafucka, you in the casino now. Boys tell me they found close to a grand on yo ass.

He raises his hands in the air.

—Yo! Yo!

The crowd noise lowers.

—Yo! Check it! White boy say he got the fever! Got a G he want to put on my bitch! Who up for that action?

Papa raises his cigarette holder.

Digga points at him.

—There you go, Pitt, you down for a G with Papa.

He raises his arms again.

—A'ight, muthafuckas, let's get this bread and circus shit on!

The crowd howls and shakes the chain-link, the dogs howl through their muzzles. Somewhere, a DJ fires up his turntables and bass thunders, turning the tiled cavern into a giant sub-woofer.

Digga dips his head at the men in the pool. Simultaneously the handlers jab their dogs in the neck. Instantly the dogs start to tremor, voiding their bowels. The handlers whip the dogs' muzzles off. The rot snaps and his handler loses a finger. The dogs gnash and foam, clawing at the floor of the pool, trying to chew their way up the poles to the handlers' assistants struggling to control them.

Near the stairs, a rhino stabs his needle into the enforcer's neck. A lump appears under his skin as the infected blood is forced in too quickly. His head starts to thrash up and down and vomit spews from his mouth. The rhinos release him and run for the stairs. The handlers' assistants maneuver the dogs until they frame the spastic enforcer. They catch one another's eyes and un-hook, jumping for the hands waiting to pull them up out of the pool. The gate at the shallow end slams shut. And the business in the pool begins.

He might have had a chance. If they hadn't shot him up, the en-forcer might have had a chance. The action I saw from The Spaz at Doc's was just a warm-up. That was a new fish who shot a taste too much. This is a Coalition enforcer, fed and trained, and shot full of the nastiest dope on the planet. He flails his limbs with such force, he breaks his own bones on the air. The maddened dogs, bred to the arena, retain just enough of their conditioning to stay focused on the man between them.

They jump like ticks, the Vyrus doing some unspeakable thing to their insides, warping their chemistry and powering their muscles. The enforcer dervishes on the slippery floor of the pool. Digga's bitch flies at him and one of his arms catches it in midair and sends it into the fence. The crowd jumps back, their screams lost in the hammering bass. One of the fence poles is bent by the impact. The dog drops back into the pool and goes for the man again, one of its forelegs broken.

Papa's rot stalks the enforcer. It's frustrated by the speed of its movements, driven by the unfamiliar strength in its legs to bite its hindquarters. Both dogs circle the enforcer in blinding leaps and bursts. He wails and blood pours from his nose. They attack.

Digga's bitch gets her jaws into his calf and clings there as he kicks furiously. The dog waves and snaps like a flag in a high wind. The rot comes in from behind, flying through the air and landing on the enforcer's back, sinking his teeth into the meat where his shoulder joins his neck. The rest is just time. Too much time. The bitch is kicked free. The enforcer goes down on his back, the rot under him, but still latched on. The bitch comes back and gets the forearm that was shattered when it struck her from the air. Its bones shattered, the arm comes off in the bitch's mouth. She drops it and goes for his throat. Her teeth go in, but he grabs her by the neck with his remaining arm and twists her head around. She lies on his chest, flopping.

The rot gnaws and chews. Eventually it's over. When it is, the rot is clearly ruined. One side of its chest is crumpled where the enforcer caved in its ribs and its lower jaw hangs loose, broken by its own murderous assault on the enforcer's neck.

The music changes, heavy hip-hop beats replaced by R&B, and Digga's people drift away from the pool, pairing off to dance.

Papa waves two of his men into the pool. His dog wobbles and whines, but whenever they come close it hauls itself up and snorts blood. One of them pulls an old Mauser from his jacket and tries to take a bead on the dog, but it skitters about, too quick for him to get the shot.

Digga is staring at the corpse of his own dog.

—Damn. Damn, that was a fine bitch. Damn.

He looks and sees what's going on with the rot.

—Mothafuckas. Hey! Hey!

Papa's men look up.

—Hey! That ain't how you put down the champeen.

He leaps, grabs the top of the fence, vaults up and balances there. He strips off his tie, his jacket, his shirt, dropping them all to Timberlands. His torso is knotted muscle.

—Get back from that dog, mothafuckas.

He jumps down into the pool, easily keeping his feet on the blood-slick, and approaches the wounded dog. The men in wrap-arounds look up at Papa and he signals them back. The dancing couples have returned to line the fence.

Digga walks at the dog, talking to it softly. The dog's hackles stick straight up. Digga keeps coming. The dog goes for him, jumping at his face. Digga catches the dog in the air. They go down, Digga on his back, the dog clutched between his hands. The dog's lower jaw flaps as he tries to bark. Digga flips over, gets the dog under him, opens his mouth wide and digs his teeth into the back of the dog's neck. It goes limp, recognizing a superior hound, and he twists its head, breaking its neck.

Digga's people go crazy. Papa climbs down from his perch. Digga stands, coated in dog blood.

—Papa! Don't you worry. I send the white boy's money to you first thing.

Papa turns away, strolls to the exit, followed by his men.

I'm led around the pool to the steps at the shallow end. Digga has stripped to his Calvin Kleins and is accepting several towels, mopping the blood from his skin and from around his mouth.

—See that? See that, Pitt?

I nod.

—That some shit, right?

I look at the dog corpses being hauled from the pool.

—I've killed a wounded dog before. It's nothing to be proud of.

The music keeps playing. People keep dancing. The guys in the pool keep cleaning. But the folks around us get very quiet.

Digga slips on a clean pair of trousers.

—That so? You killed a dog? Killed a muthafuckin' monster dog on dope like that sad beast down there? Like that champeen hound I just put down?

I don't say anything.

Timberlands holds out Digga's shirt and he slides his arms into it.

—Well, let me tell ya. These soirées here like this one? This ain't everyday shit. More a *special occasion* kind of thing. 'Specially some shit like that enforcer. Man on our turf, clearly in violation of the treaty? Man like that, we can use how we please. Don't always have that on the menu. But I tell you what, maybe we have another party tomorrow. Yeah, another get-together. Maybe have some barbeque this time. Yeah, that's the shit. After all, muthafucka, tonight we had him to sport with.

He points at the enforcer's mangled corpse.

—An that was a'ight.

He throws his tie around his neck and lets Timberlands drape his jacket over his shoulders.

—So maybe tomorrow night we go it again. And then we can see how *you* do 'gainst a *champeen* dog.

He points at me.

—Stick this muthafucka in a box.

Two rhinos grab me.

—See you on the morrow, Pitt. Give you a chance to go double or nothin' on that G you owe Papa.

They don't really stick me in a box; which is kind of a nice surprise. Instead, they stick me in an old shower room. I take a walk around, but there's not much to see. No windows at all. I find a vent under one of the sinks and fish the switchblade out of my boot, the fine art of the pat-down seeming to have been lost, and pry it loose. If I lost about a hundred pounds I might be able to worm in there and get trapped at the first bend. I flip through the lockers but don't find anything useful. There is a tiny panel of glass in the door they pushed me through; I take a peek and see my two rhinos in the hall smoking and trading rhymes back and forth to the beats that echo down the hall from the party in the baths. I tap on the glass and one of them looks at me. I point at the cigarette in his hand and then at myself. But he just flips me off instead of opening the door so I can stick the knife in his neck. I go to one of the sinks and twist the taps and a little cold water dribbles out.

My cigarettes are in the jacket Timberlands took off me. Sure like to get that jacket back. I bend my face to the sink and wash up, rinsing away some blood on my upper lip from when the rhinos bounced me around. I think about the enforcer. I think about being eaten alive by dogs. I think about the way he freaked when that blood hit his vein. The way he was jumping, I wonder if the dogs were a mercy. I dry my face and hands on the tail of my shirt. I look at the lockers. I could go through them again, see if someone maybe forgot their assault rifle down here sometime, but I take a pass.

I sit on the floor with my back to the wall and watch the door. I pass the time waiting, waiting for someone to come through the door and do something just the least bit stupid so I can kill them and give myself something resembling a fighting chance. I'm not holding my breath.

Figure coming up here was a mistake. Figure it was a big one.

I try to figure how long I should wait before I tell Digga I'm doing a job for Terry. Figure I wait too long and I'll have a skin full of that junk and be down in the pool with the dogs. Give it up now and he'll have plenty of time to check it out. But Terry might not like that. Figure I know for a *fact* Terry won't like that. Easiest course of action for him? *Pitt? That asshole? I don't know why he's up there. I mean, I never want to endorse execution, but that's your prerogative, Digga. You'll have to do whatever, you know, gives you peace of mind.*

Yeah, I'm fucked.

I just wish I had my cigarettes. And that jacket. I do love that jacket.

The music finally stops. I look out the window again; the rhinos are still there. Someone has brought them coffee and more cigarettes. I go back to my spot against the wall.

I close my eyes. But I don't sleep. I do that for a long time.

The door opens. I keep my eyes closed. Someone walks across the room toward me. My thumb is over the silver button on the side of the switchblade. Whoever it is stops at my feet. I smell baby powder and Bay Rum.

—We kin fix that right up.

I open my eyes.

—No trouble a'tall. Fix it right up.

The one-armed barber is standing over me.

—Fix *what* up?

—That nasty-ass haircut I wuz givin' ya. Make ya look proper.

I touch my hair.

—It's fine.

—No, no it ain't. Looks like shee-it. Fix it up right.

Across the shower room, the door to the hall is open. No sign of rhinos. The switchblade is cupped in my palm, unopened.

I watch the barber's eyes.

—Digga want you to clean me up for my big match?

—What? No. Shit no. He don't care none what yo ass look like. I care. Got me some pro-fessional pride.

—Gonna do it now?

—What? You stupid in the head? Got no time ta do it now. Got ta get yo ass out of here.

—What?

—*What? What?* Man, Digga right, you one stupid-ass white boy. Get up, we got ta get gone.

I get up. He walks over to the open door.

—*Come on.*

The rhinos are on the floor in the hall. I look at the barber.

—You do that?

—No one else here, is they?

There isn't.

—They dead?

He scratches his head.

—Well, that the million-dollar question, ain't it?

—Sure is.

He points at one of the rhinos.

—They just out. Now get that coat off him. An' that sweatshirt underneath.

I tug off the rhino's jacket and the hooded sweatshirt beneath, seeing the huge knot on the back of his head.

—Put that shit on. An walk while you doin' it.

I walk, following the barber away from the shower room, wrapping myself in the rhino's clothes and noticing the massive build of the barber's left arm and shoulder. I think about putting the knife in his ear. I should wait 'til he leads me out.

We climb some stairs; different from the ones that had been guarded by Papa's man. These are narrower; the back way in. The barber looks me over.

—Put up the hood. Yeah, that right. An keep yo head down. An yo hands in yo pockets. Yeah. OK. An keep yo mouth shut.

He opens a door and we walk onto the blacktop playground behind the Jack. I keep my head down, my hands in my pockets and my mouth shut. We walk past the basketball courts. I can hear the jingle of chain nets in the breeze. The barber tugs my sleeve.
—This way. *Keep yo head down*. Just follow me. Doan look up none. Things quiet, but still they got a watch on. Gonna climb some steps now.

We climb some steps. A lot of steps. We're climbing the concrete stairs that cut up the side of that cliff I saw earlier. The barber pauses at the top.
—OK. I think we cool. You kin look up, but keep that damn hood on.

I look up. We go down Edgecombe for a couple blocks. At the corner of 150th, he stops. There's a house with a spiked iron fence around it. He unlocks a gate and lets us in. The house is huge. It's red brick with black shingles and shutters, looks like a haunted house straight out of an old Universal horror flick.

The barber walks around a cracked stone path that takes us to the rear. We go down a couple steps to a basement door.

He looks at me.
—Place got atmosphere, doan it?
—Yes, it does.

He unlocks the door, steps in and switches on a light. I follow him in, expecting Digga and his crew to jump out and yell *surprise* and beat the hell out of me. It doesn't happen that way. Instead, the barber takes me through a small parlor, neat but dusty, and into a kitchen where most of the living is clearly done. I take my hands out of my pockets, without the switchblade.

He points at a chair. I sit. He takes off his coat and hangs it on a hook on the back of the kitchen door. He looks at me. I look at him.

He rolls his eyes.

—Well?

—Well, what?

—Ain't you got no questions?

—Sure. What do you want?

He shakes his head.

—Stupid white boy. Ain't figured it out?

I shake my head.

—I'm Percy, asshole.

He bugs his eyes and wiggles his fingers at me.

—The craaaaazy one-ahmed neegro in the bazemint is yo contact.

He unbugs his eyes.

—*Now* you got any questions?

—You got a smoke?

—Funny thing 'bout cigarettes.

Percy sticks a Pall Mall between his lips. He fishes a book of matches from his breast pocket, folds a match around 'til the head rests against the strip of rough paper on the back, and flicks it with his thumb. The match ignites and he offers me the flame. I lean forward and light my Pall Mall. Percy lights his, waves the match out, pinches it from the pack and drops it in the red-and-white tin ashtray between us.

I take a drag and exhale.

—What's that?

He smokes some.

—Funny thing 'bout cigarettes and the Vyrus. Vyrus attacks anythin' bad yo ass could care to stick in yo body. Booze, junk, rat poison, whatever it is, it can't hurt you none. Got no stayin' power whatsoever. No boozehound Vamps. Can't get hooked on shit. But cigarettes.

He blows a ring of smoke.

—They always good. Just as good as if I was still jonesed on the nicotine. Which I know I ain't. Still I crave 'em. And still they always good.

I take a drag.

—Never thought about it.

—Uh-huh?

I take another drag.

—But you're right.

—Yep. Funny, ain't it?

—Yeah, it is.

We smoke.

—So what you need up here?

I've smoked my cigarette down until the cherry burns my lips. I stub it out.

—That shit they stuck in the dogs and that enforcer.

—Yea-huh?

—What the fuck is up with that?

He puts out his own cigarette.

—That a good question.

The ceiling of the kitchen has a big, brown water stain above the sink. He stares at it.

—A good question. Lemme ask you somethin'.

—OK.

—See that man at the pool? Papa Doc?

—Yeah.

—What you make of him?

—Looked like the competition.

He gets up and walks to the refrigerator.

—Competition.

He opens the fridge, pulls out two cans of Schaefer and takes them to the sink.

—Let me tell you somethin' 'bout competition.

He takes a couple glasses from a cupboard.

—Digga, he Luther X's warlord. When the X got taken out, Digga, he step in, declare martial law, move his rhinos out on the street. Say, *We in a state of siege. Coalition agents done assassinated our fearless leader.* That two years back.

He snaps one of the cans of beer open and empties it into a glass.

—An' he prove it. Brings us the heads a two enforcer types he say was the ones stabbed Luther in the eyes. Good enough. All the peoples think it a good idea: Close the border and tighten the belt. Digga, he gets support from all over the Hood. Harlem, Washington Heights, Spanish Harlem, shit, even the Dominicans up Inwood come to the meetin' and stand with Digga. But, like the man say, that two years ago.

He pours the other beer.

—Time pass, people want to know, *When martial law gonna end? When we have elections? When we get a new elected president?* People agitatin'. Now these people agitatin', they mostly come in one flavor, they Papa's *ton tons macoute.* Them boys in the shades.

He brings the glasses to the table and sets one in front of me.

—So for 'bout a year now, they do this little dance, pokin' and proddin', seein' how far they push things, see if they break. Digga, he nobody's fool nohow. He see the pressure risin', he look for ways to let it off. So sometimes he think it a good idea ta get the dogs in the ring. Let the dogs bleed so the people ain't got to.

He sips his beer.

—But lately, that pressure keeps climbing. Heat stay on. Know why?

—Nope.

He wipes some foam from his lips, lights a fresh smoke and drops the pack on the table.

—On account that shit you askin' 'bout. On account that shit comin' in up here an fuckin' up some our young people. On account Digga say it comin' from across the border, from the Coalition as part a they plan to poison us and take the Hood back. He talkin' war. Papa, he preachin' we don't need no war. Everythin' cool, need diplomacy. Need elections and diplomacy. Need some normalized relations with the Coalition and everythin' be cool.

I drink some beer. He watches me.

—Well, boy, what you think 'bout that? What that all sound like to you?

I pick up the pack of Pall Malls and shake one out.

—Sounds like Digga killed Luther X himself and he's thrashing around trying to keep his office. Sounds like maybe he's the one behind that shit.

He lights another match and holds it out to me.

—Yeah, it do *sound* like that, don't it?

I light up.

He blows out the match.

—Let's fix up that haircut.

—See that picture up on the wall next to the phone?

I sit in a chair in the middle of the kitchen, a tablecloth draped over me, newspapers spread under the chair.

—I see it.

—What you see?

What I see is a black and white photo of a group of people at some kind of meeting in a school gym or someplace.

—Looks like Luther X and some other folks back in the day.

—That right.

He runs a wet comb through my hair.

—That man off to Luther's right, that his original warlord. Man gonna come to be known as Papa Doc. Gonna form his *ton tons macoute* an *challenge* Luther's leadership one day.

He starts to clip my hair.

—Holdin' Luther's hand, that his wife. Good woman. Long gone.

He pushes my head to the side and snips at my sideburns.

—That big nasty negro to the side, the badass with the shotgun? That me.

I look again. The man in the picture has two arms.

—Back before shit happened. Move yo head back.

I move my head back.

—An' that weedy thing with the glasses? That Craig Jefferson Wallace. Soon to be known as DJ Grave Digga.

I look again. He was a weedy kid.

—That boy born in Scarsdale. Come down here to do community work. A more Oreo negro you never met in yo life. Got hisself infected first month he here. Luther brought him in. Saw somethin', made him over. Spread stories how he a hardass De-troit niggah. Groomed him for warlord when he saw Papa sneakin' round tryin' to make some moves. Not many left know that story now. Just us old folk. You say natural in the back?

—Yeah.

He pushes my head forward.

—Yep, far as the man in the street know, Digga just what he seem: ex-gang-bangin' roughneck that muscled hisself into the throne. A wartime ruler. An' lots them folk like that just fine. Got a focus, got a *reason to be*. Got a cold war with the Coalition. Got a enemy. Life always easier with a enemy. But behind all that?

He walks around in front of me and tilts my head this way and that, inspecting the cut.

—Behind all that, he one sneaky mutha.

He snaps the tablecloth off of me.

—You done.

I stand up and move the chair back to the table.

Percy gathers up the newspaper, careful not to drop hair clippings on the linoleum.

—Yeah, he sneaky.

He stuffs the paper in a garbage pail under the sink.

—But he sure as shit did not kill Luther.

He comes back to the table and lights up.

—Luther done that to his own damn self.

He looks at the clock above the stove.

—Let's go see 'bout makin' you a place to sleep.

We're in the parlor. I help Percy tuck a sheet into place on the couch.

—Why?

He pins one end of a pillow under his chin and works a pillow-case around it.

—Why what?

—Why'd Luther kill himself?

—Don't know.

He drops the pillow on the couch.

—Tired of livin', I guess.

He goes to the closet and pulls down two musty afghans.

—Know how that is, don't ya?

I take the blankets and spread them on the couch.

—Not yet.

—That so? Don't get tired of life yo ownself?

He sits on the old recliner that faces the TV. I accept the cigarette he holds out to me.

—Yeah, I guess sometimes I do.

—Sure you do. Me, I feel that way most all the time now.

We light up.

Percy touches the remote. The TV blips on. He flips a couple channels, then turns it off. I lean over and knock some ash into the tray resting on the arm of his chair.

—How'd he do it?

—Like they say, stabbed hisself in the eyes.

—How'd he manage that?

He looks at me.

—Ever meet the X?

—Nope.

—Man had willpower.

—Why you think he did it that way?

He pulls the lever on the side of his chair and it tilts back until he's looking at the ceiling, blowing smoke at the fixture above his head.

—Didn't like what he saw no more. Didn't like what he saw comin'.

He talks to the ceiling.

—See, back when that picture was taken, we had us a time. Had us a fight. All this up here was Coalition. Till the X. He made it happen. Revelation. Revolution. Once that was done, once we was our own masters, things still wasn't easy. No more of that Coalition welfare blood comin' in. Had to work, find new ways to keep people fed. Had to integrate the brothas and sistas with the Latinos. Havin' the revolution, that was just the start. But we got there, the X made damn sure we got there. An' for a while then, things was easy. People start forgettin', don't remember what the cost was. Got people like Papa sayin' it time for a change. Sayin' Luther had his time, now we stable, now we at peace, now we start communicatin' with the Coalition again. Time to let bygones be bygones. War was war, but now we got prosperity. Hook up with the Coalition and it be even more prosperous. Bull. Shit. They just comfortable. Want to be *more* comfortable. Ask me, Papa's on the Coalition tip. Ask me, that spook Dexter Predo whisperin' in his ear.

Saying Predo's name, he turns his head and spits at the floor.

—So maybe Luther looked at all this. Saw his people getting fat, saw his old friend gunnin' for him, saw another fight on the way, maybe he saw all that, and he decided he didn't want to see no more. Maybe he said to hisself, *Time to go out. Go out on my terms. Go out and maybe leave a little gift behind, something my boy Digga, my smart boy Digga, can turn to his hand.* So maybe that why he did it that way, the hard way. Man's got daggers in his eyes, ain't no way no one gonna say he did it hisself. Somethin' like that, it like to cause an outrage when Digga stand up an' say, *Coalition did it! White devils assassinated our king!* That a rivetin' image: a king with knives in his eyes. That rallied the troops alright.

He picks up the ashtray and hands it to me.

—Put that on that table there.

I put it on the table.

—Yeah, Digga got us back on that war-foot. Galvanized the people. Got they's heads right again. But that talk comin' back now. That appeasement talk. Digga can throw as many dogs as he wants in that pool. Bite as many as he want. Keep puttin' on a show. Sooner or later, boy gonna have to show the people the devil's face. Prove to them they got enemies outside they borders. That enforcer comin' up here was a help, but he need more than that. Need to show that poison comin' in for real. An' it comin' from Predo. He show that, no one gonna take his crown nohow. He show that, Papa gonna have to mind his P's and his Q's.

I start another smoke.

—How you know all that about Luther?

He sighs.

—I cut the man's hair din't I? Now switch off that lamp.

I switch it off and we sit in the darkness. Just some light coming from the luminous dial of an old clock on top of the TV and from the tip of my cigarette.

—You stay up an' smoke you want to. Gonna get me some sleep.

He settles deeper into the easy chair.

—Percy?

—Huh?

—What's your end in this?

He turns his head to face me.

—Shit, boy, I'm Enclave. Just doin' a solid for Daniel.

I study his black skin by the glow of my cigarette.

—You don't look it.

—Well, theys Enclave and theys Enclave. Man can be a Baptist without he got to be no holy roller.

He closes his eyes and turns his face away.

—The can is down the hall you got to take a piss.

—Pitt.

—Hmmn?

—Wake it and shake it. It time.

—Hn?

I feel like I just closed my eyes. I open them.

Percy is sitting on the edge of the couch. I boost myself up.

—What?

—It time. Here.

He hands me an unopened pack of Pall Malls and a book of matches.

—Now doan forget what we talk about.

—OK.

—Things ain't always what they look like they is.

—I know.

—When the man give you a proposition, you take it. Right?

—What?

—Take the proposition.

—What?

He glances at the door.

I hear them.

I'm off the couch and down the hall. Behind me the door is kicked in. I'm past a bedroom, past the bathroom. Ahead, there's

one more door. I open it and a vacuum cleaner falls out. Foot-
steps are behind me. I turn around.

Timberlands is coming down the hall followed by the two rhinos from last night. I reach for the switchblade in my pocket.

Percy yells from the parlor.

—Careful, he got a knife.

Timberlands pauses as I pull the switchblade and pop it open.
He puts his hand in the pocket of my own fucking jacket and
pulls out my own fucking .32 and points it at me.

—Gonna put a hole in yo ass, you doan drop it.

I drop the knife.

He steps to the side to make room for the rhinos. I try to fight
them, but they make me stop. They drag me back down the hall
and through the parlor.

Percy is talking.

—Take you long enough. How long a man supposed ta entertain
the white boy?

Digga is standing in the open doorway.

—Just as long as it take, Percy.

—They not happy with you, Pitt.

I'm sitting in the backseat squeezed between the two rhinos.
Timberlands drives. Digga sits in the front passenger seat.

—Why's that?

—Could be cuz they had ta go down like that. Had ta take a rap
on the back of the skull from the one-armed man. Not the kind
of thing a man likes gettin' 'round. Course, it ain't gettin' 'round.

—No?

—Shit no. What gettin' 'round is how you fooled they asses into
openin' the door and then took 'em both. *That* the story gettin'
'round. An *that* the real reason they not happy with you.

—Too bad.

—Too bad for you, they get a chance to dance on you.

I look from one rhino to the other.

—I like dancing.

Digga turns himself around and looks at my face. He points at it.

—Not done yet. Mark him up a little more.

The rhinos toss a couple quick elbows at my face. My lips split open. A knot starts to grow over my right eye. My nose breaks for about the twentieth time in my life. It's OK. Pain is relative. You never stop feeling it, but have enough of it inflicted on you and you get kind of accustomed to it. It'll all heal. If they don't kill me.

—Enough.

They stop.

—See what I mean, Pitt. They just not happy with you.

My right eye is swelling, closing up. I squint at Digga.

—What about you, you happy with me?

—Me? Well, I say this, you playin' yo role.

I spit blood onto his upholstery.

—Still happy with me?

Digga snaps his fingers at Timberlands.

—Pull over.

—Know what that is?

—A park.

The Hummer is pulled over on Morningside Avenue at 123rd.

—Look like a park, don't it?

—Yeah.

—But it ain't. That a outpost. That a Coalition outpost.

The park is overgrown and abused. Dirty snow from our last big storm is dotted with unclaimed dog crap.

Digga points.

—Look.

I look. He's pointing at the paths that climb up the park, climb up a cliff face like the one that backs Jackie Robinson. But it's different here. At The Jack, the cliff is native stone, raw and worn from when it was first cut. Here, the heights of the park are defined by a massive barrier. Huge blocks of dark stone are masoned into a wall topped by an iron fence. Two paths cut back and forth across the park, climbing to two great staircases, one at either end of the park.

—See what they got up there?

Morningside Drive runs atop the wall, lined with luxury apartment buildings and a tower of Columbia student housing.

—That was part of the treaty Luther made when we got independence. Had to leave them this turf. They *settlement*. They *Gaza Strip*. They presence up here so no one forget this was all theirs once. All those sweet blocks around Columbia, that still Coalition turf. That where it comin' from.

—What's that?

—That shit. That poison they pumpin' into our blood. That shit you say croppin' up downtown, too. You think that a coincidence? Some dangerous-ass new drug, only drug can get a Vampyre hooked, just happenin' to drop on Society an' Hood turf? That sound likely to you, Pitt? Or it sound like a conspiracy?

I look behind us to the east, where the sun will soon be rising.

Digga grabs my face and turns it back toward the park.

—Don't you be worryin' 'bout that sun. It rise all on its own. This what you came up here for, ain't it? This what Bird sent you to look into?

—Nobody sent me. I'm here on my own.

—Uh-huh. Up here investigatin' this shit cuz you got a social conscience.

—I care about the little people.

—Uh-huh. A'ight. That good to know. Mean you won't mind

doing a little service for yo black bruthas and sistas. Let's stretch our legs.

Timberlands and the rhinos stay by the Hummer while Digga leads me to a bench.

—Percy talk to you?

—He said some things.

—He one alchemical niggah.

—If you say so.

—Trust me on that, he is. So, you got a little picture 'bout the political climate up here?

—Volatile.

—*Volatile*. You got some words on you, son. Yeah, *volatile*. Right now, it more volatile than usual. That because of you. Word out you on the loose. I put that word out. While you rappin' with Percy, I been talkin' with Papa Doc, tellin' him how you busted out. Now he say you a *Society* agent. Cross Coalition territory without no passage, come up here with an enforcer on yo ass; do all that to create friction when he be wantin' ta make peace with our neighbors to the south. Wants to call Dexter Predo, tell him we got nothin' to do with somethin' nasty happened to his man. Wants to call Terry Bird, tell him we want compensation for the trouble you cause us. *Whatever* you up here for, Predo and Bird? Neither them muthafuckas gonna be happy with you. But don't worry, I talk Papa down. Told him. *First things first: got to find the muthafucka.* Then we can worry 'bout who first in line to fuck yo ass. Now, *ton tons macoute* out looking for you. *Ton tons macoute.* Named for the secret police down in Haiti. Bad news. Man 'tween a rock an' a hard place, he be glad he not you right now.

He looks at the sky.

—'Course, soon enough they gonna stop lookin'. Everybody gonna sit out the day. Start it up again come sundown. Think I can keep them from callin' on Predo or Bird 'til then. Give you maybe enough time ta do somethin' 'bout your situation.

—Any ideas?

He turns his face to the heights above us.

—Go up there.

I look up at the old, well maintained buildings illuminated by ornamental street lamps and security lights.

—You go on up there where the white folk live.

—And when I'm up there?

—See if you can't get taken in. Them settlers got people watch that border all the time. They spot you, probably got yo picture in a face-book. Gonna want to talk to you. I be surprised they don't grab you up an' get you inside before you can burn.

—Then what?

He faces me, lays his arm along the bench behind my shoulders.

—Get me some fuckin' proof they sendin' that shit down here. Find it. Bring it out. Do that? I fix all this other shit. Get me proof and I put Papa where he belongs. And I put you on yo way back home. Don't say boo to Predo or Bird 'bout shit.

—Or?

He takes his arm away.

—You goin' up that hill, Pitt. We gonna sit down here in the Hummer behind all that UV tintin' an watch. You try to come back down, we gonna have yo ass. Once you up there, only so many things can happen. Sun gonna kill you, or maybe they gonna kill you. Nothin' lost on my end either way. They take you in, you either gonna do my job or you ain't. You shine it on, manage to get back home on yo own or work out some deal they send you home, we gonna know sooner or later. An' we *gonna* make them calls to Predo an Bird 'bout how you makin' troubles up here. Stir shit up, make life uncomfortable. Bird gonna want nothin' ta do with you on his turf no more. Once you off Society land, we gonna come for you. Makin' you a proposition, Pitt. Oughta take it.

I take a look at Timberlands and the rhinos. They're not far enough away for me to kill Digga before they can get to me. I think about what Percy said about propositions. Guess this is what he meant. Nice of him to give me a heads up. Sort of.

—Being awfully generous with me, Digga. Why's that?

He shrugs.

—Different reasons. Mostly, you white. Need a white boy ta go up there. Other than that, Chubby Freeze vouch for you.

—Yeah, imagine my situation if he hadn't.

Digga laughs.

—That no lie, muthafucka. That no lie.

He stops laughing.

—So what it gonna be?

I look at the sky again. Getting lighter with every minute.

—Well, like you say, I'm going up that hill. Once I'm up there, we'll just have to see what happens.

—That right, we will see what happen.

He stands up and heads for the Hummer. I follow him.

—Say. One thing.

He has the door open.

—What that?

I point at Timberlands.

—Suppose I could get my jacket back?

Digga creases his forehead.

—Doan ask me, it his jacket now.

I look at Timberlands.

He looks at me.

—Fuck off, it my jacket now.

—Uh-huh.

I look at Digga.

—How 'bout my gun and my knife?

Digga looks at me, looks up the hill, looks at Timberlands.

—Man should not go unstrapped.

Timberlands shrugs. He hands me my switchblade and I slip it in my back pocket.

—My piece?

He takes the .32 out of my jacket's pocket. He weighs it in his hand.

—Gat a piece a shit anyways.

He hands it to me. I take it from him and stick the barrel in his mouth.

—Suppose I could have my jacket back?

The rhinos take a step. Timberlands stays where he is, but his eyes go to Digga.

Digga shakes his head.

—Me, I'd give him the jacket, niggah.

Timberlands takes off my jacket, carefully. He holds it out. I take it, remove the barrel of the .32 from his mouth and wipe it on the front of his shirt. He and the rhinos close in.

Digga holds up his hand.

—Uh-uh, no time now. Sun gonna be up. Man's got walkin' to do.

The rhinos get in the Hummer. Timberlands walks around to the driver's side.

—Gonna settle with you later, muthafucka.

—Yeah, yeah. Wait your turn.

Digga gets in the Hummer and sits there with the door open.

—Someone special musta give you that jacket.

I put it on, take my Zippo from the pocket and use it to light one of Percy's Pall Malls.

—Yeah, pretty special.

The asphalt path climbs through pools of lamp light. Down here, just off the street, they're cast by ugly gray industrial lamps. Up higher, around the wall, they have the same ornamental lamps you'd find in Central Park.

The sky is low and sickly. I walk beneath it, the wall looming closer. Plastic bags are snagged in the bare branches of the trees. They look like scraps of dead skin. The park lights go out, letting me know daylight is on the way. The hovering storm clouds will give me a little time, blocking out the worst of the sun. But I need shelter, I need it fast. I look down at the street. Digga's Hummer cruises slowly, keeping pace with me, making sure I don't make a break. Making sure I don't run for God knows what.

Figure Digga's right about the border patrol up there. Probably spotters in that big dorm. Get someone installed up there near the top floors and they can spot for miles. And I *will* be in their face-book. If they're up there, and figure they must be, they have my face. Digga's probably right about what that means, too. Means they'll try to snag me off the street and bring me in. Only question left for me is how to play it at the top. The paths bends again, cuts, and I'm looking up the southern staircase. Wide, the wall on one side, a view of the Hood on the other, a gate at the top.

I climb.

Figure I let myself get hauled in, at least I don't have to worry about the sun. For the moment. Soon after that, I'll probably be hearing from Predo. That's what Digga doesn't really know about; that damn hard-on Predo has for me. Figure that's gonna make it pretty difficult for me to fish for any information on the shit. Difficult as in impossible. I make a break for it, I might make it to that 1 stop. And if I make it to the train, get my ass back downtown in one piece? Figure Digga's right on that count, too: gonna be hell to pay. A Rogue at odds with both the Coalition and the Hood? Count my remaining days on one hand and you'll have some fingers left over when you're done. I come to a landing halfway up the staircase. I stop and look at the view. I light up.

Yeah, this one's a bitch alright.

I turn around and look at the wall. It's right in my face now. I have to crane my neck to look up to the top. Big stones with deep cracks at the joints. Yeah, I would have held on to this turf, too. If hell ever does break out between the Coalition and the Hood, this will be the turf to have. I smell something on the wind. I look up at the gate at the top of the stairs. They're up there, two of them, waiting.

I look back down through the park. The Hummer is still down there. I think again about the enforcer: a skin full of that shit and being eaten by frenzied dogs. I touch my left shoulder where a dog once bit me. I didn't like it. I look back up at the guys above: silhouettes against the blank sky. I drop my smoke, grind it out under my boot, and climb.

They're young as hell and armed to the teeth. The ones at the top of the stairs flash me the tiny black machine pistols that dangle from their shoulders. One of them latches onto my arm and jams his weapon into my back. If he pulls the trigger the bullets will spew out and slice me in half. He pushes me away from the wall as the other one stays at the top of the steps making sure no Hoodies are following me. Once he's sure his rear is safe, he follows us to the curb and raises his fist in the air. A black SUV pulls out from between two parked cars, zips up and stops on a dime. The back door opens and another young guy with a machine pistol grabs me by the shoulder and pulls me inside. The door slams, a bag is dropped over my head, my hands are yanked behind my back and bound with wire, and I'm finally given a proper pat-down that finds both my revolver and my switchblade. The only real pisser is that they take my smokes and my Zippo as well.

They don't talk. The SUV jerks around a corner, taking a left. Another quick left, and another. And one more for good measure. Then some more of the same. Jesus, they got most of the snatch right, but this is just embarrassing.

—I can tell you're driving in circles.

Another left.

—I mean, if you're trying to disorient me, you might want to throw in a right turn every now and then.

Another left.

—See, like right now, we're on the south side of that same block you grabbed me off of.

Another left.

—East side.

Another left.

—If you don't want to change it up, you can also try giving a guy a whack over the head or something so it's harder for him to know his left from his right.

WHACK!

I shut up and let them do it their way.

The boys are young. The woman is old.

—What did he have?

One of the black leather jacketed muscle boys hands her a Ziploc bag full of my stuff. She unzips it. She opens the cylinder on the revolver, ejects the shells, sees the one spent round and sniffs the barrel. She empties the smokes into a bowl and hands it to one of the boys, who grinds them up and sifts the tobacco and paper through his fingers. She pulls the inner workings of the Zippo out of the scratched chrome sleeve. She undoes the little screw at the bottom and shakes the lighter 'til the flint drops out. She uses her fingernails to pinch out the piece of cotton at the bottom and unravels the long, Ronsonol-soaked wick inside. She places the gutted lighter beside the gun. She gives my keys and the change that was in my pocket a quick glance. She pops the switchblade open and squints into the slot the blade folds into. She taps the handle against the table and hears that it's hollow.

She hands it to the boy who ruined all my smokes. He sets it on the floor and stomps on it and the plastic grips shatter. She bends and looks through the pieces. She looks at me.

—His clothes?

One of the boys who grabbed me shakes his head.

She frowns.

—Do it now.

One of them pulls wire-cutters from his pocket and snips my hands free and they strip me to my skivvies. They run their fingers over seams and inside pockets. They tap the heels of my boots. She passes my jacket through her hands, finding flakes of tobacco in the pockets along with a couple movie ticket stubs and a poker chip I got at a bar as the marker for my second drink during a two-for-one happy hour. She flexes the chip between her thumbs and forefingers, it snaps in half.

I scratch my balls.

—That was good for a drink at HiFi.

She doesn't look up, her fingers probing at an irregularity in the collar of my jacket. She picks up the switchblade with the broken handle.

—There's nothing in the jacket.

She presses the tip of the blade against the collar.

—Ma'am, I'd really prefer if you didn't do anything to that jacket.

She shoves the point through the leather and jerks it to the side, tearing a small hole in the collar. She puts the knife down, works her fingers into the hole, gets a grip, and rips the collar wide open. She looks at the filleted leather. She throws the jacket on top of the rest of my clothes.

—He can dress.

I dress. I look at the ruined collar. I remember the day Evie gave me the jacket. It was my birthday. The day she thinks is my birthday, anyway. I look at the old lady and put the jacket back on.

—Can I have my poker chip back? They might still accept it.

She picks up the two halves of the poker chip and hands them to one of the boys.

—Make him eat it.

They don't really make me eat it. What they do is, they get me on my knees and stick the barrel of one of those guns in my neck and I open my mouth and they shove the jagged edged pieces of plastic inside and force it closed and punch my face a few times and the broken chip cuts up my tongue and gums and the soft insides of my cheeks. But, no, I don't actually eat the chip. When they're done I look at the old woman, still seated on her couch, wearing that very practical sweater and slacks combo and equally practical walking shoes, gray hair back in a bun, reading glasses dangling from a neck strap, machine pistol-armed boys arrayed around her. I open my mouth and the broken chip and some bits of skin and a large quantity of blood falls onto the parquet floor.

—I don't suppose your last name is Predo, by any chance?

She brings the glasses to her eyes and looks me over. Inspects me. Takes my measure. I don't like it.

She lowers the glasses.

—If Dexter Predo were my child, I'd cut out my womb and throw it on the fire.

I wipe blood from my lips.

—Well, we have that it common. Minus the womb.

—One lump or two.

I scratch my cheek.

—If I say three, are you gonna whip out a mallet and hit me over the head with it?

She wrinkles her forehead at me, tiny silver tongs still poised over the sugar bowl.

—Excuse me?

—Nothing. Sorry. No sugar.

—Milk?

—Black is fine.

She lifts the delicate cup and offers it to me. I take it and give it a good sniff. Nothing but the strong scent of Earl Grey.

She watches me through the steam drifting off the top of her own cup of sugary, milky tea.

—Tell me, Mr. Pitt.

—Yeah?

—What is it about the manner in which you've been treated here that makes you think we'd resort to anything so subtle as drugging your tea?

I take a sip.

—Nothing. Habit.

She nods.

—One may assume then that you do not often take tea with friends.

—If one wanted to, sure.

I look over my shoulder at the window.

—It makes you nervous?

I look back at her.

—A big, east-facing picture window with nothing covering it but a drape? Yeah, I'm a little itchy about it.

—It's a very heavy drape.

—Imagine my relief.

—And we certainly wouldn't consider throwing it open on you while we are all here together enjoying our tea.

I look at the four boys standing about the room. They're taking their tea in shifts; two of them sipping while the others keep their guns on me.

—Sure. But you never know when someone on the street might shoot out that window and tear that rag to shreds. You should nail up some plywood at least.

The corners of her mouth drop.

—Plywood. It would ruin the room.

She stands and walks toward the window.

—And I would lose my view.

She fingers a fold in the burgundy drapes.

—True, I cannot enjoy it during the day. But at night it is still quite spectacular.

She stares at the curtain, looking beyond it to the sprawl of the Hood below Morningside Park.

—Even if it does remind one of what is out there.

She turns back to me.

—Of what is living in homes that were once ours. On land that we rightfully own.

She spreads her arms wide.

—No, Mr. Pitt, I keep this window so thinly covered for a reason. So that I might open it that much more quickly when the time comes to watch the things down there being burned out of their nests.

She returns to the couch.

—That day will come soon enough. I can bear waiting for it a little longer. Just now, we should talk about you. And what is going to be done with you.

I swirl the last of my tea around the bottom of the cup.

She points at the cup.

—Anything of use to you in there?

I look at the tea leaves. They don't tell me the future. They don't tell me anything at all. But I don't really need them, I already have a pretty good idea of what's going to be done with me.

—Nothing I can see.

She holds out her hand.

—May I?

I hand her the cup.

She gazes into it.

—Hmm.

—'M I gonna hit the lotto?

She sets the cup on the tea tray.

—No, just as you said, nothing. But I can tell you your future nonetheless.

—That would be a relief about now.

She arches an eyebrow.

—A relief? Well then, allow me to relieve you. I will soon call Dexter Predo and inform him that we have you in our custody. He will immediately make arrangements for your rendition, which will most likely take place as soon as the sun has gone down. You will be transferred to Coalition territory proper, and Predo will begin a lengthy interrogation. When he has extracted every last scrap of useful information you possess, you will be executed. In the traditional fashion. Having not seen the sun in . . . many years, I could almost envy you the view you will have.

I cross my legs.

—But not really.

She shakes her head.

—No, not really.

I play with the frayed hem of my jeans.

—So what's holding up you making this call?

She slips her glasses on and studies me again.

—Dexter Predo will do what is best for the Coalition at large. Or rather, what is best for the Secretariat and for his chances of advancing to that body. I, on the other hand, will do what is best for our settlement here. This final scrap of our great northern territory, which is all Predo retained for us when he negotiated that abominable treaty with the animals on those streets.

She gives it a rest for a second.

I have nothing to say. So I don't.

She picks it back up.

—Seeing as you have just come from our occupied territories, I am very curious to hear about what you have seen there.

Another rest.

Me, I still got nothing to interject.

—Predo will offer as little of this information to me as possible, keeping the most useful details for himself.

I look at the mixing bowl at the edge of the table, the one still filled with the remains of those cigarettes.

—And I intend to extract as many of those details as possible before I must call him and report your capture. Using the same tactics he will use.

I cough.

—Lady, if you're offering me a chance to avoid being tortured twice, just say so. Tell me what you want to know and I'll spill it. Just maybe one of these guys could get me some rolling papers so I can put my cigarettes back together and have a smoke while I'm talking.

She looks at one of the boys. He comes over and puts a box of Marlboro Lights and a yellow Bic on the table.

I light up.

She takes my empty cup off its saucer.

—You may call me Mrs. Vandewater. I prefer it to *lady*.

I blow smoke.

She slides the saucer in front of me.

—I'm afraid I don't have a proper ashtray.

More smoke.

—And now that you have your cigarette, I would like to know what you saw while you were below. How many soldiers, what arms, defenses along the border, these are the details I am most interested in.

I heave out another lungful of smoke and knock ash onto the very-expensive-looking Persian rug that her tea table rests on.

—Fuck off. Mrs. Vandewater.

*   *   *

I expect to be given a few good raps on the back of the skull and hauled away to a basement or some other place where the floors aren't as nice and the bloodstains won't matter so much. But all that happens is the Vandewater lady gives a little sniff, lets her glasses drop to the end of their neck chain, gets up and walks out, two of her boys trailing her. The others don't even slap me around. They just stand there and keep me covered, both of them staying on the same side of the room so there's no chance they might shoot each other if they have to open fire.

I make the most of it, smoking the rest of the Marlboros and grinding the butts into the rug. It passes the time.

An hour goes by. I run out of cigarettes. I stand up and the boys don't shoot me. I stretch. Still no bullets. I take a step in their direction. They both take their fingers from the safe position alongside the trigger guard and wrap them around their triggers. I take a step back. They unwrap. So I guess this is my side of the room. I take a look.

I had the bag over my head when they brought me in, but I'm pretty sure we stayed on that same block they were driving around. There or very nearby. They drove us down a ramp into an underground garage. The elevator went up express, opening right into the apartment. The way Vandewater talked about the view, figure we're anywhere from the sixth to the tenth floor. I can't hear anything from the other rooms of the apartment or the apartment above. Probably prewar, brick walls. The wainscoting and the molding around the ceiling have never been painted over white like in most old Manhattan buildings. Yeah, this is one of those places on Morningside Drive, one of those castles right at the top of the park.

I take a look at the walls: a couple nice prints, some of van Gogh's sunflowers, a Remington. Nice stuff, but not my style.

There are a few plaques, dark wood with brass, the Vandewater name engraved prominently. Awards. Acknowledgments for efforts. Thanks for donations. That kind of thing. Some sheepskins, too. A yellowed diploma from Columbia when it was still King's College. Several more, also from Columbia. Men and women, all Vandewaters. Most very old, some that are new.

I look at the new ones. All the degrees taken in the sciences. Biology mostly. I think about that. I think about that school right around the block. I think about the kind of people who go there. And I file those thoughts away. I get lucky, I can maybe follow up on them someday. Think I have an idea who one of those thoughts might lead me to.

I look some more.

There are some photos. Silver-framed, sitting on a table at the end of the couch, a shaded lamp illuminating them.

I look. Blink. Look again. I pick one up.

Vandewater. Predo. Terry Bird.

The door opens. Vandewater comes in. Her boys come after, a sagging, head-bagged body between them.

She takes the photo from my hand.

—I have no idea why I keep this.

She lifts her glasses to her eyes and peers at the photo.

—To remind me of happier times, I suppose. Although I hate to think of myself as being nostalgic. Nostalgia rivets you in the past. It keeps you from looking forward. It is good, I think, to be proud of your history, to honor it, but one should never wallow in it.

She taps a very short nail against the glass covering the picture.

—That is what I tried to teach those boys.

She has smudged the glass with her finger. She pulls the cuff of her sleeve down and uses it to wipe the smudge away.

—I'm not certain Bird ever quite got it.

She sets the photo back in its place.

—While Predo, I fear, has taken it much too far.

* * *

—Have you ever wondered about the name *Coalition*?

—Not really.

—It never occurred to you that it was an odd name for an organization that shows such unanimity?

—Like I said, never thought about it.

—Yes. You strike me as one who does that frequently. Someone who fails to think about things. Some history then, while they prepare.

Two of the boys are moving furniture from the middle of the room. The guy with the bagged head is slumped in a corner.

—The Coalition was once just that: a Coalition of smaller groups. Over the years those groups *coalesced*; they became a single, unified entity. For the most part.

The furniture out of harm's way, the boys begin spreading a sheet of plastic over the floor.

—This is what I mean when I accuse Terry Bird of nostalgia.

She points at the photo.

—He was apt at recruiting. And so there he is, Downtown, trying to repeat the lessons of the past. Assembling a coalition of disparate groups, with the goal of creating a single, unified whole. He will fail. The historical moment is different, time has marched, while he remains in the past. What worked once, will not work again.

They begin taping down the edges of the plastic.

—Predo, it is true, looks forward. But to what end? He sacrifices territory, maneuvers behind the scenes, probes for weaknesses in the uninfected world that he might manipulate, looks always to the future. To adapting to the future. But only for himself. Only out of a desire for power. He is craven. And he disguises this, hides it from himself, by cocooning himself with influence. But I have seen him cower. From the back of my hand.

They pick up the guy by the wall and carry him to the middle of the plastic.

—Bird, at least, went off on his own, attempted to forge his own kingdom. It will crash down around him, but he has a sense of vision beyond himself. Predo is narrow.

One of the boys has a briefcase. He opens it. Inside there are works: needles, syringes, plastic bags, loops of rubber hose.

—Predo is selfish.

She walks over to her window. Daylight glows at the edges of the drapes. It hurts my eyes to look at it.

—That is why we are caged up here, surrounded by filth. Robbed of our heritage. Unable to exert our influence as we should. Unable to shape the future.

The boy pulls the bag from the guy's head. It's a young guy. Hispanic. Close-cropped hair, a hoop piercing his left eyebrow.

—Except by using the tools of the past.

One of the boys on the plastic sheet draws a scalpel from the briefcase.

Vandewater moves to the edge of the plastic, standing over the boys who kneel on either side of the Hispanic kid.

She looks at me, sitting over here on her couch, arms once again wired behind my back.

—Have you ever infected anyone, Mr. Pitt?

—No.

—Then this will be an education for you.

One boy opens his mouth. He sticks out his tongue. The other, the one with the scalpel, places the tip of the blade against his partner's tongue and cuts. He pushes the scalpel until the blade has disappeared inside the healthy pink flesh, then he draws it downward, slicing it open to the tip. Blood begins to gush. The boy with the butterflied tongue bends forward, he opens the Hispanic kid's mouth, and covers it with his own. Blood seeps out around the seal created by their lips.

Vandewater looks at me.

—There are other ways to do it, of course.

The Hispanic kid starts to jerk.

—But this is one of the surest.

His heels kick the floor.

—Ultimately, it all depends on the subject.

His palms slap the plastic and his fingers clench and unclench.

—You see, not everyone can accept the Vyrus.

The boy lifts his mouth away, blood still leaking from his tongue. He looks at Vandewater. She watches the Hispanic kid for another moment as greenish yellow foam begins to erupt from his mouth and nose. She shakes her head.

The boy with the scalpel places it against the Hispanic kid's neck and shoves it deep into his carotid, cupping his hand around the entrance wound to keep the blood from spraying the room. The Hispanic kid's tremors subside. In less than a minute he is still.

The boy with the sliced tongue wipes at it with a cotton pad. The wound has stopped bleeding and a scab is forming. The other boy puts his tools aside and the two of them begin to roll the plastic sheet with the Hispanic kid inside.

Vandewater steps out of their way.

—And so we will have to try again.

The door opens. Another head-bagged kid is brought in.

—A student body is an invaluable resource.

The new kid is laid out on a fresh sheet of plastic. The bag comes off. This one might be twenty. Middle Eastern. Khakis and a button-down.

—Away from home for the first time, they become depressed, alienated. Their behavior may be uncharacteristic. They get in-volved with drugs. Run away from school. Walk into dangerous parks after midnight. Commit suicide.

The two boys prepare to repeat their procedure, switching roles so that the one who last wielded the scalpel will now be cut.

—This is especially true of freshmen. They drop like flies.

More tongue slicing occurs.

—And even more true of the racial minorities. So driven. I'm speaking particularly of Asians, East Asians, and Middle Easterners now. The internal and external pressures to succeed, it can be unbearable for a youngster.

This one tremors and shakes, but no foam spews. Instead, his throat works as he sucks the infected blood out of the boy's split tongue.

Vandewater bends to observe.

—There, we have a match.

After several seconds the boy pulls his mouth free. The Middle Eastern kid's mouth opens and closes and his own tongue runs around his lips cleaning them of blood. His eyes are open, but they stare unfocused and sightless at the ceiling.

Vandewater moves closer, stands over the kid, looking at his face.

—Now he has great potential. He could accomplish remarkable feats.

The boys have begun assembling the works from the briefcase.

—With nurturing and care, with a firm hand to steer him, he might become something worthwhile. A scholar of our kind, one who might someday unlock all the secrets of the Vyrus. A statesman, to unite the Clans. A poet, to write verses of our plight. An able soldier, to take arms in the coming battles.

One of the boys takes the kid's arm and inserts an IV needle into a vein.

—But it is not to be. I will not have him.

The blood cup is fitted to the hose and the blood begins to fill one of the pint bags they have at hand.

—I will not have the brown, black, and yellow in my land. Once, yes, they had a place. But they proved treacherous. And they will not be given a second chance.

The bag is full. One of the boys closes the valve at the end of the hose, slips the full bag free, and connects a fresh one. Blood flows.

—Do you know what you are looking at?

I shake my head.

—There is no reason you should. You are looking at a weapon. A very old weapon.

Another bag full, another attached.

—Although it has never been used as such before. In the past it has always been simply a vice. Albeit a very dangerous one. And very exclusive.

Another bag.

—One wonders where the original inspiration came from, who it was that stuck their finger in the air and declared, *eureka!*

She picks up one of the full bags.

—I suspect it was an accident.

She walks toward me.

—I suspect it was a Vampyre, crazed with hunger, attempting to feed on someone who had been very, very recently infected. Through some odd set of circumstances, this Vampyre fed only for a moment. And made a discovery.

Behind her, another bag is filled.

—That, when consumed, the blood of one freshly infected will induce the most remarkable sensations. Remarkable, and addictive.

She raises an index finger.

—An unbelievably expensive addiction, mind you. For who can afford to be addicted to blood twice over? Who can bear the risks of hunting not just for sustenance, but for pleasure? Thus the exclusivity.

They're massaging the kid now, rubbing their hands over his legs and arms, as if squeezing dry a tube of toothpaste.

—That expense lies also at the heart of the secret as to why something like this has laid buried for so very long. Of course, I say *something like this,* knowing that nothing else like this exists. The point being, our lives are difficult to say the least. And they can be very long. And, if one does not have resources, very boring. An effective distraction from the basic needs for survival would be compelling in and of itself. Even if it were not addictive.

Another bag.

—It was decided some time ago, some very great time ago, that this was an indulgence that could not be afforded. It was declared anathema by the body that governed the Clans. When there was such a thing. In fact, that was the name it was given.

She shows me the bag in her hands, holds it in front of my face so that my nostrils are full of the stink of it.

—*Anathema:* the name for both the substance itself, and the habit of indulging in it. It was forbidden. The addicts were hunted and slaughtered. It became a crime so heinous, no one even knew of its existence. And so you see my personal values employed.

She turns to face the kid being wrung dry on the floor.

—Employing something of the past in a new manner, in order to shape the future. It flows out of these sacrifices.

She points at the window.

—And we send it onto the streets below. To wear holes in their unity. To create dissent and expose weaknesses. To drive their children to hunt to excess and endanger themselves. Thus, it is a weapon.

One of the boys has hoisted the kid by his ankles. A bag fills in fits and spurts.

Vandewater turns back to me.

—A weapon that, given time, will spur a war.

The kid is dry. They begin to bundle him in the plastic sheet.

—It will drive the Hood to threaten war on the Coalition. Predo, clinging to the status quo as he does, will attempt to avoid this. But he will have no choice. The chaos reigning in the Hood will force him to take action. Especially once I have assured him that I will be taking action whether he does or not. He will not risk losing this settlement. Particularly not when he sees how vulnerable to attack I have made the Hood.

She points at the two plastic wrapped bodies.

—Put them in the kitchen for now.

Two of the boys haul them out of the room.

She shows me the bag of blood again, holds it balanced on the open palm of her large hand.

—And that is what you are looking at.

I look at her.

—Me, I thought I was looking at a lady who's crazy as a shithouse rat.

She nods.

—Vulgarity. Of course. The refuge of the weak-minded. Scoff if you like. But there is more.

The boys come back and begin replacing the furniture they had moved. She raises a hand and one of them brings a chair. She sits.

—Once the Hood has fallen. Once we have reclaimed our territory and these boys and their brothers and sisters know the security they have never known. The security that would have been theirs if the Secretariat had never bowed to those animals. Once that is secure, my attention will turn south, to our lands below 14th Street.

The room has been put back together. Two of the boys continue to stand watch over me while the others gather together the anathema and pack it in the briefcase.

—In fact, that project has already begun. Gradually, much as we did here, the anathema is being introduced. Which, I would imagine, is the reason you have come so far away from home in the first place.

She looks at me through her glasses again.

—Another thing.

The boys come over to the couch, one of them carrying the briefcase full of anathema.

—While in modest amounts anathema's effects are essentially euphoric, larger amounts are quite agonizing, if not lethal.

She hands one of the boys the pint she's been holding.

—It takes an experienced and steady hand to administer the perfect dosage to inflict that agony without inducing an undesired fatality.

The boy unwraps a clean syringe.

—But if done properly, such a dose is every bit as effective as the most savage torture.

He begins to draw anathema into the syringe.

—Minus the mess and inconvenience.

She holds up a finger. The boy stops filling the syringe.

She points at it.

—This, I believe, would be your *ideal* dosage. If I were to inject you with this, every muscle in your body would warm and relax. A slight sweat might break out over your face. The worries of your everyday life would cease to have weight. Music would fill your ears such as you have never heard before. Images would light the undersides of your eyelids. Shapes, colors. Fantasies, but also more concrete hallucinations. Communal visions that are shared by all who have experienced anathema. Visions that some would say prove conclusively the spiritual nature of the Vyrus. Though I am not among them. But perhaps you are, Mr. Pitt?

Again she lifts the glasses to her eyes.

—I have heard that you sometimes associate with Daniel and his followers. Are you one of them? I've long suspected that Daniel's interests are not so ephemeral as he claims. It would not surprise me to discover that you are in fact *his* agent. Predo and Bird running you for their ends, but all the while, secretly, you are an instrument of Enclave concerns. It might be so. It might be so and you might not even be aware of it, Daniel being so subtle as he is. Would you care to have such visions? Unlock a deeper level of meaning within the Vyrus? You've been infected long enough to ask questions, haven't you? The first years of infection being filled as they are with simply learning to cope, deciding if you want to live this life at all. The next several with learning the tools of survival. The next several with learning to fit in, to adapt to being infected in an uninfected world over the long term. And finally, if you have the endurance, the cleverness, some set of tools to keep you alive, you begin to ask questions. *What is the Vyrus? What are the Vampyre? How long have we been here? Where did the Clans come from? Are there more of us out there in the world? How many? Do they all live as we do?* And, of course: *What am I?*

She lowers her glasses and waves them at the syringe in the boy's hand.

—This might hold answers for you. They would come with a price, naturally. You would arise from my couch with a new hunger, a second need. You would find yourself distracted from the hunt, contemplating how best to use your victim's blood. Consume it? Or have another Vampyre infect it for you? You can't use as anathema blood you've infected yourself, it will only make you ill. Nor can you use blood infected by the same Vampyre, not more than once or twice. You see how the complexities of this addiction multiply.

She points at the boy again. He pulls smoothly on the plunger.

She tilts her finger upward. He stops.

—With this amount, you will still be granted visions, likewise universal in their nature, but far more unpleasant. And accompanied not with warmth and relaxation, but muscles contracted so tightly they sometimes tear from the strain. Fever. Pain. In your bones. Particularly in the sternum, the spine, the hips, and the femurs. Odd, yes? And when it is over, you will be left not with the same addiction, but with one that demands these higher doses. An addiction that can only be sated through misery.

She moves her finger. More blood enters the syringe. Stops.

—With this amount, things become simpler. Agony. Harrowing phantasms. Blood at war with itself. And a lengthy, wracking, death.

The boy pulls the syringe free, wipes the needle. Offers it to Vandewater.

She takes it.

—Predo wants you. Knowing that, and knowing that I cannot afford to thoroughly alienate him, we can dispense with this dosage as an empty threat.

She presses the plunger, squirting a thread of the blood onto my chest. The smell burns my nostrils.

—Having done so, it only remains to decide.

She holds up the syringe.

—Will it be this? In which case I will save my questions until after you have recovered and are begging for further torture.

She holds her fingernail against the side of the syringe, indicating a smaller amount.

—Will it be this? In which case I will still hold my interrogation, waiting until you have suffered sweetly, and crave yet more sweetness.

She lowers the syringe.

—Or may I begin my questions now? Secure in the knowledge that you are aware I will not brook the barest shadow of a falsehood in your answers. Knowing you understand the price that will be paid.

And she shows me the needle again.

I rub my chin against my shoulder.

—Well, Mrs. Vandewater, it took you a while to get there, but you finally managed to say, *tell me what I want to know or I'll fuck you up forever.*

She waits.

I roll my eyes.

—I don't know what you're waiting for, I already told you once to fuck off.

There's a knock at the door. One of the machine pistol boys answers it. He nods at Vandewater.

She sets the syringe on the tea table. The boy assisting her closes the briefcase full of anathema.

She stands.

—Of course, one of the components of anathema's effectiveness as a weapon is its brief shelf life. It must be distributed immediately after it is harvested. This batch is meant for the Hood. And the courier is waiting.

She walks to the door.

—But not to worry, the dose in that syringe will last more than long enough to serve its purpose. In fact, a few minutes' aging will make it much more effective.

She leaves, escorted by Briefcase Boy and one of the machine pistols.

I look at the syringe sitting on the table and then over at the machine pistol boy and the tongue slicer that remained behind. I look again at the syringe, secure in the knowledge that when the time comes, I will beg like a child to keep her from sticking it in my arm.

I'm a dead man. And not just in the way that I'm always sort of a dead man. Once I'm in Predo's hands there will be considerably less talking and much more thrashing and questioning. And after that, I'll get to see my first sunrise in a quarter century. That should be worth something, but I expect I'll be distracted by the sensation of my eyelids melting. Being addicted to this shit will be the least of my concerns. Hell, the smart play here is to volunteer for the light dose. Lady wants to offer up a last gasp of nirvana, who am I to say no? That or just answer her damn questions outright. Figure I got no one to protect. Not like I owe anything to Digga. Not like I can tell her a hell of a lot about his setup anyway. Figure she won't stop with questions about the Hood. That's her obsession, but she'll get around to asking about the Society, too. Figure I don't much care about that either. Why should I? Only reason I ever stuck on that turf is because I like the neighborhood. Sell Terry out? Yep, no problem. The thing to do here is let her shoot a little of that shit into me and go out with something soft on my mind. And who knows, maybe there are some answers in that needle. I don't really believe that, but a lie can be just as sweet as the truth. Sweeter, nine times out of ten. Yeah, all in all, I got no good reason to be hardass here. I'm a dead man and the lady is just giving me a chance to decide how hard I want to go out. Most guys, they'll never be so lucky. No reason to be a hardass at all. No secrets worth keeping. No one worth protecting. Just me. Figure a better deal ain't gonna come around for a long while.

Vandewater comes back in alone.

She takes her seat. Lays a hand over the syringe.

—You've had ample time for thought?

I shrug, feeling something that resembles freedom.

Her fingers curl around the syringe.

—If, by any chance, you should need any additional incentive to make this easy and less time consuming, I could point out to you that our distributor in the Society tells me you have a girl whom you are—

She doesn't get to finish. It's hard to finish what you're saying when a guy lunges at you and bites one of your eyes out.

The boy who wired my hands together in the car knew what he was doing. He looped it around each wrist several times, then crisscrossed it back and forth between both wrists, drawing them tightly together, knotting the loose end and mashing that knot with a pair of pliers. The boy who rewired them after they had clipped me free for tea time? He didn't take the same class. Probably the one who drove around the block over and over. He should have started with fresh wire. But he didn't. He should have made sure my wrists weren't flexed when he bound me. But he didn't. No, he used the same wire that had already been stressed by all my wiggling and twisting when I was figuring out how good a job the first guy did. He wrapped it around my flexed wrists so that when he was done I could relax those muscles and have a little slack so the wire didn't bite so deeply into my skin. And he took those loose ends and twisted them together like the bit of wire used to close a bag of sliced bread.

If I ever find out which of them it was, I'd like to give him my thanks. Because it's his shitty job that makes it possible to wrench my hands free and keep this crazy witch from clawing my ears off when I spit her eye in her face.

I'll give it to her, she doesn't scream, much.

The one by the window is circling, looking for an open shot, a shot that won't have to go through Vandewater. The tongue slicer is closer, his hand is inside his jacket, going for a weapon that is less indiscriminate than the machine pistol the other boy has. Vandewater is blind, one eye somewhere on the floor, the other covered in blood, she's still raking her nails at my face. I throw her at the tongue slicer. He has his hand out of his jacket, holding a tiny automatic that looks like a mechanical wasp. The old lady is coming his way. He lets the gun fall from his hand and holds out his arms to catch her. I don't watch what happens next, I'm busy picking up the tea table and throwing it at the boy with the machine pistol.

He's young and he's well trained, but he hasn't had too many opportunities to put that training to use, so he's worried about getting hurt. Dumbshit little boy, he hasn't been around long enough to develop new reflexes, his brain is still living in a world where large objects fly at you and you flinch; doesn't get it that pain doesn't matter. Something hits you, it's either gonna kill you or it ain't. The table doesn't kill him. I do.

He puts his arm up, easily knocking the table out of the air, but I'm right behind it. He wastes time trying to bring his gun back down, centering his aim on my torso instead of simply pulling the trigger and waving it around. I'm on top of him before it can matter. The gun is out of his hand. He's on his back. My knee is slamming into his crotch. He's strong, keeps going for my face. One of those other boys is gonna come in here any second. I put my hands in the boy's armpits and heave, sliding him on the wood floor, and his face disappears under the hem of the burgundy drapes.

The room instantly reeks of rotted meat being scorched by a blowtorch. I hold him there for a couple seconds while he shrieks and tries to pry my hands loose. When he stops struggling I'm off him and turning to see what's become of Vandewater and the tongue slicer. He sits up. The drapes tent around him for a moment, flashing sunlight over his body, before they swish back into place. Then he sits there, the hole that used to be his mouth oozing cancer, his hands clutching at his peeling scalp, pushing at the tumors that have erupted across it, trying to force them back inside.

The tongue slicer is on his back, trying to restrain Vandewater, trying to keep her from mauling him while not hurting her. That pain thing again. If he'd been around a bit longer he would have pounded her unconscious by now.

The door is opening.

I look at the floor, see the syringe, pick it up. The door swings wide, two of the boys coming through it, weapons up. I bend over and loop my left arm around Vandewater's neck and bring her up. She's still blind, still trying to hurt someone. The boys are in. The tongue slicer is picking up his automatic. I've got the old lady in front of me; windpipe caught in the crook of my elbow, toes just grazing the floor. Her remaining eye is open, blinking the blood away. She sees her boys.

—Shoot him!

Yeah, she knows about pain, she knows what it takes. She's ready for a few bullets.

I bring up the syringe and show it to her.

Her remaining eye rolls around and fixes on the syringe. The boys are circling, looking for the shot that will harm her the least.

I stick the needle in her empty eye socket, my thumb on the plunger.

And apparently some things are worse than pain.

—Don't! Don't shoot!

They don't.

The room is quiet. We can all hear each other breathing too hard. Some of Vandewater's blood drips off her face and hits the floor. The guy by the window hisses and gurgles like a pot of something viscous boiling over. The room stinks of his cancer and the lingering tang of the anathema.

I put my mouth close to her ear.

—Tell them to drop their guns and fuck off out of my way.

—Allow him to—

I clamp my arm tight.

—That's not what I said.

She gets it right this time.

—Drop your guns and fuck off out of his way.

They drop their guns and fuck off out of my way.

I glance at my possessions scattered on the floor. The .32, the broken switchblade, the gutted Zippo, the broken poker chip, and the spilled bowl of tobacco and shredded cigarette paper. I'll miss that Zippo, but more than anything, I wish I could have those cigarettes back.

The service elevator's just off the kitchen. There are also a couple plastic wrapped corpses and more of the boys. The boys drop their guns and fuck off just as well as the others.

I frog-walk Vandewater to the elevator, watched by the boys.

There's a keyhole just above the call button.

—You got the key?

She nods.

—Use it.

She takes a key ring from her pocket, sorts the proper one, twists it in the keyhole and pushes the button. We all wait a moment. The blood in her eye socket congeals a little more. The boys have brief wet dreams about what they'll do to me when they get the chance. The elevator creaks in the shaft. If we weren't all otherwise occupied, we'd be staring at the numbers above the door, watching them light up one by one.

—How long this thing take?

She twists her neck a little, getting some air. Her voice rasps.

—It's old.

—No shit.

More creaking.

I remember something important.

—Who's your dealer downtown?

The muscles of her neck tighten slightly. She's smiling.

I give her throat a squeeze.

—Something funny?

She coughs.

—I thought you'd forgotten.

—Yeah. Well.

I uncurl my index finger from the syringe and point at the boys.

—All this ruckus, it slipped my mind for the nonce.

The elevator creaks closer.

She smiles again. But keeps her mouth shut.

I push the needle a little deeper into her eye socket.

—Who?

Knowing the name, wanting to hear it.

She's still smiling.

—You won't believe me.

—Try me.

Smiling. Croaking.

—Tom Nolan.

OK. Not the name I was expecting.

I squeeze her tighter.

—Bullshit.

The elevator clanks into place.

—Tell me the truth.

The words rasp out of her mouth.

—That is the truth.

The door clicks. The boys aren't looking at me anymore.

Fuck.

I step to the side as the door slides open and the boy inside sprays his buddies instead of me, some of them hitting the deck, some of them riddled before they can react. I slam Vandewater against the wall, forearm across her throat, syringe in front of her face.

—Who?

She laughs.

—Tom Nolan! Tom Nolan!

The boy in the elevator stops shooting. I shove the plunger down, spurting the anathema into the old lady's dead eyehole.

She screams and I shove her in front of the elevator. Bullets tear up her belly and she's blown back into the uninjured boys who are getting up from the floor. The boy in the box stops shooting. I reach in and get a fistful of his jacket and drag him out.

Vandewater is freaking out like the enforcer did in the pool. The boys forget about me, trying to get a handle on her, trying to keep her from killing herself as she trashes the room. I throw the boy from the elevator at her and she latches on to him. I grab the key from its slot, step inside and hit the button for the garage.

As the door slides closed I see Mrs. Vandewater with the boy from the elevator in her clutches, dealing with him as the enforcer dealt with the dogs, the rest of the boys trying to bring her down.

I have the key stuck in the elevator control panel, turned to *express*. The boy's machine pistol is on the floor. I pick it up. The elevator hits bottom and the door opens. No one is waiting. I flip the key over to *hold,* leave it there and get out. The garage is small, a dozen very expensive cars for the very expensive tenants of this building. The entrance is gated, a dull gray glow filtering through it. I turn away. There's no attendant. I look at the cars. Really, it's no contest, the Range Rover with the all-around tint job wins hands down.

I walk over and press my face against the glass to get a look inside at how serious the alarm is. I get my look. I jump back and bring up the machine pistol. Nothing happens. I take another look.

Motherfucker. You can't be serious.

I try the door. It's unlocked. I open it. His head is hanging to one side, mouth slack, one sleeve rolled up, syringe still in his hand. Couldn't wait to fix, could you? I shove him to the passenger's seat, climb in and check the back. The briefcase of anathema is right there. I look at his sorry ass.

—Dealers should never use, asshole.

But Shades doesn't say anything, not nearly as talkative as he was when he was working the door at the Jack. He just stays right there in dreamland.

I put the machine pistol on the floor, close the door and give Shades a pat-down. I find his gun and phone, gloves, and a ski mask. I put on his gear, turn the key and the engine rumbles up. I pull the Rover over to the gate. As the light gets brighter, the tinting gets darker. Still, my eyes water and burn. An electric eye triggers the gate and it slides open. I scoot as low as possible in the seat, sun visor dropped, and drive like hell.

There's a reason they call it Morningside Park. That cliff is actually a part of the Manhattan schist, a long rift that runs along the upper end of the island. West is high ground, east is low. And the park? That's facing east. I come out of the garage headed into the sun. But the tinting was worth every dime Shades paid for it. I know this because my eyes don't turn to steam. I head north on Morningside Avenue, the sun on my right, hidden by the clouds. I follow the avenue around the block and it drops down a slope to Amsterdam. Another right, and the slope grows steeper as the buildings grow taller. I'm driving in shade. A right on MLK Boulevard and I'm dropping down to the Harlem Plain. Back in the Hood.

Frying pan?

Fire?

Who's keeping track anymore? They both burn. And tinting or no, I'm gonna do the same if I stay out here. A blast down the West Side Highway is tempting, but it'll most likely be gridlocked this time of morning. Traffic jam? With the sun climbing? No thanks. Across Hancock Square I see the big mall they built a few years back, part of the economic recovery in Harlem. It already looks shabby, but it has a public garage. I swing in, roll the window down, stick out my gloved hand, snatch a ticket from the dispenser and pull into the deep darkness. It takes a few minutes to find a space big enough for the Rover, but I don't mind.

The backs of my hands are blistered. They caught a few rays when I had that boy under the drapes. The burn runs up my forearms. I'll live. For the moment. Getting to the moments after this one, that's the trick now.

I look at Shades. A muscle in his cheek twitches. If he's dosed like the girls at The Count's place, he should be rousing pretty soon. I give him another pat to make sure he's not packing any other weapons. I give the interior of the car a once over. Just me, Shades, and the briefcase full of anathema.

I wonder what the expiration date is on that shit. If this stooge was taking a break to fix, it must be at least several hours. He probably wasn't gonna be driving all over the Hood making drops in the sun. It might be as many as twelve hours. I take one of the bags and slip it inside my jacket.

Time to call Digga.

The anathema, that's the evidence he wants. Shades alive and available for questioning, that's a bonus. Play it cool, there should be something in it for me. Blood or money. Skin in the game.

I flip open Shades' phone and make a call.

—Chubby.
—Grand to hear from you, Joe.
—Good to hear your voice, too, Chubs.
—Something I can do for you?
—Well, kind of embarrassing, seeing as you already did me a solid recently.

He grunts.

—Vouching for you, Joe? That's wasn't a solid, that was merely good business. Someone calls asking me for a reference, it's only good business that I tell them the truth. That is all I did. Happy to do it. Happy to. But there's something more?
—I need a number.
—Mmhmm?
—On account.
—Mnn.
—But I'll cover it when I get back.
—*Get back?* Still in the northern latitudes, my friend?
—For the time being.
—Well then, if I can be of assistance in bringing you homeward, I must do so.

He gives me the number.

—Thanks, Chubs.
—A pleasure. As always.
—By the way.
—Yes?
—Never knew you were quite so connected.
—Caution, Joe, use it in liberal amounts.

He hangs up.
I dial.

—What up?
—The sun.
He's thrown.
—Get it, Digga? *What up? The sun.*
He gets it.
I tell him where. I tell him to come alone. He's says it'll take him a couple hours. I tell him he has fifteen minutes before I risk the commute. And I hang up.
I set the phone on the dash just as Shades moans. I look at him. He brings a hand to his face and rubs it around. Moans again. Shit, that stuff must be good. He opens his eyes. Blinks. Sees me.
I wave.
—Peek-a-boo.
He makes a move for his piece. It's not there. I show him the machine pistol in my hand.
—Best thing for both of us, you should maybe just fix again and take another nap.
Seeing how thoroughly fucked he is, he seems pretty happy to oblige.

—Muthafucka!
—It's a bitch, ain't it?
—Mutha!
—Got to hate finding a Judas in the house.
—Fucka!
—Makes you want to lash out at people who got nothing to do with the problem.

—Muthafuckingfucka!

—Otherwise I wouldn't be pointing this thing at you.

—Shit.

He looks from Shades slouched in the passenger seat and across the Rover's cab to me. He sees the gun in my hand. Shakes his head.

—Shit. Put that thing away. Like I give a fuck.

I keep it where it is.

—You cool?

He points at Shades.

—*Cool?* You *think* I'm cool with this shit? Muthafucka, nothin' ever gonna be cool again. This some serious shit. I knew Papa was playin' games. But this? This gonna have repercussions.

—Yep.

—Wave the fuckin' gat 'round all you like. I got bigger fuckin' problems.

I put the gun down.

He slams the passenger door. Opens the rear and climbs in.

He looks at the briefcase.

—This the shit?

—That's it.

—Tell me.

So I tell him.

—That some crazy shit.

—Uh-huh.

—Old crazy lady on the hill goin' off Predo's talkin' points. That is some *crazy* shit.

—Uh-huh.

—*Uh-huh.* Pitt, anyone ever tell you you got this gift for some fuckin' understatement?

—Uh-huh.

—*Sheeit*.

We sit there. Digga still in the back, me in the front. He's gone casual today: beige boots, baggie camos, silver Ecko parka. Once he pulls on his ski mask, gloves and sunglasses, he can go for a little walk.

He points at Shades.

—How long he gonna be on the nod?

—Don't know for sure. Been down for about fifteen. Maybe fifteen more. Maybe less. What the lady says, the more you hit from one batch, the less you get from it.

He grunts.

—A'ight. You see my ride?

He points at a silver Lexus parked a few slots away.

—We gonna get this punk-ass mutha sequestered. Take him up to Percy's shack and let the barber put the razor to him. Percy starts quizzin' muthafucka's ass, ain't no stone gonna be unturned. Once we have all the details, we'll go to work on Papa. Sort out his ass good.

He puts his hand on the door.

—Follow the Lex. Stay close. We gonna be at Percy's lickity-split.

—Uh-uh.

—What?

—Uh-uh.

He leans forward.

—That don't sound right. Before, you was all, *uh-huh*, like in the affirmative. That there, that sounded like, *uh-uh*, like in the negative. That what I heard?

—Uh-huh.

A sharp line draws itself between his eyebrows.

—You best start findin' some extra fuckin' syllables to 'splain yo-self, muthafucka.

—No.

He makes a move.

I bring up the machine pistol.

—Digga, we're not in your barbershop. We're not in The Jake. We're not at Percy's. You don't have a gun in your hand. And I do. Sit back and relax.

He sits back, but he doesn't relax.

—You wanted proof. You got it. In abundance. You want to take jerkoff here and cut him to ribbons, be my guest. You're planning a big unveiling, gonna show up Papa Doc in public, put him in his place? My blessings. Me, I'm going home. All I need from you is you call off the dogs and get me my passage.

He looks out the window, shakes his head.

—*Call off the dogs. Get me my passage.* You take a look outside? You see the time of day? *Call off the dogs?* Muthafucka, they ain't my dogs. Peeps out there spottin' for you, sittin' behind shaded glass with an eye on the street, they all Papa's. *A passage?* Where to? Gonna go home now? Want me to arrange a passage for yo ass 'cross *Coalition turf?* That what you want? Shit. That takes time. 'Specially seein' how Predo all on the warpath for yo ass. What you think been happenin' all night an' all that time you been up on that hill. Phone been ringin' off the damn hook. Check this shit out.

He pulls out his phone, flips it open and scrolls to the incoming calls screen.

—Look at this shit.

I look.

PREDO

PREDO

PREDO

—The fat is in the fire. The man knows you crossed his yard. Says you went runnin' through his flower bed, trampled some prize shit. Says one of his gardeners went MIA, last seen heading in this direction. Has an APB out. Here. There. Everywhere. An' now you tell me you just laid a smackdown on that crazy witch up on the hill? You know who that grandma is? That is one of the truly last of the old-old skool. She an original piece of work. Word from the X, she the one used ta wipe Predo's ass when he was little. Now, things X told me, things you just shared, sounds like they had something of a fallin' out, but that doan mean he gonna be pleased 'bout you makin' a mess up there. You want to go *home*? Muthafucka, there *ain't* no home for you. Not now. Terry Bird gonna want nothin' to do with yo ass down there. Not till this shit gets sorted fully out.

He leans back, runs a finger over his moustache.

—You come with *me*. Kick it up at Percy's place. Nobody gonna mess in Percy's shit. Not Papa. All the shit in the world can rain from the sky, not a drop gonna land on Percy's roof. That's truth. Kick up there for a few days. I need it, maybe you bear a little witness to some of the shit been going on. Predo gonna kick and scream, but when I drop the knowledge on him, he's gonna have to back down. Gonna give up some shit. An' I tell him so, he gonna lay off yo ass. Once that happen, yo boy Bird gonna welcome you back with open arms. Hail the conquering hero an' all that shit. All you gotta do? Sit tight. Give this shit some air to breathe. It all gonna sort out just fine. Cool?

He puts out his hand.

I don't take it.

—Yeah. Trouble is. I got a date tonight.

He raises his eyebrows.

—*Got a date*.

I shrug.

He keeps his hand out.

—Know, Pitt, that shit ain't funny. Man's here in front of you of-ferin' his hand, offerin' a way out of some shit you in, offerin' to pull you up out of it, an' you makin' jokes. Best thing you can do here, stop bein' a fuckin' comedian an' take what's bein' put yo way. Kiss this shit off twice, it doan come back around.

I look at his hand. I think about the sun and all the hours of daylight between right now and sunset. I think about those couple pints I drank before I came up here and the one left at home and the punishment I've been taking. I run my tongue around the inside of my mouth, feel the last traces of the cuts Vandewater's boys put in there when they tried to make me eat that poker chip. I look at the man who sent me up that hill, the hand he's holding out to me. I think about pulling the trigger on the machine pistol in my hand and watching the bullets disintegrate his face.

He sees my eyes.

Not a stupid man, he sees I don't like him. He takes his hand back.

—Have it yo own damn way, Pitt.

I put the gun down.

—That's kind of the point.

I pull Shades' ski mask over my face. I slip on his gloves and his shades.

—That the A stop across the street?

Digga watches me.

—Yeah. Got the train fare?

—Got that grand you bet for me on your weak-ass dog?

He fishes his hand in his pocket and comes out with a roll.

—Here's the G.

I take the money.

He thinks about something, licks his thumb and peels off another thin sheaf of bills.

—Here's another G. For yo trouble.

I take it.

He puts his roll away.

—Kind of throwin' good money after bad on my part. Seein' as how you ain't gonna live ta see nightfall. But you did yo part. Guess you deserve to least hold it for a while, 'til whoever takes you down pulls it off yo corpse. That train takin' yo ass nowhere, Pitt. Only place they can watch with the sun up is the hole. 'Tween here an 14th, gonna be nothin' but hell to pay.

I open the door.

—Got no choice. My girl, she hates to be stood up.

I get out of the car and walk into the daylight.

It's the direct UVs that get you. Uncovered skin gets hit by the direct rays of the sun, you cook like that boy got cooked in Vandewater's apartment. Keep covered, stay in the shade, get lucky, and you can get by. You'll burn alright; you'll burn, and the more you burn the more you'll push the limits of the Vyrus. But stay covered and you can get by. I am far too well protected by my covering for the sun to do any permanent damage here. I would have to walk in the direct rays, unshaded, for blocks before the UVs could do serious damage through all these layers.

And yet.

One step out of the garage, walking in the sun-protected lee of the mall, I feel it. Its pressure and heat. Like a Russian bath, a Russian bath that causes cancer. I feel the heat straight through the mask and gloves and every other stitch of clothing on my body. Sweat erupts across my scalp and rolls down my sides. My mouth goes dry and I feel a hot flash that ripples out from my gut, rolling through my organs and my blood. The Vyrus writhes inside me, confused, threatened, ready to kill me, kill itself, rather than endure the sun.

Crossing the street, trotting between the cars so I don't have to stand on the corner and wait for the light to change, I remember something. I remember being a sixteen-year-old runaway, how

I spent that summer, every day in Tompkins Square. I remember sprawling drunk and shirtless on the brown grass and waking, my skin so deeply burned it radiated heat. The girl I was with that night, holding her hand an inch from my stomach, warming her fingers. I poured ice-cold beer over my chest. For days the skin flaked and peeled. I picked at it, teasing off leafs of it and burning holes in them with the tip of my cigarette to gross out my friends with the smell. When the burned skin was dead and gone, I was browner than the grass in the park. That winter I was infected.

I look at the subway entrance just ahead. All things being equal, I'm going to die down there, somewhere between here and home. I stop at the top of the stairs.

I look up at the blue sky.

And pay for it with boiling tears and blurred vision.

Half blind, I stumble down the stairs into the hole in the ground, cursing myself.

The platform is crowded. My vision is still clouded, but I run my eyes around, looking for any of Papa's *ton tons macoute*. Nothing.

I pull up the ski mask. Doesn't matter who sees my face. The ones I'm most concerned about will smell me anyway.

I stand on the platform, shifting from foot to foot and rubbing the tears from my eyes, blinking away the blur. The platform grows more crowded. I put my back against one of the green girders that lines the platform. I breathe deep, smell the rats on the track along with all the other stinks of the station. I watch the faces, not caring if I catch anyone's eye. Never certain if I have because of my fogged vision.

I squint at a map of the system. It's a jumble of wavy lines: blue, orange, yellow, red, and green. Meaningless. That's OK, I know the tunnels, I know the lines. I can picture the A in my head. The express down to 59th, to 42nd, to 34th, to 14th. I sniff again. Still smells clean, clean of what I'm looking for anyway. If the *ton tons macoute* want me, they'll have to do it here, make their move in this station. Then again, they could try it on the line, move close to me on the packed train and . . . and what? What are they going to do on a packed train? Nothing. Nothing that won't cause a scene. No, it has to be here.

Or.

Or Papa could have a deal with Predo. Percy said Papa might be dealing with him, might be *on Predo's tip*. Figure it could be that bad. Figure *ton tons* could ride with me right onto Coalition turf. They could hang back, wait till we're below 110th and show me their colors; do it just to drive me, herd me off the train, right into Predo's enforcers.

The air moves in the station; a stale breeze blowing in from the tunnel, pushed ahead by the train. This is a bad play. I should be above ground. Duck into a bar and call a car service. Get a limo with tinted windows. Yeah, sit in a bar on Hood turf and wait for a car. Bad call. A cab? Traffic, clear windows. *Excuse me, cabbie, but would you mind driving exclusively in the shade? I'll make it worth your while.* No. A bus? Jesus fuck, what am I thinking, a bus? This is the way to go. It's this way or it's Digga's way, on *his* tip. And enough guys got a handle on me, I don't need anyone else thinking he can give me a ring whenever things go shitty on him.

The train squeals into the station. People cram themselves up close to the doors, staring at the folks on the inside, also packed at the doors. All of them sizing each other up, challenging one another for space. The doors slide open, the speakers crackle, there's a brief free-for-all as the people on the train and the people on the platform trade places. I wait for the last possible second, looking for some danger more obvious than what I know is already out there, and push my way aboard.

The doors snap shut and the train jerks and rolls. I scent the air in the car and find it safe. My eyes are clearing quickly now, my vision all but normal. I look around and catch sight of a service advisory, a sign telling me at once why the platform had been so crowded. Telling me the C and B trains are out of service and that all express trains are running local. Local, as in hitting every stop between here and home. Slow and steady all the way.

A long slow train through the gauntlet. And me, no cigarettes at all even if they would let you smoke down here.

Stopping, starting, pausing in the middle of the tunnel for a red signal, rolling. The train takes its own goddamn sweet time. 116th, a college kid with a sketchbook in his lap, drawing the passengers seated across from him, just their feet. 110th, last stop in the Hood, people cramming on and off. No *ton tons macoute*. 96th, back on Coalition ground, a guy walking the center aisle, a display of Duracells in his hand, incanting, *Battery one dolla, battery one dolla, battery one dolla*. No enforcers. 81st, a DJ and his crew, still coming down from last night's gig, shoving each other back and forth, showing off for a cute girl in their midst. 72nd, the speaker squawking, endlessly repeating its message that this train is running local. 59th, a homeless guy that reminds me of the Renfield that fingered me on the way up, but it's not him. 42nd, man with a baby carrier on his chest, the baby's eyes returning again and again to my face. 34th, a woman overloaded with Macy's bags. My eyesight clear by 23rd, I see a subway card above the seats; a stanza of Dylan Thomas:

> *Dead men naked they shall be one*
> *With the man in the wind and the west moon;*
> *When their bones are picked clean and the clean bones gone,*
> *They shall have stars at elbow and foot;*
> *Though they go mad they shall be sane,*

> *Though they sink through the sea they shall rise again;*
> *Though lovers be lost love shall not;*
> *And death shall have no dominion.*

And I ride the rails, straight down to 14th Street. Straight down and free and clear. And I just know that it's gotta be bad news.

At 14th, my nerves shot to hell, I get off. I transfer to the L line, cross over to First, and walk out of the station and back into the day.

The sun presses on me just the same as it did Uptown, but here it is almost a relief. As if it were a different, more familiar sun. I walk quickly to 10th, stopping in at my deli. I grab a six-pack and a carton of Luckys. The guy gives me a book of matches and I light up. I walk the last half block to my front door. I step into the vestibule and check my mail. Just a couple things for *occupant,* same as always. I go down the hall to my apartment, unlock the three deadbolts, go inside, turn off the alarm, close the door, snap the locks, rearm, and lean my forehead against the wall. I stay like that 'til I know I have to move.

I walk past the couch, wanting nothing half so much as to sink down onto it, drink my way through the six and smoke Luckys one after another. Instead, I go down the stairs into the basement apartment and get my other gun.

There's nothing wrong with the 9mm I took off Shades, it's just that I know this gun, I trust it as much as a gun can be trusted. Being a gun, it's more than likely gonna end up in someone else's hand being pointed at me someday, so I don't trust it too much. But it's mine and I've used it to kill people before, so I know it works. I leave Shades' piece in the gun safe and pocket my own. Then I crack the fridge.

The bag of anathema is still in my jacket. I take it out and give it a sniff. I have no way of knowing for certain if it's still potent, but it sure as shit smells like it is. I stick it in the fridge. I don't want anyone smelling that stink when I come through the door. I look at my own last pint. The blisters on the backs of my hands throb. My whole body feels baked and dry, skin bright pink. Once it's gone, it's gone. Fuck it.

I pop the pint open and suck it down. Once it's in me, I wonder what the hell I was debating about. Of course I'm drinking it now, you should always drink it now. Drink all of it you can whenever you can. Anything that makes you feel like this, you should drink it. I drain it, slice it, lick it clean. It's good. The blisters don't go away, but they feel a fuck of a lot better. Everything feels better. We'll see how good it feels in a couple days, if I'm still alive and haven't scored. I toss the empty into the biohazard bag and close up.

In the can I give my face a good splash, wash away the last bits of scab clinging to the inside of my mouth. Some of Vandewater's blood is on my shoulder. I towel it off. I see the hole she ripped in the collar of my jacket. I stick my finger in it. Gonna take a pro to make that look OK again. I put the jacket back on. I toss all of Shades' sun-gear in the trash and dig out my own, tired of the stink of someone else's sweat in my pores.

I slam one of the beers and put the rest in my normal fridge, the one with actual food in it, or stuff with mold growing on it, anyway. I grab my picks and I stick a couple extra packs of smokes in my pockets. Wishful thinking on my part, hoping I might actually get to smoke all of them. I leave.

The Count's place is where I left it. I could lurk outside, wait 'til someone goes in and slip in behind them. But lurking and the sun don't go together. Instead, I go next door to the El Iglesia de Dios.

Churches don't bother me. Some guys, they do. Some make a big show of it, avoiding places like this, part of the scene they think. Some are genuinely freaked out. Those are the ones that are sure we're all cursed. They may not say it out loud, but they think it. Most of those kind, they don't last. Who can last walking around thinking their immortal soul has been consecrated to damnation? Except the folks who think that way and really dig it. Those ones are out there, too. They bug me. Who'm I fooling? They give me the willies. But churches don't bother me one way or another. Just four walls and a roof. And maybe a big wooden cross with a guy nailed to it. Nothing I haven't seen before.

I go into the church. There's a couple old ladies in there, kneeling, heads bowed on folded hands. Could be praying. Could be junkies on the nod. Churches are good for that also. I walk past them, right up the aisle and through the door behind the altar. There's a corridor. At one end an office door, at the other a stairwell. I take the stairs.

I run into a guy in a coverall. He's carrying a toolbox. He gives me and my ski mask and sunglasses a look.

I point up the stairs.

—All done?

He looks blank for a second then nods, hooks his thumb back up the way he came.

—Yeah, yeah, all set. Where's the?

—In his office. He'll have your check.

—Oh. Really? OK. Thanks.

We edge around each other and I keep climbing, going past a couple landings and whatever he may have been repairing in here. The door at the top is padlocked. I don't bother with the picks here, just grab the lock and give it a good yank and the screws holding the hasp fast to the door frame tear loose. I push the door open. Jesus, it's bright out there. I go out on the roof and close the door behind me.

There's a gap of about six feet between me and the fire escape next door. I jump it. I don't need a running start. I come down on the escape, making a lot of noise, and have clambered up the iron ladder to the roof before anyone can peek out their windows.

No shade at all. I scoot around on the verdigrised copper sheeting. I find a window that looks in on darkness. I break it and go in. It's some kind of hut, a storage and service unit of some kind. Cobwebs and boxes and gardening tools, of all things. But no door into the building.

I sit in the darkness and smoke. I drop the spent butt and stomp on it. My foot lands on a trapdoor. Fuck, Joe, take a better look around next time. It's one of those spring-loaded jobs. I give it a push. No luck. It's locked on the other side. I stomp on it. Something gives. I stomp again. Something rips loose and the trap swings down and a ladder unfolds and bangs into the floor. Subtle. I go down. Just a tiny landing at the top of the stairs. One door. No one looks out of it to see what the noise is about. Lucky them. I fold the ladder and close the trap and go down a couple floors.

The Count's door is locked. Well, no shit. I take out the picks. They're good locks. It's an expensive building, they should be good locks. But I'm up for the game. Fresh pint just down the hatch, I can feel and hear every pin as I tease them into align-ment. I pop the first. I pop the second. I draw my gun and go in-side.

They're all on the nod, heaped half naked or more in Poncho's door-walled room. If they hadn't been high when they crashed, they would have woken up the second I came through the door. Or maybe that's just me. Maybe when you live like this, with peo-ple, lovers, maybe when you have a Clan to watch over you, you sleep easier. Maybe I'm the only one whose eyes snap open five or six times a day, when a car with an odd sounding engine drives past or a rat rustles the garbage out front or a kid laughs on the sidewalk. Maybe that's it. Maybe my life sucks just a little more than everybody else's. But I doubt it. I think all our lives suck about the same amount. Just in different ways. I look at The Count, Poncho's legs wrapped around his, Pigtails and PJs jumbled next to them.

This guy, I'm about to make his life suck in all kinds of brand new ways.

I nudge the sole of his foot with the toe of my boot. He stirs, they all stir, but only his eyes open.

—Wha? Hunh?

—Morning.

—Whan? Joe?

—Yep.

—Hey. What's up, man?

—You.

He cracks a tired smile.

—Not really, man.

I show him the gun.

—Count. Get up or I'm gonna start shooting your girls.

Poncho's eyes fly open at that.

I level the piece at her face.

—Stay there.

She stays there. The Count gets up. He's wearing blue and white briefs and a girl's T-shirt that rides too high on his skinny belly, Buffy silkscreened on the front.

I point at the girls, all of them stirring now.

—Tell them to stay put.

He runs a hand through his tangled hair.

—Yeah, no problem.

He looks at them.

—Chill, ladies. This is cool. Just a misunderstanding. Nobody lose it. Me and Joe are gonna figure this out.

He looks at me.

—Right, man?

—Sure.

I let him lead the way over to the kitchen. Behind us, the girls press their eyes against the cracks between the doors that screen Poncho's room.

The Count points at a coffeemaker.

—You want some?

—No.

—Cool if I make some?

—No.

—OK. OK. So what's the deal?

He leans his skinny butt against the counter, arms folded, rubbing sleep from his eyes.

—This a jack? You after my stash?

I point at his shirt.

—That supposed to be funny?

He looks down at the picture of the vampire slayer on his chest, shrugs.

—I don't know. I guess so, maybe.

—I hate that shit. That self-aware, ironic, pop culture Vampyre shit. I hate it.

—I.

—Like it's a game.

—It's not supposed to mean anything. Just a shirt.

I bang the barrel of my gun across the bridge of his nose. The nose breaks and bloods runs out. He barks, goes to his knees, hands over his face. Another of those kids who hasn't figured out the pain thing.

—Fuck! Oh fuck!

—That funny, Count? That fit in with your hipster Vampyre lifestyle?

I kick him in the gut. He rolls onto his side, curled in a ball.

One of the girls hisses. I don't bother to look. I put the gun to The Count's head.

—Stay in that fucking room or the gravy train goes off its rails right here.

The hissing continues, but quieter.

I grab some of his hair and pull his face out of his hands.

—Those supposed to be your brides, those girls? They complete the scene for you? Help to polish your image, Count?

I knock out a couple of his teeth with the pistol butt, knowing they won't grow back. Happy about it.

More hissing.

—Fuck you. Fuck your stupid games. Come down here. Like the vibe, do ya? Uptown not your style? Columbia not for you? I get it. Me, I was just Uptown myself. I see why you wouldn't be into that. All those boys the old lady keeps around, I can see where you wouldn't want to join that scene. So, pre-med wasn't what you wanted. Tell me. Tell me about Columbia. Was she saving a spot for you on her wall? Old lady Vandewater, she got a place all picked out to hang your sheepskin next to the others?

—Don't.

I put the barrel in his mouth, make it harder for him to talk.

—Come down here where people live their lives. People try to get by. Try to make this fucked up shit work. Come down here playing games and drawing attention and making life harder than it already is. You fucker.

He dribbles some blood from his mouth.

—Dunht!

I take the barrel out.

—What?

—Don't. Oh fuck. Don't fucking. Don't kill me, man. Don't.

I drop him.

—You stupid fuck. You'd be lucky if I was the one to kill you.

—Just. Please. Don't.

—And besides, nobody tell you yet? You already died.

He coughs blood.

I drop a dish towel on him.

—Get your shit together. I want to hear about Tom. Tell me again how he was the one sponsored you. I want to hear about you and Tom.

The door busts in.

I hesitate for less than a second. That finishes me. I had time to get one round off. Trying to decide whether to use it to kill The Count or slow down Hurley finishes me. I do manage to get one in on him, one punch in the gut. It doesn't do anything. You can't fight Hurley. He puts me down, Tom right behind him.

They're pretty surgical about it, almost as clean as Vandewater's boys. They chill the girls, get me and The Count wrapped tight, and have us out and into a van before anyone in the building can take an interest.

Figure we'll end up at one of Tom's personal safe houses. Someplace private where he can ice The Count until they have their story straight. Me, I'm way past icing in Tom's book. I'll be lucky if this hood ever comes off my head. Actually, I'll be luckier if it never does and they just put a couple in me and sink me in the river. Figure there's a chance of it. Tom may have enough heat on him that he won't take any chances, just waste me and get rid of me. Figure that's wishful thinking. He's had a hard-on for me for too long. He wants to get his licks in before the story's over. He's such an incredible dick he won't be able to resist torturing me one last time. Figure that's about the way things work out. I ain't got any better coming to me anyway. I've done my share of this shit. What goes around, it comes around. Figure it's my turn.

And figure I'm pretty fucking surprised when the hood comes off and the first face I see is Terry's.

He's not alone. Far from it.

They get me strapped to my seat. When the bag comes off my head, I'm expecting to see Tom's fist coming at my face. Wrong. There's Terry, sitting at the kitchen table in the Society headquarters, sitting there with some notes and shit in front of him, looking at the papers. There's Tom, pacing back and forth behind him, a few of his partisans standing around the room. There's The Count, taped up to a chair right next to mine. Looks like Hurley must have given him a good one 'cause he's out. Dry blood covering his lips and cheeks and chin, snuffling through the scabs clogging his nose. He's better off. There's Hurley, right off my shoulder, making sure I don't try to do fuck knows what. And there's Lydia, sitting next to Terry, not looking happy to see me at all. Terry, Tom and Lydia in the same room. Me on the other end of their hard looks. Not the first time I've been here. But it's never a good thing, having the senior council of the Society all in one place looking at you like your head coming off is a foregone conclusion and they're just deciding who gets to swing the ax.

—Hey, guys. What's up?

Terry takes off his glasses, rubs his eyes, making a big show of how run down he is.

—I need your help, Joe.

Tom starts waving his arms around.

—Fuck that, *his help*. We don't need his help, he's already helped plenty, already fucked himself. It's time for sentencing. I move waiving the inquiry and going straight to the sentencing.

—Yeah, Tom, once we're officially convened and the whole council is here, that'll be cool. But for now, I'm just kind of passing the time with an old friend here.

—Bullshit! That's favoritism, Terry! That kind of crap, that shit is over! You can't get away with, with protecting him anymore. He's done. And, man, your time, your time is coming to a close. As soon as we're convened, as soon as this *spy* has been executed, I'm calling for a referendum on your chairmanship. You harbored his ass, you kept this serpent in the garden, man. This shit is down to you as much as it is to him.

Terry starts to open his mouth. I get ready to enjoy seeing Tom put in his place, but it doesn't happen. Terry just shakes his head and holds up one hand.

—Yeah. Yeah, you're right. That's right. And I, man, I thoroughly expect something like this, my chairmanship has to come into question. That's, you know, that's just the price. But I am going to invoke some privileges, I am going to serve as Joe's defense in the inquiry.

Tom shakes his head, arms folded over his chest.

—Not gonna be an inquiry.

Terry nods.

—Yeah, OK, if you have your way, in the sentencing phase I'm still gonna serve as his defense. And, you know, as such, I have a right to talk to the man. Right here, in front of everybody.

Tom taps his index finger on the table right in front of Terry.

—No. Fucking. Way. No way does this guy get any more special treatment.

Lydia leans forward, putting her elbows on the table, her biceps stretching the fabric of her black sweater.

—You're wrong, Tom.

He moves his eyes from Terry to her.

—What?

—It's due process. He may be a shit, and Terry may be on his way out, but due process is due process. He can talk to him if he wants.

There's a little stare-off. Lydia could tear Tom a few new assholes at will. If he didn't have his partisans here. But it hasn't come to that yet, it hasn't come to an open coup of Society leadership. Yet.

He nods, throws up his hands.

—OK, OK, *due process* it is. But if Terry can ask questions, we all can.

Terry shrugs.

—Sure, sure, if that's what it takes. Sure.

He looks back at me.

—So, like I was saying, Joe, I can use your help. As I guess you can kind of see, the shit's been hitting the fan.

—No kidding?

—Sure has.

—How hard?

Tom sits on the edge of the table.

—Not as hard as I'm gonna kick your balls into your throat if you don't stop being a smartass.

I look at him.

—How's the leg, Tom? Get that bullet out?

He laughs.

—Yeah, be funny. Take it all the way. Sure, I got the bullet out. Got it in a plastic bag. Gonna be exhibit A when we sentence your ass. That alone, fucker, that alone is gonna get you executed. Before we do it, I'm gonna take that bullet and shove it through your ear.

I look at Terry.

—You gonna let him talk to me like that?

Terry fingers his papers, gives them a flip.

—Well, right now, like you kind of been hearing, there's not much I can do. I mean, you ask how hard the shit's hit the fan, let me tell you, hard enough to stick on everything.

—That's pretty hard.

—Yeah, yeah it is. Hell, Joe, once we got tipped off you were on your way back down, the shit would have to be pretty hard to get Predo and us to agree to let you pass all the way without no one getting in your way. 'Cause, you know, no one wanted a big scene with you getting dragged off a train or anything. And still, getting Predo to agree to let us take you into custody, that took some doing. Wouldn't you say that's some shit hitting hard?

I don't say anything. I don't really have to. Because he's right, that's some shit hitting the fan pretty damn hard.

—You got to admit, whatever it was made you go wandering around the Hood, trailing one of Predo's enforcers, whatever that was, it'd have to be pretty damn important to get you off the hook at this point. And, well, that's even assuming the enforcer hadn't gone missing. Then we got.

He looks at his papers.

—We got one of Digga's people, Papa Doc, sending word through Predo that you escaped custody and beat on some guards. All and all . . .

He looks at the papers again.

—Looks like you've been making some noise all over. And, you know, shooting Tom, well, that was a bad call, too. So.

He drops the papers and looks up.

—So, I don't know. You got anything to say about all this?

Anything to say? Anything to say about Terry being the one who set me off poking in the first place? No. Not yet.

And Tom's just playing his angle. Hand it to the shit, it's a bold play. We'll see how far it gets him.

—I got nothing to say.

Tom hops off the table and goes to the fridge.

—And how 'bout this, asshole, got anything to say about this?

He drops a bag of anathema on the table.

—Got anything to say about this being in your apartment? You fucking poisoner. You motherfucking dealer piece of shit.

Terry gives me a look.

The look goes from the anathema to me and back again. A shake of the head goes with it.

—Of all things, Joe. This stuff? I never thought I'd see it again. Been so long, I had to explain it to Tom and Lydia. You know it's killing kids out there? You know what it's doing right now to our kids? Let alone the Society cause, man. Stuff is trouble. Got to say, Tom's right on this one, it's poison.

Lydia points at the bag.

—That shit. That shit. That kid you took care of at Doc's? That fish you put down? That fish was one of mine. He was in the Alliance. You. You fucking. You what? You hooked him and what? He was gonna talk to someone? Tell someone where he got it? Was that it? Did you give him the hotshot that sent him over? You. Jesus. You fucking.

She looks elsewhere, happy not to have my face in her field of vision.

Terry picks up the papers.

—All this stuff, I don't know, man, this stuff. Maybe, maybe we could have worked some of this out. But that.

He waves the papers at the anathema.

—That is . . . I don't know, Joe.

He drops the papers.

—Help me here, man. Tell me something that will help.

Tom sticks his face in mine.

—No. He's got nothing to say this time. He's in it now and he knows it. Don't you, asshole? You are in the shit. Know better

than to open your mouth this time, don't you? Know if you open
your mouth this time it'll fill right up with shit.
—It's Tom! He's the one!

It's funny. Sometimes, you'll be thinking something, thinking it
over and over and over again. You'll be thinking it and just waiting
for the absolutely perfect moment to say it when you know it will
have the most impact and really fuck somebody's shit up. And
then, right when you're all set to say it, someone beats you to the
punch.

We all look at The Count.
  He says it again.
—It's Tom! He's the one! He's the dealer. Not Joe. It's Tom.
  Tears are running down his face, cutting tracks in the dry
blood.
—It's Tom. He. Oh, God. Don't let him hurt me. Don't let him
hurt me anymore. It's Tom.
  Not surprisingly, Tom does try to hurt him.
—You shit! You little fuck!
  Terry doesn't need to move.
—Hurley.
  Hurley scoops Tom up before he can touch The Count. He
puts him on the floor and puts his foot in his chest as he pulls out
his twin .45s and points them at Tom's partisans. They stop think-
ing about whatever moves they were thinking about and get busy
thinking about staying very still.
  Hurley looks down.
—Sorry 'bout dat, Tom. You OK?
—Get off me, you fucking moron!

—Sorry, Tom. Not till Terry says so.

The Count, his legs strapped to the legs of the chair, is rocking and lunging against his bindings, trying to get farther away from Tom.

—No! No! Don't let him up! No! He'll kill me! No!

Terry stands, arms held out.

—Cool it! Everybody just needs to cool it. Kid! Kid! Count! Dude, cool it. No one is gonna hurt you. Just cool it.

The Count freezes, eyes big in his head. He's stopped screaming. Mumbling now, whispering.

—Oh, shit, oh shit. I'm gonna die. I don't wanna die. Oh shit.

—Cool it. Calm down, man.

The Count goes silent except for the crying.

Tom is another matter.

—Get your fucking foot off me, you fucking stupidass retard.

Hurley looks at Terry.

Terry walks over and looks down at Tom.

—Be cool, Tom. This is a tense situation, I know, but we're gonna sort it. Don't take it out on Hurley.

—Fuck you, Terry. Get him the fuck off of me.

—You gonna be cool?

Tom opens and closes his mouth a few times, takes some deep breaths.

—Yeah. I'm gonna be cool. Now. Get. Him. Off. Me.

Terry nods.

—OK, cool. Let him up, Hurley. And those guys are OK, you don't have to cover them.

Hurley takes his foot off Tom's chest and lowers his guns. But he doesn't put them away, just moves to the door so no one can get out without going through him.

Tom jumps up and takes a step toward The Count.

—You fucker.

Terry comes between them.

—Cool. Remember?

Tom turns and walks to the other side of the room, closer to his partisans.

—Yeah. Cool. Fine. Long as I don't have to hear more of that shit.

Terry nods.

—Sure, sure. But, you know, let's just look into this. See where The Count is coming from.

He faces The Count.

—What's it about? An accusation like that, that's a pretty big deal, you know? Could get you in a lot of trouble.

The Count rolls his eyes.

—Trouble? I'm *in* trouble, man. What do you think? Man, that's why. Don't you know what?

—Cooool. Easy. Breathe a little.

—Little lying fucker.

—Tom! Cool it.

The Count breathes.

Terry puts a hand on his shoulder.

—So what's up here? What's got you spooked enough to try a story like that?

—Story? Man. Story? You want a *story*? OK, try this. Tom is the fucking dealer. Tom is the hookup for all of downtown.

—This is such fucking!

—Hurley.

Hurley holds up one of his pistols and presses it to his lips.

—Tom, shhhh.

Tom shuts up.

Terry pats The Count.

—And?

—And. And. Oh shit. You guys. You're gonna. Just. Look. All I want is. I'll tell you everything, man. It's gonna come out. All I want is, keep him away from me. And. And when you do me. Don't let me burn. Just. Not the sun. Something. But not the sun.

—Hey, hey. We'll talk about executions, all that, you know, later. But, we're not gonna burn *anyone*.

—OK. OK. I'm. OK. So. I, you know, I have some money, I like a good time. The other fish, they know that. So I have a lot of *friends*. Tom, he, you know, he's the guy who gets the shit. Me, I'm the guy helps to hook him up with other fish, other kids.

Tom's not even trying to talk now, just staring, jaw hanging, face going from red to white and back again.

—Tom brings it in, and I help to hook up the customers.

—OK. So Tom brought it in. You helped. Why? You don't need money.

—No. It's. Oh shit. It's for the Coalition. Tom's a fucking mole for the Coalition.

Tom coughs. Laughs. Laughs some more. He shakes his head. Starts to breathe normally again. It's too outrageous. Hearing it, it's too much to believe.

The look The Count is getting from Terry is the look you give someone when the lie they're telling is so over the top you have to listen out of sheer awe.

—Wow. OK. That's, wow, that's pretty big. That would be a pretty big deal. So he, what? He told you? He told you he was a Coalition mole and he was, I don't know, bringing this shit in to undermine the Society. Is that how this stuff works?

—No. I. No.

—No. OK. OK. You, like, you found out. You found out and you were outraged and now you're telling us, that it?

—No.

—OK. Well, I don't know, man, you tell me what the story is. How'd you find this out?

The Count starts to cry again.

—Because I'm a spy, man. I'm a fucking Coalition agent. Don't you. Maaaan. You're being sold out. There's a deal. Tom helps to bring you down, man, he does that, sets up an alliance with the Coalition and they let him run the turf. I know. I made the contact, man. I'm a spy. I'm a spy. Just don't. God, please. Don't burn me, man. Don't burn me.

Terry straightens up. He looks at Tom.

—Wow. How about that?

Tom is shaking his head.

—Fucking spies, man. What a load. That, see, that's how the Coalition works. That's how they fucking plan to undermine us. By attacking our unity. That kind of creepy bullshit.

The Count isn't done.

—He told me. He said I was supposed to tell a story about Joe. Say Joe was the dealer, say he was the spy. I was supposed to do it here. In front of the council. He told me to act like I was unconscious until the council was in session. Then tell this story. Tell it in front of everybody, that it was Joe, and that *you knew*. Tell 'em that *you knew*. So he could, he could have you removed. Have you executed and take the chair, man. He. He would have killed me after. He would have. He's a fucking.

He turns his eyes on Tom.

—You fucking sadist! You sick son of a bitch! That shit you did to me! You fucking! You die! I don't care anymore! Burn me! Burn me! Just burn him next to me so I can watch!

It's more than a guy like Tom can take.

Terry takes care of him this time, has him on the ground almost as quickly as Hurley did. The partisans want to help their leader, but what are you supposed to do with Hurley and Lydia in your face?

The Count sobs.

—I'll burn. Ungh, God. I'll, Jesus, I'll, hngh, hngh, hngh, I'll burn just to watch.

Tom raves.

—Off me! That fucking spy. Both of them. Don't think this is gonna get you off the hook. You know it's bullshit. Everyone in here can smell it.

I clear my throat.

—Um, I don't want to stick my nose in family business, but that is pretty much what the old lady told me.

Terry swings around.

—Old lady?

—Vandewater. She said her name was Vandewater. Lives Uptown. Ever hear of her?

First, things come to a halt as Terry tries to get Digga on the phone. That takes a while. Seems he's been pretty busy smacking some ass up there. But once he does, once Digga confirms that I did some *muthafuckin' fine recognizance* for him up on Morningside Heights, once it is confirmed that I was up there and met the old lady and came down with the anathema and a witness, once that all gets said? The shoe gets on the other foot in a hurry. Figure some of that speed has to do with a sense of justice needing to be done in a hurry. Figure some of it's because Terry doesn't want me talking too much about some of the things Vandewater had to say. Figure six of one, a half dozen of the other. But mostly, figure it's the other: Terry being the private sort and all.

The partisans get to stay. Once they see the new wind that's blown through the room, they opt for roles as official witnesses to a hastily called tribunal. Terry and Lydia sit. Under normal circumstances Tom would have sat next to them as head of security, loving a good tribunal as he does, but things being a bit out of joint, Hurley sits in for him.

It's an intimate affair. The Count gives testimony. I give testimony. The partisans give testimony as to what they just heard in this room. Tom tries to give testimony, but the tape Hurley wrapped around his face keeps it to a minimum.

The verdict comes in fast.

Terry, Lydia and Hurley each write a word on a scrap of paper and show them to each other.

Terry does the honors.

—Tom Nolan, on charges of treason, espionage, distribution of poisons, murder, corruption of the principles of the Society, abuse of office, and any and all additional charges that might accrue to you posthumously, you are found guilty and will be executed.

He shuffles the scraps of paper.

—Further.

He takes off his glasses, blinks.

—Further, due to the nature and, well, the extent of your crimes. We've decided. Hell. You're going out in the sun. You have to burn.

He puts his glasses back on.

—You sorry son of a bitch.

—There's gonna be some fallout.

Terry comes back from the fridge and hands me a beer.

I take it, set it down.

—Figures.

He offers one to Lydia.

She shakes her head.

—Beer companies peddle male domination fantasies to twelve-year-old boys.

Terry sets the beer on the table.

—My bad.

He sits next to me.

—Some of Tom's people won't accept it. You know. So. We're gonna have to work fast. Make sure things don't get out of hand. Get our ducks in a row.

Lydia grabs the beer.

—Fuck it.

She opens the can and takes a long drink.

—We're going to have to kill some people, Terry.

He shrugs.

—Yeah. Yeah. I guess, I guess that's what I'm getting at. And we're gonna have to kill them now. Today. Before, you know, before word gets out.

He looks at me.

—Before word gets out about what was said and, you know, by who.

I look at my own unopened beer.

It's not like it's a shock. Situation like this, guy like Tom with all those fanatics behind him? Execute a guy like that after a kangaroo court, some people will get up in arms.

Terry drinks.

—I'm not big on covert operations, but we gotta be quick, I think. And quiet. On this one? The less people know, the better. Not gonna increase anyone's confidence in the Society knowing the head of security was a spy.

Lydia frowns at her own beer.

—I'm more worried if the other Clans find out. Some of the smaller Clans, some of those guys below Houston could take it as a sign, start picking at our turf. The Bulls and the Bears, those money-grubbing pigs, they'd love to move their turf closer to the Coalition, get hooked back up. We need to keep it in-house. Make sure everybody knows we can clean our own mess. And

we need to send a message Uptown. Let Predo and that Vandewater woman know they can't get away with this shit.

Terry nods.

—Yeah. Yeah.

He looks at me.

—That's why, what we're doing with Tom, that's why we felt we
needed to do that. Make sure people know we're serious.

I take out a smoke.

—I know you're serious, Terry.

He takes a drink of his beer.

—Well, OK, if you say so.

I go to light my smoke.

Lydia puts a hand on my arm.

—No smoking in Society buildings, Joe.

I look at her, look at Terry, one on either side of me.

Figure it was gonna come to this. Figure I don't like it. Figure it's this or the other. Figure it's take care of the list, or end up
on it.

I move Lydia's hand and light my smoke.

—Guys, stop fucking around and tell me who you want me to
kill.

They start me with Tom.

—A case like dis? Da hardest part is just knowin' da poor fooker.
Ever seen it bifore, Joe?

—Nope.

—Ain't fookin' pretty. It's not dat hard, mind. It's easier if ya start
at night. Stake 'em out an' let da sun rise and take care of 'em. Dis
way is harder. But it's still not dat hard.

I drive Tom's van while Hurley lectures me on the logistics of
burning someone.

—What we'll do, when we get ta da spot, we'll unwrap him here in da van. In da back der. One ah us, you or me, don't matter none to me, one of us will open dat back door, da udder'll shove da fooker out. After dat it don't take too fookin' long. Once he's done, I got a snow shovel.

Way at the end of 14th, past the power station there, away from the projects and the playing field of the park, we find a square of asphalt littered with broken bottles, tiny, empty glassine envelopes, and used condoms.

We climb into the windowless back of the Econoline. My hands have been getting too much sun, wrapped around the wheel, exposed to the rays. The blisters that had been soothed by the pint I drank are starting to bubble back up under my gloves. We take off our shades and look at the writhing log of black Hefty bags.

Hurley grunts.

—T'aint no use puttin' it off. Got lots more ta do after dis.

He grabs the plastic and heaves, ripping it open, revealing Tom, bound and gagged in rolls of duct tape and spools of wire.

—Futchkthers!

Somehow he's managed to bite through most of the tape over his mouth.

—Futchking futchkthers!

Hurley shakes his head.

—Jaysuz yer a sad fook, Tom. Look at ya. Ta tink I called ya a friend. Ya sad, sorry fook. Well, ya got no one ta blame but yerself. Fer da sake a our history, I'd put ya out before tossin' ya, but Terry said ya need ta be awake. An I got ta say, I'm not feelin' dat charitable just now after da way ya called me a retard an' all. Just cuz a fella's not da brightest in da bunch, dat don't mean ya gotta . . . Well, fook me anyway, ya don't wanna hear dis shite.

He looks at me.

—Ya want da doors or da shove?

I look at Tom, he's chewing at that gag, clearly hoping to get in a last word before it's over. I think about all the grief he's caused me. That time he had me in chains.

—I'll do the shove if it's all the same to you, Hurley.

—Taught ya might. Taught ya might.

He moves over by the doors.

We put our shades back on.

—Fuchkers!

He's almost through the tape.

—Futchking! Pitt! Pitt!

Hurley puts his hand on the door.

—Ready, Joe?

—You're an asshole, Pitt!

I take a seat on the floor, just above Tom's head.

—Just a sec, Hurl.

—But you're not a complete fucking idiot!

I plant my feet on his shoulders.

—Hurley's an idiot! But not you.

I look at Hurley.

—Think about it! Fucking me a spy?

I nod.

—You're a tool, Pitt!

He pushes the doors open.

—You're being used!

Sunlight claws at us.

—He's using you!

I shove, putting everything I have into it, my legs pistoning and sending him sliding across the floor of the van and out into the day.

—You're Terry's fucking tool!

Hurley grabs the lengths of rope he's tied to the door handles and gives them a yank.

—You fucking asshole!

The door slams shut. The screams quickly cut off as tumors fill Tom's throat.

There's a hole drilled in the door, a circle of steel the size of a quarter hangs from a single rivet above it. Hurley swings it aside and looks out.

—Jaysus.

He lets the cover swing back into place and looks at me.

—Ya want ta see dis?

I crawl over and take a look. One is more than enough.

I smoke while we wait.

I think while I smoke. I think about how I got here, how I got to be in this van with Hurley, doing exactly the kind of job for Terry that I told myself I'd never do again. I think about how this got started.

I think about The Spaz at Doc Holiday's, one of my regular hangouts. That kid spazzing on Evie's night off, a night I could be expected to be there. I think about hotshots and how easy it is to slip one to a junkie. About how the jobs had all dried up, how I couldn't score a gig to save my life, how the only place to go looking for a job was Terry. And that little confrontation between Tom and Terry the day Terry gave me the gig. The hostility in the air. The smell of the young wolf circling the old. The threat to Terry sprayed in the air. I think about the job Terry offered me, looking into the shit that was going around. A job like that, sooner or later I'm going to be squeezing Phil for scraps. And everyone knows Phil is my snitch. And Phil, I think about how he knew The Count, already. How that slimy Renfield had been let inside the biggest secret on the street. Like maybe someone wanted him to see it.

I think.

I think about how I ended up with Tom's name. Tom the zealot. Tom the patriot. Tom the Coalition-hating fanatic. I try to square that up with Tom the spy. I think about setups and betrayals and backstabbing and power plays, and being a tool.

I think, and the back of the van fills with smoke.

And then Hurley flips a coin to see who has to use the shovel. I lose.

The sun is bad. I've gotten far too much of it today. It's gonna age me. Getting sun, it always sticks another year or two on your face. But that's not the bad part. The bad part is what I shovel off the ground and dump in a pile on top of the shredded Hefty bags.

What I would have done to die without seeing that, it's a long list.

Hurley has another list.

Seven names. It could have been worse. It could have been longer. Or some of them could have been friends. That's happened. Back in the day, working for Terry, I've had a piece of paper in my hands with friends' names on it. But not this time. Could have something to do with my not keeping friends anymore. Whatever. We still have to go to work.

None of them are expecting anything. Middle of the day. Sun in the sky. They're all fully pledged members of the Clan and they're in tight with the head of security. What do folks like these got to worry about? Except folks like me and Hurley. And really, nobody's expecting folks like me and Hurley.

It's all pretty easy and clean. As these things go. Double park the van a few times, run across the sidewalk, get into whatever squat or tenement these guys are jungled up in. The ones who even have their eyes open, the ones who see us coming, they wish they hadn't. No one wants to take the last trip seeing the two of us coming for them. But we don't make it any worse than it has to be. Say that for Hurley, he's a professional. And me, I just don't see any sense in making a mess that you're gonna have to clean up yourself.

When it's over, we make one last stop. We wheel over to Tom's favorite safe house, the old Society headquarters on C, the basement he still used for meetings of his Anarchists.

And we leave him there. In the middle of the floor. For them to find. For them to see should any of them meet down here to talk about options and retaliations. A look at that, they'll be lining up to stop by Terry's one by one and pay their respects. One look at *that,* they'll be A-OK with anything Terry Bird has to say.

How nice for Terry, the way things turned out.

It's well after sundown by the time we've finished the last of it. Every name is checked off the list, Hurley licking the tip of a pencil as he draws a line through each one, one by one. They've all been gotten rid of, mortal, or not so mortal, remains tucked away.

Hurley's behind the wheel now. He bums one of my smokes and takes a huge drag.

—Keerist, but dat is lovely.

I nod, smoke my own.

—Got some place you want ta be, Joe?

—Just drop me back at headquarters. I should have a quick word with Terry.

—Sure, sure.

He drives me over.

—Say, Joe.

—Un-huh?

—A little like old times, eh? Me an you deliverin' da mail, like.

—Uh-huh.

—Fer da record.

—Yeah?

—It ain't true what some people say.

—What's that?

—Ya ain't gone soft. Shite, ya ain't no softer dan a fookin' stone.

—Thanks.

—Cheers.

And off he drives.

Me, I go up the steps and hit the buzzer.

Terry answers the door himself.

—Hey, Joe. Everything go alright?

He's not surprised at all when I punch him in the mouth. Just gets off the floor and wipes the blood from his lips and walks down the hall away from me.

—Come on in, Joe. If we're going to talk personal, we should do it inside.

—Everybody needs something at some time or another. That's just the way it is. And, you know, sometimes, you can't always get what you want, but you can get what you need. So we may work at cross-purposes, some of the Clans. You know, especially when it comes to the majors, the Society, the Hood, the Coalition. We all have different mission statements, opposing philosophies. So there's conflict. But, you know, everybody knows it's no good for anybody if the balance is agitated. What I'm trying to do down here, what we're trying to achieve, that's very long term, man. It requires some finesse. I truly believe in radicalism, we wouldn't have broken free of the Coalition without it, but it has its place

and time. A guy like Tom, an avowed Anarchist, he doesn't necessarily have the right attitude for the times. That was my bad, I
thought he did. I thought he was a natural for security. I was
wrong. Hey, power corrupts. The guy didn't take to it. He started
seeing some things he didn't like, started thinking he could do
better. Next thing you know, he's got all these new faces turning
up under his wing. New fish. Too many of them. I mean, can you
imagine, Joe, the guy was infecting them on his own? When I realized what he was doing, I was, man, I was blown away. Unthinkable. To hell with the threat it posed, you know, to me. Predo
or Digga or any of the Clans finds out about that, we would
have all been in the shit. That could have started an all out arms
race. Clans infecting left and right to keep the balance of power.
Man, something had to be done. But it had to be done, you
know . . . with finesse. So. I started putting out feelers. Just kind
of looking to see if I could catch the vibe. There are, I don't know,
back channels for this kind of thing. Ways for Clans to communi-
cate without it being a big deal. Just rapping, kind of. Seeing how
things are, checking the weather. And the vibe I was getting? It
was unhealthy, man. Things were agitated all over. And, you know,
like I say, sometimes, everybody needs something.

He takes off his glasses, sets them aside.

—Safety. Stability. Security. That's what was needed. I, we, the
Society, needed Tom discredited. And, when you get down to
it, killed. And we needed it to happen before he could start making trouble with all his new fish. Digga, as Luther X's handpicked
successor and the voice of the Hood, needed Papa Doc off his
ass so he could continue to consolidate his position. Dexter
Predo, acting for the Secretariat of the Coalition, needed Mrs.
Vandewater's secret campaign to destabilize and invade the Hood
crushed. All the major Clans needed to remove a threat to their
integrity and the integrity of their members. Not to mention the
infected population at large. Any one of those threats could have

started open hostilities like we haven't seen since the sixties and seventies. Back then, we had protests and riots and high crime rates to kind of disguise what was going on. If it happened again? We would all be at risk. The climate out there in the world today? The distrust and hostility between peoples? Imagine if they found out there were people they might be able to claim weren't really people at all. People who feed on other people. That ground needs to be seeded with great care, man. I mean, that's what I'm all about. War between the Clans is unthinkable today. Revolutions like the one we had, never gonna happen again. So once we had a chance to talk, once we got it out there in front, we all put something in to make it happen. We needed a, I don't know, man, we needed a *catalyst*. All these people, Tom, Papa, Mrs. Vandewater, they all have followers. That's why they're a threat in the first place. So it has to look like the weather, like something that just happened. And, this time out, you were the weather, man.

He picks up his glasses, starts to give them a wipe.

—What really got the ball rolling was when Predo got hip to Vandewater's plans. Once he was on to that? Once he knew about The Count being down here? Once that happened, there were some pieces to start moving around. Like, Predo tells me about The Count, about him being a plant down here, Vandewater's pet project. *Predo* sacrifices that pawn, and I flip him. I act like I just ESPed him out, and put him in a corner. I give him a little clarity about where he is and how he can save himself. *I* use *him* to point *you* uptown. All that took, once he knew what to do himself, all that took was making sure Philip Sax knew him a little. Something goes down, Joe, you always start shoving Phil around. That kind of, I don't know, street corner imperialism, it never works to the oppressor's advantage, you know.

I stare at him.

He shrugs.

—Anyways, once you were headed up, there were only so many ways for you to go. And we were watching, covering the routes. And Digga was waiting. Except.

He pinches his lower lip.

—What went down with you and Daniel. I didn't call that one, you going to him. I thought, you know, you'd come to me for the passage. What was that about? Daniel give you a name or something?

I watch him, his line in the water, fishing.

He raises his hand, glasses dangling from his fingers.

—Cool. Cool. You got business with Daniel, that's not the kind of thing to go public with. No problem.

He puts the glasses back on.

—It all worked out anyway. Predo had all the lines covered. And, hey, I don't, you know, saying I don't like the man is an understatement, but Predo, he kicked in. Sacrificing that enforcer, just to, you know, help set the scene and give Digga some leverage, that was commitment to the good of the whole.

—If you say so.

—Well, just one man's, you know, opinion. So then Digga. *Digga* catches you up there. Plays some scenes, works a little on your head. Makes an impression. Once that impression is made, he makes sure you know what you're after, points you at *Vandewater*. And, well, the details are *complicated,* but you got worked into *her* plan.

—Say what?

—Her plan. She's, you know, doing *her* own thing *completely separate* from our gig. Mind you, man, there was a time, not too long ago, there was a time she would have been onto us from the start. But she's gotten too narrow-minded, too focused on that whole racism thing. How's that supposed to work? How's that not like willfully blinding yourself to the big picture? She just doesn't see the whole anymore. Anyway, what she thinks is, she *thinks* she's letting you go to come down here to rock *my* boat.

—*Letting me go?* Lady got a stomach full of bullets.

—Uh-huh, I hear you.

—I pumped her full of anathema.

—Yeah.

—Terry, I bit her fucking eye out.

—Sure, sure, I know.

—She did not *let me go*.

—Well, you know, like I said, it's *complicated*. And you shouldn't feel bad about the way you handled yourself, but, yeah, she let you go.

—Bull.

—Let's just agree on that one for now, man. The real point is that she's so blinded by her narrow mindedness, she can't see that letting you go is not gonna rock my *boat*, it's gonna rock her *whole world*. 'Cause she just handed you the evidence Digga'll use to take care of Papa. Now, did she know Papa's man would be lame enough to shoot and nod off in her basement? No. But that's just a bonus to the fact that you have witnessed the whole scene up there. *Digga* is all set up now to confront *Predo* about the anathema in a public forum. And once public pressure is on *Predo* to deal with this, with the reemergence of anathema on his watch, he can publicly reprimand *Vandewater* and strip her of some of her powers. Curb her independence and install some of his own people up in the Morningside Settlement. And that leaves the Society's needs. Digga puts you on a train. Truth is, he wanted you up there a little longer to corroborate some of the details of what was going down. You wanting to roll so soon threw things a little, but we got it back on track. Predo cleared the rails. I held Tom off until you could confront The Count. The Count played his scene for you. And I sent Hurley along with Tom to make sure you both ended up back here in one piece. After that, it's just a matter of The Count doing his thing and waiting for you to chime in with the truth. Or, you know, the truth as you know it to be. Which is kinda, when you get right down to it, all the truth ever is anyway.

He lifts his hands from the table and drops them back down.

—And that's how things work sometimes. Not always. Just sometimes. Believe me, you don't want to be trying to keep all those balls in the air too often. But sometimes the stars align. And sometimes, this picture we're trying to put together, this image of the infected in the world, sometimes it takes a different kind of cooperation than most people want to know about. It's not that people don't believe in what they say they believe in, it's just that sometimes you need to bend so you don't break. The weather isn't always what you want it to be, Joe. Sometimes, got to make it yourself. Got to make the rain to get the crops to grow. That's just pragmatic.

I think about Tom, the true believer, his final legacy being that he was a spy.

—That it is.

I look around the room.

—And Lydia?

He shakes his head.

—No way, man. Lydia is pure. She, you just know she could never take this kind of scene. Moral absolutes, that's her thing. It's right or it's wrong. No, Lydia played her part, but she didn't know she was.

—Where is she now?

—She's out rallying her people. They're, you know, pretty neutral as far as intra-Clan issues go. We thought it'd be a good idea if they kind of helped get the word out. Make sure, I don't know, that the message being heard is the right one. That kind of thing.

—And what's the message?

. He raises his shoulders, lets them drop.

—Well, you know, man, you were here. We're not really trying to hide anything.

—What's the message, Terry?

—The message is, *Everything's cool. There was some trouble, but now it's all cool.*

—What kind of trouble?

—Well, we thought it best to leave out all the Coalition stuff. That kind of thing's just gonna stir up bad feelings. So, you know, *attempted coup.* Not pretty, but an internal matter. No hard feelings to anyone or anything. Something that happens in any revolutionary movement.

—Sure, sure, just the price of doing business.

—The price of politics, anyway.

I fit a cigarette to the corner of my mouth.

—Yeah, politics. Politically speaking, you came out of this in pretty good shape.

—Well, I don't know if I'd say that. Narrowly averting a coup. Discovering a Coalition plot at the heart of our Clan. Losing one of our highest placed members. I don't know that that adds up to a good day for the Society and all.

I light up.

—Yeah, taken that way, I guess maybe not. However.

I look for a place to drop the spent match, settle on the floor.

—Taken the other way, it worked out pretty well.

Terry bends and picks up the match.

—What way is that, Joe?

—The way where the truth is involved.

He walks to the sink and drops the match.

—Well, it's a realpolitik world. The truth doesn't always *will out,* you know.

He goes to the fridge.

—Tell me, Terry.

He opens the fridge, back to me, lips zipped.

—Was this the way you had it figured from the top? I mean, when I came wandering in here looking for a gig and you sent me looking for the anathema, was this the way you had it in mind?

He looks at me over his shoulder.

—You need some?

I flex my hands, the dry white skin over my knuckles cracks.

—I'm not thirsty right now.

He sighs.

—You're a better man than I.

He comes back to the table, a pint of blood in his hand.

—Me, I need a drink.

He takes a penknife from his pocket and pokes a hole in the bag.

—I need it something fierce.

He takes a drink.

I blow smoke.

He points at it.

—That's not a habit you should be getting into, smoking in here. It's special circumstances tonight, but in general, not the way we do it.

I keep smoking.

He nods.

—Joe, it did get a little more complicated than I thought it might. I mean, you heard the story. I'm, you know, still waiting for a loose end to come around and get me.

He drinks. A little shudder runs down his body.

—Never get used to it, you know? Never. No matter how long it's been, no matter how many times I've felt it, I've never gotten used to how good it goes down. How many other things are like that? How many things in life that you just don't get tired of?

—You tell me.

He takes another drink.

—Not too many, man, not too many at all.

He drains the rest of the bag, folds it neatly, sets it on the table in front of him.

—So. How I had it figured, what I knew I could count on?

He looks at me.

—How I had it figured was you'd dig around. Being you, you'd, you know, keep digging. Dig and dig and dig until you hit something that stopped you, and then you'd try to dig through it. Knowing that, well, I, you know, guessed it'd be just a matter of time before you dug up Tom.

I smoke.

—Yeah, I get that. A matter of time seeing the way you guys had things all set up, anyway. Pretty fucked up, Terry. All the way around.

—You know what, Joe? You got that right.

He scratches the side of his nose.

—Know what else is fucked up?

—What's that?

—Think about it.

—About?

He taps his forehead.

—Think for a second. It won't take long.

I think. I think about the story he just told me. And I get it.

I have my gun. Terry gave it back before I went out with Hurley. I've used it since then. I reach for it.

I hear a noise. Terry shakes his head. His hand under the table, holding the sawed-off double-barrel that's taped there. The one I've just heard him cock.

—Easy, Joe.

I take my hand off my gun.

He nods.

—Cool, man. That's it. Let me show you something.

He brings up his hands. Brings them up empty.

—Nobody here, man. Just me and you. You want to hold your piece on me while we talk, go ahead.

I do want to hold my piece on him. So I pull it and point it.

He smiles.

—Well, shit, what did I expect, right? Offer a guy like you a chance to invest in some mutual trust, I get what I deserve, right?

—What the fuck, Terry? What the fuck with telling me that story? That's like a goddamn death sentence.

He runs a hand over the top of his head.

—Just trying to get your attention, Joe.

—Trying to get my? Fuck that. You're trying to. I don't know what you're trying to do, but it's fucked up whatever it is.

—Well, that is one possible interpretation of events.

—Fuck you. I'm a Rogue. I can't get away with knowing that shit.

—Yes, you are. You are a Rogue.

He puts his glasses back on.

—Then again, what if things were, you know, different?

I start to smell it now. He sees me smelling it.

—No.

—Just hear me out. Just, you know, give this a listen.

—No.

—Joe.

He leans forward.

—You have the gun, but you're in my place. Hear me out.

Shit.

I put the gun away. For as much good as it will do me now.

He rubs his hands together.

—OK. OK. That's cool. Now we can really rap, really get into it. OK. So, you've been asking some interesting questions here. Some deep stuff. Stuff that gets right down there in the roots, down where you don't go swinging away, hacking things to bits. Cut the wrong bit, the whole tree dies. Thing is, being around as long as you have, you've ended up mixed up in some pretty serious stuff the last couple years. Gotten some pretty deep knowledge on your own. That's what happens. You last long enough, you're going to get sucked into some stuff. Period. Can't get around that. There are only so many of us. Only so many who have some staying power. Sooner or later, you're going to get involved. Just, for just a second, just think about who you met the last couple days. Think about the people you met last year. Think about the kind of juice those people squeeze. Think about, about the things you know now, about how stuff works, the things you didn't know last year. Seriously, think.

He shuts up and watches me.

And I think.

I think about it. And it scares me.

He nods.

—Right? Got it? See what I mean? Hey, man, not everybody spends their time rapping with DJ Grave Digga and Dexter Predo and me and old lady Vandewater. And let's not even talk about how you have something going with Daniel. Any idea how many people get a repeat audience with him? How many survive the first one? That is, you know, a very short list. You're, whether you like it or not, and for lack of a better word, you're becoming a player.

He raises a finger.

—And check this out. For every little detail you've picked up, there's a whole mosaic attached to it. You just can't see it yet. Keep going, you're gonna see more. But, you being a Rogue and all, not everyone is going to be happy about your growing understanding of, you know, how we do things. A Rogue has no loyalty. You don't know where he's going to go, which way he'll jump.

That puts people, I don't know, on edge. Joe, I'm not gonna lie, it harshes my mellow, too. A good mellow is hard to come by. Security, can't pay enough to have it. And, well, that's kind of it. If your knowing things, combined with your being a Rogue, if that unsettles people? Sooner or later someone's going to deal with that. Screw the metaphors, someone's going to put you in the sun. Like Tom. And for the same reason: because he was harshing everybody's mellow.

He leans back.

—Which is why I can sit here and offer you a job I know you don't want.

—I said, no.

—Joe, man, it doesn't have to be like the old days. I mean, today, yeah, man, that was bad karma all the way around. But it's not really like it used to be. Mostly, it's just showing yourself in the neighborhood. Keeping an eye on things. Pretty much the kind of stuff you do on your own. And, you know, if someone does get out of line, sure, that would be down to you. But you make the call. With this job, you have the license to, well let's just say it like it is, you have a license to fuck people up. You employ it as you see fit. Straight up. Tom sucked at the job. You, you're a natural. We both know that.

I pick up my gun. Put it back in my belt.

—No.

I stand up.

He stands up.

—Joe, come on, I know you, man. You like to know what's up. You got to pick a scab, man. Well this job puts you on the inside, where things happen.

I turn to the door.

—No.

Like that, he's in front of me.

—Please, man. I'm telling you, it's not, like, a threat or anything, but I'm telling you, it can't go on like it has. Not now. Me, I can play it as loose as you. I dig that. But Digga? Predo? They won't have it. Not like this. You have to come back inside, Joe. It's down to that. In or out.

I think about trying to go through him. I think about going out like that, taking the head of a Clan with me. My old buddy.

I pull another smoke from my pack and light it with a match.

I think about the gutted lighter I abandoned at Vandewater's. Have to get a new one. They take weeks to break in, to get the action on the hinge loosened up so it will pop open with a snap of your fingers. The old one was just right.

I smoke.

Terry stands there, watches me. I watch him back. He's in no hurry. There's a clock built into the face of the stove. I look at it. It's getting late.

I think about last year. How close I came to dying. Dying ugly. I think about the last forty-eight hours. How close. I think about how it's hard enough day by day without this kind of crazy shit blowing up in your face. I think about that lousy fucking job. *Security.* What that job was like when I had it before.

The whip in my hand.

I think about the part of me that likes the way it feels. The part my father and mother cut into me.

Terry, waiting.

Shit.

—No.

He sags, nods his head.

—I did my best.

He steps aside.

I go for the door.

—Joe.

I stop.

—You want to buy a little extra goodwill down here, you can do me a favor.

I turn my head.

—What's that?

He goes to the fridge, comes out with the bag of anathema.

—Drop something off for me.

It's not an errand I'm looking forward to. But I'll be needing every last scrap of goodwill Terry's willing to dole out. Every scrap while I figure where to run to.

Also, I have a couple questions left. Terry left some gaps around this part. The part where everything connects.

And he was right, I do like to pick a scab.

One of the girls answers my buzz. She doesn't want to let me in, but he tells her to do it. I take the stairs. Poncho is there at the door, holding it open. She stands aside to let me in, giving me a nasty look as I go by.

He's on the couch, Pigtails on one side, PJs on the other, taking turns bathing his face with a damp cloth. Ignoring the fact that everything that's gonna heal has healed.

Poncho walks past me. She goes around the couch and stands behind him, hands on his shoulders.

He gives me a little finger wave.

—Hey.

I nod.

—Hey.

He tilts his head.

—So we cool?

—Yeah. We're cool.

—Cool. Cool. Have a seat, man. Ladies, don't be rude. Offer the man something.

Pigtails sniffs.

—I offered last time. He didn't want it. And then he was mean to you.

She hops off the couch and flounces over to me, bends low from the waist.

—But that doesn't mean I won't offer again.

I hold up my hand.

—Maybe just a beer for now.

She straightens up, puts one hand on her hip and points a finger at me.

—You are no fun.

She turns her back, looks at me over her shoulder.

—But I'll get you a beer anyway.

She skips to the fridge.

PJs has put her head in The Count's lap. He strokes her hair.

—Sure you don't want something stronger, man?

He points to the fridge. Pigtails is standing in the kitchen, fanning her hand in front of the open fridge, displaying the contents like a model on a game show. Blood. Lots of it.

—Just the beer for now.

He shrugs.

—Whatever you want, man.

Pigtails skips back over with the beer and an opener. She pops the top, takes a sip, and hands me the bottle.

—Yum.

She points at my lap.

—Mind if I sit?

The Count snaps his fingers.

—Come here, love. That man isn't playful.

She giggles and goes to him.

—I knooooow. I'm just teasing. I like to tease.

She takes her place next to him and puts her head next to PJs'.

—And be teased.

He pats her cheek.

—Naughty.

I point at his nose.

—You might want to straighten that out before the cartilage knits. It'll stay crooked if you don't.

He touches it with his index finger.

—I thought I'd leave it as is. The girls like it.

—Sorry about the teeth. Those won't grow back.

He smiles, shows me the gaps.

—Well, it wasn't fun getting this way, but I'm gonna make the most of it. Thought I'd get some gold caps. Do the gangsta thing. Work on my street cred.

He flexes his shoulders, arms akimbo, hands flashing in front of his chest hip hop style. He laughs.

—Anyway, it's no big. I had a role to play. I played it. Gotta admit, I played it all the way.

I nod.

—Yep.

—Terry fill you in on the whole thing?

—Most of it. He said there were some details I could get from you.

—Cool. That's cool. So, where do you want to?

—Vandewater?

—OK. So, this is pretty fucked-up shit, funny fucked up. You're gonna love some of this. OK.

Poncho has been rolling him a smoke, she puts it between her lips, lights it, moves it to his. He takes a drag and she removes it, his hands occupied with petting the girls' heads in his lap.

—So, do you know what she does up there?

—Besides make anathema and spin fucked-up plots to stir up shit that will get us all killed? No.

—She makes enforcers. Really, man. That's what she's there for.

Predo sends them to her. Sends her the raw recruits, and she
sends back little order-following assassin robots. She's the chief
programmer. She's been doing it forever.

—You mean that literally?

He shakes his head.

—Well, no, man. But a long damn time.

—Uh-huh. And you?

He grins.

—Me. Well, that *was* me. Funny as it sounds, man, I'm an enforcer. Anyway, I was supposed to be. She, like, handpicked me.
I mean, I was really up there, pre-med and all, and she has these
scouts, kids on campus, recruiters like? Mostly they're looking for
kids they can snatch, for the, you know, for the stuff?

—The anathema.

—Yeah, man. Like, raw material for the anathema. But sometimes, if they spot someone promising, they may try to recruit
them. Nothing too obvious, right? No, *Hey, man, what do you think
of vampires?* But she's got a profile she looks for, something she's
put together. Traits she thinks you need to have. If you have them,
and if you're vulnerable to a snatch, she has you snatched. Has
you infected. Or, tries to anyway. Sometimes it just don't take.
You know.

—But it took with you.

—Oh, man, did it ever. All of it. I don't know what it is she looks
for, but I have it. I took to this shit. The life. I know that bugs you,
like the way you went all *Raging Bull* on my head, I know you
don't want to hear that kind of thing, but it's the truth. I just plain
took to it. And, I got to admit, I like it. I like the way it makes me
feel. And, sure, I got it easier than most. The money, that makes
a difference. And that shit I told you about mom and dad cutting
me off? That was bull. Mom and dad divorced years ago. From
each other and from me. All they want is not to know I exist. It

might remind them of how old they really are. My trust fund ain't going anywhere anytime, not unless people stop buying gas. I'm set. So, yeah, I'm spoiled fucking rotten. And I love it, by the way.

Poncho feeds him another drag.

—So I had whatever kind of crazy she was looking for. Not for, like, the standard enforcer thing, but for this special gig she had cooked up. This infiltration.

He moves his hands like cat's paws.

—A lone *agento secreto* in the heart of the Society, carrying out a plot to subvert the youth of the Clan. Cool, huh? I mean, who wouldn't love a gig like that?

I light a cigarette of my own.

—So what went wrong?

He takes a drag, blows a ring.

—What went wrong is I likes to party! I likes to have a good time. And one thing the enforcers do not get to do is have a good time. Also, according to Vandewater, I happen to be the most amoral kid you're likely to ever run across. Besides being, you know, a spoiled little shit. When I was down here, it was, like, the bomb. Secret agent on his own.

He raises his arms, indicating the room.

—Sweet pad, nice threads, piles of money.

He looks up at Poncho. She bends and kisses him. He looks at me.

—Beautiful ladies. Like James Bond, man. But cooler.

He frowns.

—But then I'd have to go see M. Go Uptown like I was going to class, stop by her place. Have tea for fuck sake. Give my report. Man! That is not the kind of Vampyre action I was looking for. Then this thing came up.

I finish my beer.

—Tell me about that.

—Man, talk about your blessings in disguise. OK, so I'm down here. I mean, she's had me down here, but laying veeeeery low. Don't want to get scented. Once I've kind of established residency, I open a vein one night. Actually, one of her boys opened it for me, but that's just details. The good part is when I stumble into a place we knew Tom liked to hang at. This agro-vegan joint on C. I come in bleeding, the staff, it was like raw meat to them, they freak out. Tom is all over me, saying he'll get me an ambulance and shit. I'm pretty sure he thought a free meal had just landed in his lap. Then he got a good smell. Once he realized I was infected, I moved up from meal to recruit. Not his fault he didn't know I'd been infected for years. I did the whole act.

He puts his hands to the sides of his head.

—*Vyrus? What Vyrus? Vampyre? You're crazy! Crazy! It can't be! It just can't be!* Well, you saw my act a couple times today. What can I say? I got talent! So I played it freaked out, but not for *too* long. Then I played quick study, but not *too* quick. Then I played true believer. I played that all the way. Tom loved it. I was his star pupil. All the Anarchist meetings, calling on me to answer questions about doctrine and shit? A total drag. But I'll give the guy this: He was sincere. For whatever that got him.

I take a drag, having witnessed what being sincere got Tom.

—What about Terry?

—Terry! Now that man, he is the mac. Me, I think he had me pegged the first time Tom brought me in for vetting. He sat back, let Lydia and Tom and some of the other council members drill me on my story and my *compatibility with the goals of the Society.*

He makes his hand into a puppet and flaps its mouth open and shut.

—All that crap. He barely asked shit. But I think he knew then. Not that I had a clue. I thought I was smooth. But, man, well, you know, Terry is the smoothest. I had no idea he was on to me until he showed up here with Hurley and gave me the score.

—What was the score?

He shakes his head.

—What do you think it was? Man, the score was tell him every fucking thing he wanted to know or Hurley would start chopping stuff off of me until I was a biscuit. No problem, man, I squawked. And I got to say, greatest piece of luck I ever had. I spilled it all. Spilled who I was, where I came from, where the anathema was coming from, all of it. And Terry? He watched me, just like he watched during my vetting, and when I was done spilling, he made me an offer I couldn't refuse. Man, an offer I would never refuse.

I hold up my empty, start to stand.

—Mind if I get another?

Poncho waves me back down and gets it for me.

I take it from her hand.

She gives me a hard look, still pissed at the way I beat on her squeeze.

I drink the beer.

—So, Terry's offer?

The Count takes Poncho's hand as she circles back around him.

—Well, here I am, right? I play my part in this show, and I get to stay down here. No more Mrs. Vandewater. No more *sieg heil*. No worrying about when I'm gonna get called back and told to put on a suit and act like all the other little robots. Freedom, man. That was the deal.

—So you told Vandewater Terry's position was unstable.

—Yeah. Told her he was having trouble with Tom. Told her we could rock things down here, maybe start an outright revolution *if* we could make it look like *Tom* was behind the anathema. But I told her it couldn't come from me, Terry wouldn't buy it from me. It had to come from someone he had a history with.

—Me.

He points at his nose.

—Bingo. Terry was looking to ditch Tom. He said he needed a

witness for a trial. He said he needed two. He said I was good because I was one of Tom's guys. But he said the other one needed to be old school. He said it needed to be someone Lydia would accept. He mentioned you.

—It worked.

—Hell yeah! I sent you Uptown. Terry said not to be too specific. Said it would look weird if I knew exactly where the shit was coming from. Said to point you to the Hood and that would be close enough. Fuck it, it turned out OK. Terry said it would. You wound up in Vandewater's clutches, she messed with your head a little, you made a move, she let you escape and told you Tom was her courier as you were on your way out.

—And all she had to do was lose an eyeball and take a bellyful of bullets.

He waves his hand back and forth.

—Trust me, for her cause, losing an eyeball, taking some lead? That is nothing. If she thought it was gonna bring down *the Society,* she'd cut off her tits. If she thought it'd bring down *the Hood,* she'd cut off her tits and fuck Dexter Predo. And she hates his ass. Lady is a stone zealot. Cra-zy. Period. Funny, though, she thinks you're coming down here, gonna blow shit sky-high, gonna rock the boat. Had no idea she was helping to set Tom up for the fall. Helping to, like, entrench Terry's chairmanship. Crazy, right? All the reversals, the double-agenting, I loved it. Like *Deep Cover* and I'm all Laurence Fishburne. In too deep for my own good, flippin' and trippin'. But I had it under control. It's easy if you're not worried about right and wrong. You know, if you're just worried about yourself. Priorities, man, I have 'em.

—And the rest?

—Easy-peasy, man. Hey, I don't want you bouncing me around every day, but you made it easy to play the role. That shit was scary. And then in the *trial?* That worked out perfect. The way you were playing it all stoic set me up just right when I cracked.

I mean, the plan was, you'd be telling your story and I'd hop in with mine. But the way it played was better yet. And my cherry, just when everyone is *sure* I'm full of it, just when they *know* I'm lying through my teeth, when I pop out with, *I'm a spy!* Did you see the look on Tom's face? He shit his pants. He *must* have shit his pants. You though, you were stone cold. *That's what old lady Vandewater told me.* Snap! That was it for Tom. Game ovaah!

—Yeah. Terry said something about Lydia?

—Oh, damn, Lydia. She really a lesbo? Cuz I'm just saying, some of that? I could do some of that.

Poncho slaps the top of his head.

He looks up at her.

—There's plenty to go around, baby. No worries.

I grind some sleep from my eyes.

—How'd she go for you getting cut loose?

—Terry Bird to the rescue. After you took off to deal with Tom, Terry did some additional *interrogation.* He convinced Lydia, in a way where she was kind of thinking it was her own idea, that keeping me around was best. Double agent they could use to send false information back to the Coalition. She went for it. Plus, you know, the money. The Society is always hurting for money. Long as I'm here, I can help with that. So she agreed. House arrest. Gonna put a watch on me until I prove my loyalty. But that'll come soon enough. And, hey!

He shows off his apartment and his girls again.

—Not like it's a hard life up in here.

I look around.

—No, I can see that. Amongst all the other luxury, you got a phone?

—Sure, sure, landline's right here.

He grabs a cordless handset from the coffee table and tosses it to me.

I point at Poncho's room.

—OK if I use it in there?

—Sure, man.

I get up. So does The Count.

—Hey, Joe. We are cool, right? I mean, I am. I'm totally cool. I think you handled this shit straight up. Not easy getting played like that. You got nothing but respect from me.

I shrug.

—Yeah, we're cool. All in the way of business. And hey.

I reach in my jacket and pull out the anathema.

—Got something for you.

I toss it to him.

—From the old lady's. Fresh this morning. Terry sent it over.

He catches it.

—Oh yeah! Knew he'd come through.

He gives me a grin.

—Thought I smelled a little somethin' somethin' on you.

He gives it a sniff.

—It's a little tired, but it's good.

He turns to the girls.

—See, ladies, told you Joe is our man. Told you he knows business from personal.

Pigtails is on all fours, arching her back cat-style.

—When we gonna get personal, Joe Pitt?

She winks and hops up to help PJs get their works together.

The Count hands the bag to Poncho.

—Sure you don't want to hang, Joe? I know you don't indulge, but the fridge is stocked with regular, man. Have yourself a pint. Drink some booze. Get an old school buzz going.

He comes closer, puts an arm over my shoulder, points at Pigtails, kneeling on the floor with the other girls, getting the anathema ready.

—She really has taken a shine to you. And trust me, it's freaky good. Especially after she has a skinful. She's in another world, man.

I look at her. She catches me, blows a kiss, goes back to work.

—Maybe after my call.

He slaps my shoulder.

—That's my man!

He joins the girls. I walk into the room made of doors.

Most of it's taken up by a big mattress on the floor. Funky designer clothes from Lower East Side boutiques spill out of a chest of drawers. Three mobiles made of tin and colored glass dangle from the ceiling. I duck to go under one and graze it with my shoulder. It tinkles. One of the doors is paned with frosted glass. Through it I can see the ghosts of The Count and his ladies, in a circle on the floor.

I dial the phone.

He answers.

—Hello?

—It's me.

—Hey, Joe. What's up?

—I'll take the job.

—Wow. Well. Good for you, man. About time you stopped being just a piece of the mosaic and started to help make it. Help make, I know how this is going to sound, but help make the world a better place.

I think about the world. I think about all the room there is for making it better than what it is. I think about the likelihood that I'm a guy who can do that.

—Yeah, let's do that, Terry. Let's clean it up.

—That's the spirit. You come by tomorrow night. We'll start talking. In earnest, I mean.

—Yeah. Sure. Tomorrow. I gotta go now. Got something to take care of.

I hang up.

I walk out through the space between two of the doors, hitting the mobile again. Hearing it chime.

Poncho and PJs are already out. Wrapped in their little coma of dreams. Seeing whatever visions it is they see. Pigtails is waiting for hers.

The Count points at the fridge.

—Sure you don't?

I touch the blisters on my hands.

—A pint wouldn't hurt. Or a drink.

He gets up.

—That's the shit.

He grabs me a pint, brings it back along with a half-full bottle of Jack.

I retake my seat, open the pint, hit it.

The Count looks at me as he sets Pigtails up. He holds up the syringe.

—Want to do the honors?

Pigtails writhes on the floor.

—C'mon, Joe. Do it for me.

I finish the blood. Set the empty bag aside.

—Sure.

The Count hands me the syringe. I look at the careful measure of anathema inside. Pigtails is watching me, panting.

—C'mon, Joe.

I slip the needle into her arm. Push the plunger. She sighs, shivers, goes under. I go back to my seat, open the Jack, pour a shot down my throat. It mixes sweet with the blood.

The Count starts to fill the last syringe.

—You won't regret staying, Joe. She is wicked crazy. Start in on her when she's still half on the nod, she'll do things no girl would ever think of doing.

I take another drink.

—Where'd you get them, anyway?

He looks up.

—The girls?

—Yeah.

He looks back down, focused on filling the syringe with the proper measure.

—Hell, man, I infected them. Wasn't easy. Had to take a couple shots at it. But I followed the old lady's plan. Made a profile. You know, looked for chicks like me. Couple of them couldn't take the Vyrus at all, rejected it outright. Couple others just freaked out. But I had to have me the three brides. You were right about that, man. Totally cliché, but I had to have it. Like the ultimate Vampyre status symbol and all. I know it's weak, but, like I said, spoiled rotten. That's me.

I point at his syringe.

—Why don't you put a little more in there?

He looks at it.

—Oh no, man. You don't mess with this shit. Too much and you are fucked for life in the worst way.

—Yeah, that's what Vandewater said.

He grins.

—Hey, is it true what Terry told me?

—What's that?

—Said you dosed her. Gave her a hot shot. Said she's hooked on the bad dose now.

—Got me. I didn't even know she lived through it.

—That's what he said.

—Must be true.

—Oh, man, that is the worst. She is so messed up! Bitch's gonna be jonesin' for the bad dose the rest of her life. That's sooo F-ed in the A.

—That Spaz at Doc Holiday's. That was you hooked him up, right?

He's swabbing his arm.

—Yeah. Had to get the ball rolling. He was just a fish lost in the woods. Needed friends. Gave him a little of the needle and he was gone. I'd been haunting your background a little, looking for a good spot to open your eyes. Terry said he needed *an inciting, like, agent.* Whatever. I met The Spaz out back, by that take-out window they got. Gave him the needle good to go. Not a heavy dose, just enough to push him over the side. Told him to hit it in the can. Pow! That was that. I watched some of that through the window. Man, he was all over the place. Thought for a second I overdid it. But you, man, you handled that shit.

He has the tube around his arm.

I point at the syringe again.

—Yeah, so, like I said, why don't you put a little more in there.

He's focused on slapping a vein up.

—No joke, man, can't mess with that. Take no chances on getting a hot shot.

I take out my piece, cock it. He looks up.

—Count, why don't you put a little more in there.

He looks at the gun.

—Maaaan. Man, I thought you were taking all this a little *too* cool. I *knew* you were playing possum on me.

I point the gun at him.

—Yeah, surprise.

He smiles.

—Joe. I know you're pissed right now, but what are you gonna do? Really. I'm Terry's. I'm his guy now. You can't fuck with me. You think you can intimidate me into taking a hot shot? How? You can't lay a hand on me. Terry will freak. Kill me, you kill the golden goose. I mean, fuck all that spy shit, kill me, I won't be opening my bank account to the Society. Period.

—Uh-huh. Thing is, I just bought myself a license to fuck people up. It's gonna cost me plenty. So I need to start getting my money's worth.

He squints.

—I don't follow.

I shoot him in the foot. Blood sprays.

He stares at it, stares at the place his toes used to be.

—What the fuck?

I stand up.

—Amazing, isn't it, that moment when you don't feel any pain?

He drops the syringe, howls.

—And then it hits.

He grabs a pillow from the couch, crams it over the end of his foot.

I pick up the syringe.

—Jesus, Count, how long you been around? Give it a minute, that thing'll stop bleeding on its own. And the pain?

I slip the needle into the bag of anathema.

—That goes away, too. Stick around long enough, you're gonna have to live through no end of pain.

I draw some more of the shit into the syringe, remembering Vandewater's lesson on how much does what.

—What you should be doing is ignoring the blood and the pain. You should be trying to get away from me.

I pull the syringe free.

—That or trying to kill me.

I hold the syringe like a dagger.

—But then again, you're spoiled rotten.

I stab him in the neck.

—And you wouldn't know where to start.

For a few minutes, it's like with The Spaz at Doc Holiday's. He spins and shakes and foams a little. Finally he falls on the floor, jerking and twitching in time to the spasms in his muscles and the visions flashing through his brain. Addicted at a deeper level now. Addicted to this experience. Helpless in it. *The bad dose*, he said.

I hope it sucks as bad as the old lady said it does.

I find a little picnic cooler under the sink and fill it with the blood from the fridge. I close the valve on the bag of anathema and toss that in. In a shoe box in the bathroom, just sitting there on the back of the toilet, I find over ten grand in rubber-banded rolls. Cash from the anathema he's been dealing.

On my way to the door, I stop, look down at the girls. Generally, you don't want to fuck a guy up like this and leave him with a devoted harem that might come looking for you. Hell, this isn't their fault. None of it is their fault. But there's smart, and then there's dumb.

I put a bullet in each one, up close, in the heart.

I go out the door, a cooler of blood in my hand, a box of money under my arm. I leave The Count behind me, plagued with nightmares, surrounded by his dead brides.

Having done the job. Having started to make the world a better place.

He knew. Fucking Terry knew.

And he was right about knowing me. I don't like it at all, but he was right. Knowing me well enough to send me over there. Knowing I'd ask a few questions. Knowing what I'd do when I heard some answers. And knowing damn well I'd be ready to take his goddamn job if it meant getting away with it. And, fuck all, knowing it had to be done. The brat needed to be taught a lesson.

You don't fuck around like that and come out on top. If he hadn't been put in his place, he would have just done it again. Spoiled kids are like that.

—So what is it?

The fingers of Daniel's right hand run over the half-empty bag. He rubs a fingertip through a drop of blood that has congealed at the valve opening.

—As Maureen told you, it's anathema.

—Maureen?

He smears the drop of blood between his thumb and forefinger.

—Sorry. Mrs. Vandewater to you.

I shift my ass on the floor, stiff from sitting here while I've been telling him the story.

—OK, it's anathema. But the other thing, was she right about that? The visions.

—Well, visions.

He brings the fingers to his face and sniffs, grimaces, wipes them on the floor.

—In this batch, no. But in fresh anathema?

He shrugs.

—Certainly there are visions.

I look at the bag on the floor.

—Are they real?

—Simon, of course they're real, they're visions.

—But. Do they mean anything?

He scratches his head.

—You're making it very difficult for me to answer you. *Are they real? Do they mean anything?* A vision is a personal thing. What can I tell you about what one might mean or not mean?

—Fucking hell, man, do they have anything to do with the Vyrus? Can you learn anything about . . . about?

—Yes?

—About us? About all this shit? I.

He smiles.

—Simon, I do believe you're looking for a little wisdom this evening. How refreshing that is, coming from you. How hopeful.

I get up.

—Fuck you.

His smile gets bigger.

—Oh well, back to square one.

He holds out his hand. I take it and he pulls himself up, not needing my help at all.

He takes my arm, walks with me out of his cubicle and toward the stairs.

—I know what you're asking. I do. But I want you to know, as well. I want you to know that for each of these questions you ask me, there are any number of ways the answer might be approached. Any number of lessons to be learned. That said.

He stops us at the top of the stairs.

—I personally did not find the anathema visions to be either illuminating or useful. Entertaining. Pleasant. A distraction. But empty.

I look at him.

—You?

He looks down, shrugs.

—We were all young once.

He looks back at me.

—Really, everyone was doing it back then.

—She said it was permanent. The addiction.

He releases my arm.

—Honestly, Simon, think. Once in a great while, think. An addiction. In the blood. In the Vyrus. How do you think such a thing would be best dealt with?

But I don't need to think. I know. I've done it.

—Fasting.

He nods.

—Fasting. Starving it out. Killing it. And.

He raises a finger.

—What does that suggest?

—I.

—Think.

—I. No. I don't. Just tell me. I'm tired and I want to go home. Just fucking tell me. Just tonight. I came and visited like you wanted. Can't you just? Jesus.

He holds up both hands, palms out.

—Alright, alright. You're tired. Just this last thing.

He starts down the stairs. I follow.

—The Vyrus, Simon, it's not general. Not one thing. Not all the same. That boy you saw, the one who died when they tried to *infect* him? *He* wasn't rejecting the *Vyrus, it* was rejecting *him*. Because it wasn't *for* him. It wasn't *his* Vyrus. Each of us, we offer something to it, and in each of us, it changes, becomes unique over and over again.

He stops at the foot of the stairs, faces me, taps a finger against my chest.

—The Vyrus in you.

He taps himself.

—Is not the Vyrus in me.

We continue walking, heading toward the door.

—Anathema: The Vyrus in freshly infected blood, at its most robust as it seeks to take root. It can sustain itself for a time outside a body. But the only body it would ever thrive for, it has been killed, killed when the anathema was harvested. Introduced to a new body, one already home to another Vyrus, the two will go to war. The visions? These are the death throes of the anathema, its longings for the body it should have inhabited. The addiction, its remnants in the blood, struggling for survival. Starve it long enough? And *your* Vyrus, the Vyrus *meant* for you, will kill it utterly. This is why the larger doses are so painful. Given time, the Vyrus in its proper place, in its home, it will always win out. But the struggle can destroy the home.

We're at the door, the cooler of blood and the box of money waiting where I left them.

He points at the cooler.

—This, what's in there, it's empty. Outside of a body, disassociated from a, forgive me, but disassociated from a *soul*, it is only nourishment for the Vyrus. But it is not what it seeks. It seeks transformation. In *you*. Your Vyrus is incubating in *you*. Waiting to give birth to something more. We are cocoons for it, Simon. Each of us unique.

He spreads his arms.

—But none of us special.

I look at him.

—Daniel.

—Yes?

—None of that helped me a fucking bit.

He sighs.

—Well, I'm tired, too. So it's all I have for you tonight.

He hauls the door open.

—Go home, Simon. Get some rest. Think about it. You're always welcome.

I pick up the cooler.

—You want any of this?

He rolls his eyes.

—Not listening at all, are you?

—Just asking.

I pick up the shoe box.

He points at it.

—But you know, we can always use a few extra dollars.

I give him the two grand Digga gave me.

—Don't spend it all in one place.

He fans himself with the sheaf of bills.

—Big spender, Simon. You're a very big spender.

I step out the door.

—Daniel. What about Percy?

—What about him?

—You guys gave me his name. Was he? Were you in on?

—It's not all plots and intrigues, Simon. Sometimes, shit just happens.

I nod, turn and walk away.

—Safe home, Simon.

—Yeah, same to you.

And I'm gone.

* * *

So, it's the job now. It's the job and the whip and Terry's mosaic. And if that's it, if it's the job, then it's doing the job my way.

Anathema.

Whatever the fuck it is, figure it's a problem that's not going to go away on its own. Now that that shit is in the community, figure someone's gonna have to root it out. Gonna have a long to-do list tomorrow.

I owe Chubby Freeze. Chubby who vouched for me. Whether I really needed it or not. Chubby, who's more connected than he's let on. Figure he and I will have to have a talk about that, too.

And Predo. I'll have to talk to Predo. The job means talking to Predo. Fucker works during the day. Can't keep regular hours like the rest of us. Interacts with too many people out there in the world for that. Gonna have to talk to him about inter-Clan security issues. Wish I had thought of that. Figure that was enough of a reason to have said no to Terry right there. Fucking hell.

I'll need to start scouting some helpers. Some of Lydia's people maybe. I wish Sela was still around. But she's not. Sela's Uptown looking after the girl. That's where she belongs. I don't want to think about the girl any more than that.

Daniel. Gonna have to talk to him some more. Jesus. Ask him a question and all he does is kick up more dust. But it is interesting dust.

Like, if it's so hard to infect someone, to find a match, and seeing as we do so little live hunting, leave behind so few that have been fed on directly and left standing; seeing all that, how is the population maintained? Seeing all that, it makes me wonder about where new fish come from. Makes me wonder if Vande-water's the only one with a profile. And all the fresh faces down here? All those young rhinos up in the Hood? Maybe Tom's not the only one who was making his own new fish. Maybe Vande-water's not the only one manufacturing enforcers.

Figure there's something there. Something in there and in all Daniel's pseudospiritual psychobabble. Something about the Vyrus. Something about it being unique in the vein. About the way only some people can take it. Something about . . . Hell. Figure it's something I'm not smart enough to put together on my own. But sure as shit figure that's a section of Terry's mosaic that needs dusting off.

And figure Terry's no fool. Yeah, he knows me pretty well. Knows me a fuck of a lot better than I know him. Better than I want to be known. Figure he was right: I want to know things.

Can't leave a scab alone. A scab, for instance, like that picture up there in the old lady's place. That picture of her and Predo and Terry. The Count telling me, *She makes enforcers.*

Figure that's a scab I'm gonna want to pick at plenty. Pick it till it comes off in my hand and shows me the wound below.

Tomorrow.

Now, I got that beer at home, and all those cigarettes.

Hurley and Tom left my door unlocked when they tossed my place for the anathema. I push it open with my toe, kick it closed, and reactivate the alarm. The upstairs has been given a going over, but not too rough. They know where I live. Downstairs is gonna be a mess.

I can smell Hurley and Tom and the partisans they brought with them. But that doesn't keep me from smelling the real trouble. It doesn't even matter that the smell is always around. In the air. On the sheets.

It's different when she's actually here.

I stand at the foot of the stairs and look at her, sitting on the floor in front of the open closet, in front of the open minifridge

with the lock torn off, staring into the biohazard bag in her lap.
The room, a mess around us.

She looks up.

—You missed my reading, Joe.

My alarm clock is on the floor, near my feet. It's just after midnight.

—I know.

—That was really important to me.

—I know.

She looks in the bag. Looks up.

—Joe, what is this?

—You should put that down, baby.

—What is it, Joe?

I adjust my grip on the handle of the blood-filled cooler.

—That's the job, baby. That's what I do.

She opens her mouth. Closes it. Bites her lip. Talks.

—You need to tell me.

She holds the bag out at arm's length.

—You need to tell me about the job. Now.

I think about the new job. I think about trying to explain that
to her. I think about telling her the truth. I think about losing her.
It's a decision she should make for herself. One for which she will
need the truth.

I take a deep breath.

—I'm a courier. For organ dealers. I move body parts.

The bright red bag dangles from her hand.

I take a step. I set the cooler on the floor.

—Some people, they need money. They need it bad.

I place the shoe box on top of the cooler.

—They need it so bad, they sell pieces of themselves.

I take the bag from her.

—Kidneys.

I squat in front of the closet and stuff the bag in the fridge.

—Eyes sometimes.

My back to her, I look at the lock that Hurley twisted off.

—Lengths of intestine.

I'll need a new lock now. For my secrets.

—An artery.

I look at her over my shoulder.

—Skin.

Her face doesn't change, but tears trickle down her cheeks.

I sit on the floor, my back against the wall, keeping my distance from her.

—These things have to be moved quickly. I do that.

I take out a cigarette.

—But sometimes there's a problem. Someone balks. The money doesn't come through.

A book of matches is on the floor near my hand. I pick it up.

—Alternate buyers are always standing by. But the material has to be stored briefly while things are worked out. Held in escrow. I do that, too.

I light my smoke.

—I have to be on call. I have to go where they say when they say.

I take out my gun and set it on the floor between us.

—And it's dangerous.

I inhale smoke.

—It's dangerous to know about it.

I close my eyes and blow smoke.

—So I don't tell people.

It's quiet for a while. I keep my eyes closed. I don't want to open them, see her looking at me, know what she's thinking about me. I keep my eyes closed and listen to her cry.

She stops.

—Joe.

—Yeah.

—What's in the cooler?

I open my eyes. She's not looking at me. She's looking at the cooler.

I get up. I cross the room and get the cooler and the shoe box. I set them both in front of her. I squat and open the cooler.

She looks at the bags piled inside, an alien depth of color. Strange fruit.

She touches one, lays her hand on top of it. Looks up at my face.

—Is this for me, Joe?

I shake my head.

—Not this, baby.

I tip the lid from the shoe box.

—But I'm gonna get you what you need. Anything you need, I'm gonna get it.

She reaches for me.

Her arms go around my neck.

She puts her lips next to my ear.

—I'd rather have your blood, Joe. I'd rather have you inside me.

Something catches in my throat, snagged on the lie. But I can live with that.

—My blood's no good for you, baby.

Her hands clutch the back of my neck, they find the tear in the collar of my jacket. She works her fingers into it.

—Oh, Joe, your jacket.

—I know. I'm sorry.

She tugs my head lower so she can see the ribboned leather.

—I don't know if I can fix it.

I pull her face back to mine.

—I can live with it.

She squeezes me tight.

And it's uncomfortable, squatting there, Evie hanging from my neck.

But I can live with that, too.